THR3E

MATT STANLEY

Copyright © 2025 Matt Stanley

The right of Matt Stanley to be identified as the Author of the Work has been asserted by them in accordance with the Copyright, Designs and Patents Act 1988.

First published in 2025 by Bloodhound Books.

Apart from any use permitted under UK copyright law, this publication may only be reproduced, stored, or transmitted, in any form, or by any means, with prior permission in writing of the publisher or, in the case of reprographic production, in accordance with the terms of licences issued by the Copyright Licensing Agency. All characters in this publication are fictitious and any resemblance to real persons, living or dead, is purely coincidental.

www.bloodhoundbooks.com

Print ISBN: 978-1-917449-5-71

For Kitty

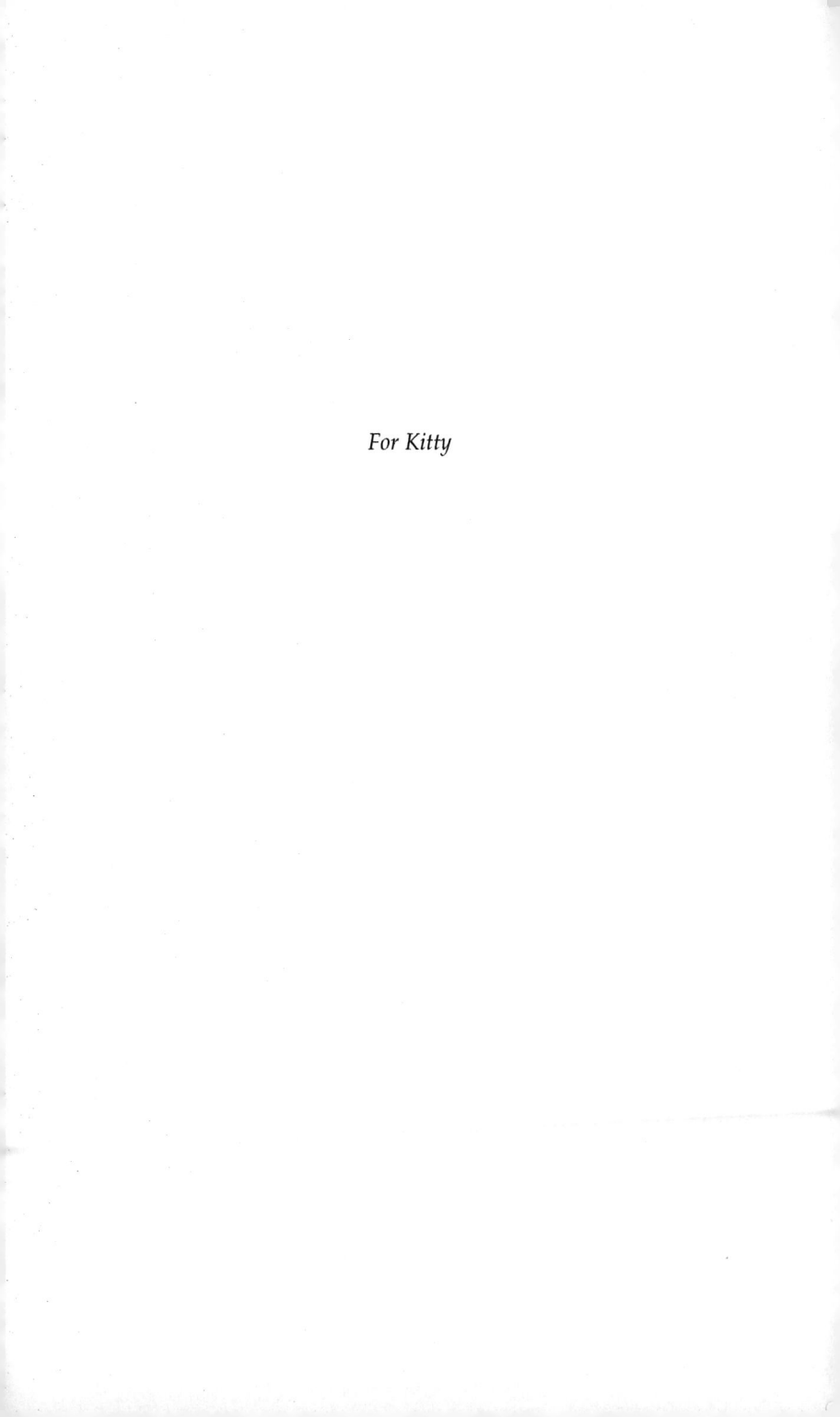

He who fights with monsters might take care lest he thereby become a monster. And if you gaze for long into an abyss, the abyss gazes also into you.

— **Friedrich Nietzsche,** *Beyond Good and Evil*

Loosely based on real events.

ONE

There's a black-and-white photo taken up on Redwood Creek in Buena Vista State Park. You know the one. You've seen it. I'm in the foreground wearing no cuffs or leg irons. The men behind me are the plainclothes officers of the Buena Vista Sheriff's Department and we're all laughing, all looking at the camera as if someone cracked wise just before the shutter dropped. A real jovial group. I was showing them where I threw the hatchet I used to cut up the first girl in my mother's tub.

It was a pretty weird day. We'd gone into Webster's Hardware together that morning – me, the two BVSD detectives and a plainclothes officer – to buy the same model of hatchet. Lieutenant Ed Schumer's idea was that I'd throw it as I'd thrown the original hatchet and they'd search in that general area of the ravine. In the end, I'd have to throw it five, six times before they found the original, a little rusty but still with microscopic bone fragments on the edge. I thought I'd cleaned it up pretty good, but I didn't know about bone fragments. Also, I didn't have a microscope at home.

Anyway, old Webster looked at us funny, the four of us buying a hatchet together. He knew me, of course – he'd sold me a gun and a couple knives – but he didn't know I'd been formally arrested. Lieutenant Schumer wanted to keep it all as quiet as possible because a rumor had got out that they'd caught the killer and reporters were sniffing around.

"You sure it was this one, Sonny?" Schumer asked me.

"Sure, Ed. This is the one." I remembered because I'd liked the hickory shaft and the gold label.

Webster didn't say anything, standing there in his flashing half-moon glasses and his leather apron. I wondered what he would've said if he'd known how I'd used that first hatchet – how slick and sticky it'd got. Later, I'd gone back to him for the boning knife that'd make the job much easier with subsequent girls.

Schumer paid for it with his own money. None of this was strictly according to procedure.

So we drove into the state park and to Redwood Creek – a lovely spot up there in the forest. Romantic. Hardly any traffic back in early '72. Just birdsong and bees and the smell of damp leaf compost. Twigs cracking occasionally under the tires. Some off-duty guys from the Rope and Rescue service were going to meet us and we smoked while we were waiting for them. The guys hadn't put me in chains because they knew I was no threat to them and because they didn't want any passing driver to guess what was happening.

At one point, a California Highway Patrol car came by and stopped. They thought we were throwing trash into the forest, which a lot of people were doing back then. Schumer told them we were up from LA scouting locations for a movie about a mass murderer. Even joked with the guys that they might appear in it, handsome as they were. It was credible enough. A film crew had been shooting near the UCBV campus about six months before. Plus, the CHP troopers didn't know any of these Sheriff's Department cops by sight. They bought it.

It was a humorous situation, all of us trying to avoid smirking. The photo happened just moments after the CHP car had gone round the bend out of sight. The other detective (Jackson, I think he was called) had a camera in his car to document the finds and he just pulled it out.

"Lights! Camera! *Action!*" he said. That was the picture.

Well, the R&R team finally arrived and we got to work, me throwing the hatchet as I'd done six months or so previously under very different circumstances, my trunk full of bagged-up limbs, looking feverishly up and down the road, listening for an engine or a human voice. (We'd go looking for those limbs later.) I'd toss the hatchet and they'd abseil down the ravine to look where it landed.

As I say, they found the original. But they also found something else and I guess this is my starting point. The catalyst, if you like. It's representative of so much that was going on back then – a version that's never been fully told because I'm the only one who *could* tell it.

The rope guys found a heavily decomposed, partially clothed women's body that had been gnawed by animals. They'd taken off the fingers and toes. The nose. Of course, the detectives immediately assumed it was one of mine.

"Are you sure, Sonny?" said Schumer. "Maybe you forgot. One more's not gonna make any difference to you."

"It's not that, Ed. It's just . . . I never disposed of whole bodies like that. And never with the head attached. I always cut 'em up. And I always wrapped the parts in black refuse bags tied off at the top. You know that. Apart from the parts I threw in the sea. The plastic would've made 'em float." I could see they didn't believe me. "Sorry gents, but it's someone else, "I said. "The MO is obviously different."

"Listen to him with his 'MO,'" said Jackson.

"I'm just trying to help you guys," I said. "You can attribute this body to one of the other killers. It's not fair that I take credit for it. I mean, I could do it as a favor to you if you want, but any criminologist'd doubt it's one of mine. It just wouldn't look right."

"I guess we'd better listen to Joseph Wambaugh here,"

laughed Schumer, cocking a thumb at me (and referring to the creator of the popular TV serial of the time, *Police Story*).

The truth – and they knew it – was that I hadn't been the only one. They hadn't even caught one of the murderers who'd been active that last twelve months. Never in US criminal history had there been such a concentration of what we now call serial killers working in one place at one time. At least forty quite brutal murders occurred – only seven of them mine. Countless sexual assaults and rapes. Statistically, evidentially, it was much more likely the body belonged to one of the others. I'd known two of them.

That's the story I'm going to tell. My story and theirs.

People usually reconstruct these things from court transcripts and newspapers. There are confession recordings sometimes. But you're always on the outside looking in. You're limited to facts and evidence. From the outside, it's like staring into darkness. You can only see so deep. You have to imagine what it's like to commit these crimes, to desire them, to live them. But you can't. Not really. You can't possibly know. You can't rationalize or empathize from the outside in.

I'll show you the inside.

It's not just about murders. That's the least interesting part of it all. You think murder is darkly fascinating because it's beyond comprehension, but the real drama is in the unnoticed, unknowable ripples outward from a killing. A woman is thirty seconds late leaving home and another dies in her place. A killer fresh from a slaying, his fingernails bloody, sneezes and the grandmother sitting next to him in the diner tells him, "Bless you, son!" A hitchhiker, mere seconds from having her throat slit, mentions her period and is delivered unharmed, oblivious, to her destination. More killings, more ripples. The intersections are where it gets really interesting.

I've been incarcerated for the last fifty years. I'll never be released. I've spent two-thirds of my life reading and studying. I teach other inmates. Now's the time to tell it all as it happened – my crimes and the others'. It's a pretty wild ride.

Remember just one thing if you choose to continue. You wanted this. You wanted to know. You can't forget evidence photos once you've seen them – no matter how much you want to unsee them. They stay imprinted on your inner vision. Enter this darkness with your eyes open. Have no illusions. I promise I'll tell it straight and honest.

But I've not introduced myself. I'm Sonny Boden. I've only ever climaxed in women I first killed and beheaded.

Pleased to meet you.

TWO

It was early 1970. I'd served my six years down at the state mental hospital in Atascadero after shooting my grandparents to death aged fifteen. I'd been released as posing no further threat to society.

In many ways, I'd been a model inmate. The 36 mandated visits to a psychiatric social worker as part of my parole agreement were merely a legal formality. Nobody thought I'd do anything else bad.

One thing: the doctors had recommended that I not live with my mother, who'd been identified as the main trigger for my earlier violence, my suppressed anger, my homicidal tendencies toward domineering or otherwise belittling women. Well, the California authorities saw fit to ignore this recommendation and handed me over to the guardianship of my mother.

That was probably the start of it.

My mother thought I might do something bad. My sister, too, who worked as a secretary at the Sheriff's Department office downtown. There were some comments.

"Don't you glare at me like that with those murderer's eyes!" my mother might say when she returned drunk at 3am on a

Friday or a Saturday night. Or any other night of the week, if I'm honest. "To think that you, my killer son, are living here in my house. Should I hide the knives?" she'd say like she was joking. "Should I put a lock on my door? I'd better not turn my back on you like your grandmother did!" And she'd laugh about it, taunting me. But she was wrong about my grandmother, who never knew I was behind her.

My sister Amber just watched me carefully the whole time, suspicious, uncertain. Like she was trying to catch me out – catch the psychopath's mask dropping for a second to reveal the monster beneath. She'd actually shiver sometimes if I passed close by her in the hallway. I saw it.

But it wasn't a big issue. Not at first. And I guess I couldn't blame them. Nobody else in Buena Vista knew about Atascadero because my record had been sealed. I was supposed to live a normal life. It was technically a juvenile case. Not even the Sheriff's Department knew, though they probably could have looked into it if they'd wanted to. We'd been living over in Alameda when I'd shot my grandparents and nobody knew me in Verdugo. Neither my sister nor my mother was about to broadcast the fact they had a convicted murderer in the family.

A bigger challenge for me was that I'd emerged from the bleach-washed corridors, pale greens and ceramic whites of the asylum into a totally different culture. I'd gone in there a kid and emerged a man to find that people my age were hippies who smoked 'lids,' dropped acid or 'bennies' and didn't dig the plastic society. I was supposed to be one of them, but I'd spent my adolescence and young manhood among the Golden State's most violently deranged rapists, torturers and murderers. I was on a different planet and, as they said, it was all 'too much' at the beginning.

My mother let me drive her old Ford Galaxie – a little beaten up, but I liked it because it was powerful, handled well and had a huge trunk. Driving around Buena Vista County and north along the coast as far as Frisco or Berkeley gave me the opportunity to join America again – at my own pace and on my own terms. I was never happier than at the wheel of that car. It was the greatest freedom I'd felt in my life until that point. The only freedom I've ever really known, if I'm honest.

The University of California had opened a new campus in Buena Vista while I'd been away and the town had changed completely with the infusion of young blood. It was coeducational and hundreds of these people my age were hitchhiking between the green-field campus, their homes in the town, and other campuses. Picking them up in the Galaxie was, I guess, my way of reintegrating and socializing.

I picked up girls, boys, girls and boys. I just wanted to be a part of it. I learned early on not to pick up the outright hippies. They didn't wash. They had lank, oily hair and their clothes were filthy. They reeked of pot and they were often incoherent if they'd dropped acid. They'd sometimes nod out and I'd have to leave them by the side of the road at their destination as if that was something groovy. I had no plans to kill any of them at this stage.

It was my very first experience of being in proximity to young ladies other than my own sister. I mean, actually talking to them. I'd maintained my heterosexuality during six years among men in the mental hospital, where being queer was considered another mental illness to be treated with extreme measures. Better to boast about a violent rape than to find human comfort in the embrace of another man. I was, then, understandably fascinated by the women and girls I picked up.

A woman, to me, was almost a different species. The timber of their voices, the texture of their hair, the softness of their bodies. Their very presence was different. They'd talk to me as if I was just a regular guy – at least initially. Some of them sensed oddness in me. I mean, I didn't know the bands they liked. I hadn't read the same books and didn't go to parties. I looked young, but I behaved old. I had short hair, lived with my malicious drunk of a mother and I was a convicted double murderer. My normality for years had been a cell that could be hosed down if shit was flung about. I'd learned to sleep amid echoing howls and screams.

My mother fixed me up with a date a few months after I got out. A friend of hers had a daughter a year or so younger than me – a recent high-school graduate – and they thought maybe it would be sweet if we met. I was judged a safe option because I wasn't a lid-toking, bennie-dropping hippie beatnik who'd corrupt the girl and lure her away into communal living and venereal disease in Haight-Ashbury. I was also known to be an inexperienced virgin. I probably wasn't going to ball her on the first date.

It didn't go well. I took the girl (I forget her name) into Buena Vista to a swanky restaurant with candles on the tables and checked tablecloths and wine like I'd seen on TV. She was pretty and more worldly-wise than me, flirting a lot with her eyes, pouting and pushing her chest out. I got the sense that she was teasing me, taunting me, like, You're not gonna get any of this, but you can look and you can imagine. Once we got to the dessert, after pretty much finishing off a bottle of wine together, she was asking, all coquettish, if I knew 'French' and how many girls I'd had.

"Are you a virgin?" she said finally, smirking. "It's cool if you are. It's just that . . . I'm interested in a guy with, you know, more experience."

I said, all casual, that sure, I'd done some balling. I gave some convincing detail to prove it. Problem was: my only experience of this kinda talk was among deviant and violent sexual predators. Peepers. Flashers. Rapists. I might not have said the right things. I didn't know the right words. She insisted on taking a taxi home and her mother called my mother the same night. There'd be no more dates with Kyla. Yeah – that was her name. Kyla.

My mother was delighted, of course. I wouldn't be surprised if she'd planned it like that, her and her friend drunkenly conspiring to humiliate me.

"Try to strangle her, did you, you oaf? You should wear a sign around your neck: *Toxic. Danger*. And what are you wearing, anyway? You look like a waiter on a cruise ship and your shoes stink of gas. Where'd you get that jacket – free with a coffin?" And she'd laughed that raspy donkey laugh until she coughed and had to soothe it with brandy or wine or paint thinner, or whatever was closest to hand.

But I was learning to assimilate. I was trying. I got a job as a forecourt attendant at the Arco gas station on the corner of Dyer and Sloat in El Bosque just a few miles from home. I was good at it. It taught me a lot. More than anything, it taught me how to become invisible. Who remembers a forecourt attendant? You're just a uniform and a smile: part of the service.

"Fill her up, sir? Regular or sport, miss? Clean your windows and your lights while you wait? If you'll just pop the hood, I'll check your oil and your radiator. Loose petcock there, sir. I'll tighten that for you and . . . Yep, you'll be due a new fan belt pretty soon. I can fit that for you before you go if you like. Rain forecast for tomorrow, madam, if you'd like a wax job. Protects the metalwork! And when's your birthday if you don't mind me asking, sir? Ah, a Taurus! I'll get you one of our promotional astrological glasses. No, they're absolutely free with each fill-up from now until December. My pleasure, miss! No, thank *you*."

I was happy at the station, my chamois rag in my back pocket, my tools on a leather utility belt. Some people hate the smell of gasoline, but I liked it. The oil, too, and the smell of new rubber. I'd practice flirting with the prettier young ladies, and they'd let me because it was safe out on the forecourt, me in my smart Arco uniform. I was subservient. I was the help. Society had placed me lower than them. I was no threat. They could drive away and watch me grow smaller, less significant, in their rearview. If they noticed me at all. I'd already vanished the moment they'd closed the car door.

Tom, the owner of the place, liked me a lot because I did what he told me to. He said I sold more spark plugs, wax jobs and fan belts than any other attendant he'd employed. I was just being observant and thorough. Before long, he'd let me do the late-night shifts on my own.

His sister, the co-owner, didn't like me so much. She was curt and impersonal whenever she had to talk to me. I once heard them arguing about me when I was in the restroom.

"He looks at me funny, Tom. There's something off about Sonny. I don't know what it is, but he gives me the creeps."

"He's just a nervous kid. He's shy. You don't have to be his friend. He's a good worker. Let me handle him if you don't like him. I don't want you pushing him away. I need to work fewer nights. Are *you* going to do them?"

"It's not only me. A few customers have mentioned it. Women."

"He likes to flirt! He's young and full of jissum, God! Like any young man."

"It's not that. It's like he's not looking at you as a person. Like he's looking at a cat or, I don't know, a can of soup that he might or might not want to eat. Like you don't really exist. He's not seeing you. He's seeing something else."

"A can of soup? Jesus, Maxine! You need to talk to Doctor Jameson about upping your dosage."

"You go to hell, Tom!"

They switched hastily to talking about till rolls when I came out of the restroom, Tom nodding a greeting, his sister reddening and avoiding my eyes. I had soup that day for lunch at the diner across the street, but I didn't think about murdering her. I wasn't ready for that yet.

I loved working nights. There was almost no custom and I had the whole place to myself. It was on nights that I started killing animals again – probably the first sign, though I didn't recognize it at the time.

There'd been a couple cats when I was eight or nine, but the real slaughter started at Grandmother's when they bought me the

.22 rifle and let me run wild. They had no idea what I was up to and they didn't care as long as I left them alone. I must have killed thousands of birds, gophers, cats and squirrels that summer. Mice. Rabbits. I'd stalk them. I'd wait hours sometimes, totally immobile, the long barrel pointing at the entrance to their burrow and the moisture from the ground soaking into my clothes. They knew I was there. They could probably smell me. But I wasn't going to let them win. They had to come out to eat at some point and . . . *BANG*. I opened their heads. I was a crack shot. I could shoot a bird right out of the sky nine times out of ten.

At the station, this particular ginger-colored cat started to come in. It was insolent, striding across the forecourt like it owned the place. One time, it did a shit by pump four, looking at me the whole time as if to say, "Fuck you, Sonny." I had to clean that up with a shovel and the hose. I didn't get it that time.

Instead, I rigged up a kinda trap for it: a balanced plank with one end over the barrel we used for all of the dirty oil drained out of pans. I put some tinned tuna fish on the end of the plank over the barrel and weighted it just right so that if the cat walked to the end to eat the fish, it'd tip the balance and drop right into the barrel.

Well, it worked perfectly first time. I kept mostly out of sight, but I could see the end with the bait. As soon as it went into the barrel, I rushed over and caught it trying to scrabble up the side, this black-bedraggled thing with its green eyes urgent. Not so insolent now, eh? *I'm* the boss of this gas station! Each time it looked like it was going to get purchase on the side, I'd push its paws away with the end of the plank.

I'll give it credit: it was a fighter. Cats usually are. But the lights of a car swept over the forecourt and I couldn't waste any more time. I hit it sharply on the head a couple times with my ball-peen hammer – difficult because it was bobbing unsupported – and left it to serve the customer. I later threw the body down a storm drain a few blocks away and called into the late-night bar on Jackson for a couple beers before going home.

THR3E

Well, that was me in early '70, a month or two before it all started. There were others. They were close. One of them – a local – was actually an occasional customer, though I didn't know it at the time. I'll get to him. Another was living a quite different life up in Frisco.

THREE

Dwight Paulson was renting a room in a flophouse in the Tenderloin and he was already insane.

These weren't the incense-scented, flower-children-happy streets of Haight-Ashbury. This was the late-nite jazz district of strip joints and prostitution, needles on the sidewalk and dealers under bridges. Every second storefront was a pawnshop. Buy-Sell-Trade. Live Nude Girls. Polk and Taylor were populated by outrageous hair fairies after midnight, screaming queens fighting with bottles, their make-up smeared bloody. Queers and sissies gravitated to the YMCA on Embarcadero to pick up young navy boys drunk on Thunderbird and curious, take them dancing and blow them in some piss-puddled alley off Turk. The residential hotels would let a room an hour at a time if they had capacity.

Skinny, pale and runtish, Dwight looked the part – like a Tenderloin junkie – but his poison was pot and acid, kept at a pretty constant dosage so he was high all the time. Like many of the long-hair drop-outs, he spent hours on a bare mattress reading astrology or the Kriya mysticism of Paramahansa Yogananda. But his real passion, then as now, was to write.

It wasn't writing as you might understand it. Not stories or diaries. What he called his notebooks were simply an obsessive compulsion to write anything and everything that occurred to him. They were a release valve for the noise inside his head. Tiny, condensed text. No errors. Each letter consistently sized and formed as if printed – madness teletyped. Disorder ordered. After he'd filled a page horizontally from left to right, he might write vertically up the margins as a frame.

MONDAY 12 January, 1970, Hyde Street Hotel, Hyde St., San Francisco, California, USA. 50°F and overcast. 10:05AM. Scrambled eggs and waffles at the Fill-Up Café. Coffee hotter than usual because, they said, the cups were steam cleaned before being filled. Maple syrup jug disagreeable and the whorish old waitress told me to f*** off when I gave her a piece of my mind...

Dwight passed his days over in hippie central: Haight-Ashbury. The Tenderloin was black leather, frayed collars and worn soles, but hippie central was velvet jackets, fringed buckskin and kaftans. Patches and paisley. It was barefoot, beards, beads and headbands. Braless girls and stoned. The kids wore orange on Haight and walked with bells around their necks or on their sandals. No orange or bells on Hyde Street unless you wanted your head kicked in.

Even in '70, there were bus tours through the district so the squares could photograph the freaks and return to Idaho or Kansas or wherever to tell their redneck neighbors about the Revolution. Maybe take a souvenir lapel button back for Uncle Todd: Trust Yourself. God is on a Trip. Fly Trans-Love Airways. "You shoulda seen 'em, Todd! These young things strumming guitars and playing tambourines out on the sidewalk, all misty-like in clouds of incense and pot smoke!" And Uncle Todd'd grunt his disapproval, never having shared his WWII bayonetting horrors or news of the tumor growing in his balls that'd kill him before the winter was out.

Dwight was briefly cool when he shaved his head and went about, Ho Chi Minh-style, in a green robe and Fu Manchu mustache. But generally, Dwight was pretty weird even among the pothead acid-droppers. He wore a sequined sombrero and torero boots one week, speaking in a fake Mexican accent and carrying a dented mariachi trumpet he couldn't have played even if it'd had a mouthpiece. Another time, he wore a rummage-store three-piece suit, strutted with a cane and said he was an English lord, accent and all (but no shoes).

One time at a party after a Turk Park happening, he'd suggested to a Chinese girl that they get married and breed – like, *right now. Tonight* – to create an oriental-occidental master race that'd combine her spirituality with his western rationality. Ying and yang. Her ylang-ylang, his wang. She got nervous and some of the other brothers had to step in.

"Like, she doesn't dig your rap, man. Leave the sister alone."

Dwight pulled a knife and started carving space around him.

"Like, aggression is not the answer, man. Don't you see that?"

They'd had to throw a blanket over him and wrestle him to the ground, hitting him as non-violently as possible until they could prize the knife from his hand and kick him out. A Puerto Rican kid offered to shank him and teach him a lesson, but instead one of the sisters took Ricardo to the love room to distract him. Nobody was going to call the police.

Dwight came back with a Samurai sword about half an hour later and tried to get in again, slashing and stabbing at the door as they watched him, distorted, through the peephole, pushing each other aside to look and wondering if this was part of a trip. God knows where he got a sword. He must have walked from home with it or gone a few stops by bus, grasping its lacquered scabbard like some bushido Dadaist. Only in Frisco. They would have shot him in New York. *Hey – you wid the sword! Freeze!*

He was arrested later that night, but for public intoxication. The sword must've been lost or discarded. He wasn't normally a drinker, but he'd drunk on top of the acid and the pot. He might have gotten more of a beating if his hair hadn't been so short after the monk phase. They threw him in the drunk tank.

Well, there was some fuss that night. Early hours, fluorescent lights stark and buzzing, guard dozing with his head back and mouth open. The other prisoners – a young black boy with a bloodied lip, a middle-aged wife-beater, a classic wino with a nicotine-yellow beard – were sleeping when Dwight walked over barefoot-silent and stood looking down at the black youth on his bunk. He knelt, touched the boy's cheek and started to kiss him.

"The fuck, man!" swatting Dwight away. "What you *doin'* Get offa me!"

"Quiet in there! You want me to come in?"

"This honky motherfucker tryna kiss me, man!"

Dwight was still on his knees by the bunk. He looked affronted, like all he was trying to do was kiss a sleeping black man and what was wrong with that?

The guard came to the bars, his nightstick out. "If I have to open this door . . ."

'Hey, fruit-fly!" called the wife beater, gummy-eyed and mean on the edge of his cot. "Wake me up for this bullshit, will ya? Come over here and *I'll* give ya a kiss."

Did Dwight really expect a kiss from the guy? Was he that stoned or naïve? He stood and ambled over into a sharp right hook that sat him on his ass, dazed, nose bleeding.

"Get up. I dare you," said wife beater, on his feet and dancing. He'd been interrupted prematurely in his earlier domestic disturbance. Fucking neighbors.

"Hit him again!" encouraged the black boy, also on his feet for the show.

"Right. That's it," said the guard. He turned down the corridor. "Guys? Wanna come down to holding one? We got a situation."

Three of them came into the cell swinging their nightsticks.

"I din't do *nuthin*, man! Why you beatin'on *me*?"

"Gimme one of them sticks and I'll take ya all," promised wife-beater.

Dwight said nothing, curled on the floor covering his head and, it seemed, singing some reedy, high-pitched tune to himself. A mantra, maybe.

The wino slept through it all.

It was easier to just release him at dawn. More trouble than he was worth. Just another acid head voyaging through interplanetary dimensions. Goddamn hippies.

Dwight was sharing his Hyde Street room with a young man from back east. Sixteen, possibly seventeen, Kenny was a junkie who'd come for the Revolution and ended up on smack selling his ass in the Tenderloin. He'd become something like a mascot among a group of Hells Angels who didn't pay him but fed him, which kept him alive whether or not that's what he wanted.

Kenny woke to Dwight rummaging in his groin.

"Leave it, man. Lemme sleep. I didn't get in until three . . . Fuck, Dwight! I said leave me alone! What's *wrong* with you?"

Kenny pushed him away and reached for the lamp, only now seeing the dried blood on Dwight's face and head.

"Shit," he said. "Cops?"

Dwight seemed not to hear, intent on pulling off Kenny's shorts.

"Stop it! Stop it! You're fucking crazy, man. Look, I'm going. I'm leaving today. I can't take any more of your shit."

Dwight stood and dropped his pants.

"Fuck. Not this again. . ." said Kenny.

Dwight took a hit on his joint and touched its glowing tip to the end of his penis, barely flinching – just staring at the ashy singe mark.

The upstairs residents banged on the floor. Sounded like a shoe this time.

"You need to see someone, Dwight. I'm serious."

Kenny left later that day. Standing in the doorway, leather holdall over his shoulder, he said, "Good luck, man. Hope you figure it all out."

Dwight was unresponsive, cross-legged on the floor and meditating, his thumbs and forefingers pinching circles atop his knees. He looked calm. Like the Buddhist monk Thích Quảng Đức aflame, but amid the invisible fire of his psychosis.

THR3E

WEDNESDAY 15 April, 1970, Hyde Street Hotel, Hyde St., San Francisco, California, USA. 61°F and cloudless. Apx. 02:41PM. A group of Hells Angels told me to dance for them and I refused. They beat me to the ground, stomping me and spitting on me until the police came and arrested all of us. I passed out before reaching the station and woke up in hospital. . .

Alone in his flophouse room, Dwight dropped acid and smoked pot and beat on the floor with his hands, screaming and trying to get through to the voices he was hearing. The landlord finally opened the door and stood there with two uniformed cops, the three of them looking at him naked and shit-smeared and tearful, asking, "Can you hear them? Can you hear them?"

He was going to the psych ward, but that was just a temporary stop. Dwight was coming home – home to Buena Vista County.

FOUR

As for Joe Wilder, he was already in Buena Vista and ostensibly the most normal-seeming – at least in the beginning. He was off work, recuperating at home after a pretty bad auto wreck in which he'd gone clear through the windshield and out onto the road, lying there unconscious amid the tail light glow and shattered-glass glitter. He had a broken collarbone and was a mass of bandages when he woke up. Also, he was blind.

The docs said his sight should come back in a couple weeks if he was lucky. So he lay in bed and his young wife Sally brought food and fed him like he was a baby, feeding their new baby the same way and sometimes at the same time, the infant propped between Joe's arm and ribs. "Like a momma bird coming back to the nest and finding the chicks with their mouths open, cheeping," she said.

He hated being an invalid. He'd never been a momma's boy, never spoiled or fussed over. He looked like the mechanic he was: burly, square-handed, thick-armed. He had tattoos back when only sailors, prisoners and bikers had tattoos – a legacy of his delinquent days. Sally'd ask him about his ink and he'd lie about what they meant or where he'd got them. The whore that gave him clap. His father's car. The buddy they'd beaten to death as he watched, cowardly, from that corrugated rooftop, pissing himself with fear and trying to stop it running down to give his position away.

The attraction between Joe and Sally had been mutual and instant, though she'd been married at the time and working at the diner across the street from McGraw's auto shop, where Joe fixed cars. He'd go in lunchtimes and she'd bring him a coffee right away (cream, two sugars) without him having to order it. It was an animal thing, neither of them talking about it much until they were practically living together.

Joe had night terrors at the start, waking up sweating, hyperventilating, crying, struggling to break free of the sheets. Sometimes he'd shout, but it was unclear what. He also wet the bed for the first three months. Sally didn't ask. She guessed there was a lot of stuff in his past and she waited. It'd come out in good time. When he was ready. All she had to do was love him enough.

The sleepwalking was a little more worrying. He kept a Smith & Wesson .38 in the top dresser drawer to protect the family. He'd sometimes try to get it in the night, muttering and fumbling at the curved wooden lip of the drawer.

"Come back to bed, Joe," she'd say, sitting up in bed, and he'd look at her without seeing, saying something that might have been addressed to her or to someone in a dream or in the past or in the ground. He was a different person when he sleepwalked – his face different. Tense. Anxious. There was an urgency to him in the darkness, his naked body pale in the slats of streetlight through the blinds.

Funny thing, though. Blind as he was, he could navigate the house perfectly fine in his sleep, skirting the furniture like he had 20/20 vision. In daytime, he'd be barking his shins and walking stooped over, fingers out probing for edges and seatbacks, cursing.

They were a week into his blindness when he woke up with the terrors, the mattress hot and wet. Sally placated him.

"I . . . I need to tell you something, Sal."

"Tell me, hon. Anything." Talking quietly to not wake the baby.

"I'm afraid you'll leave me if you know."

"You know I'll never leave you."

"You might. You left Robert for less."

"He was worthless. You're a man." Wondering meantime what would be a reason to leave Joe – something he'd done that'd provoke this confession and the rest. There were things you couldn't forgive a man. Anything to do with kids. Torture.

"I killed a guy."

"Come on, Joe. You wouldn't do that. I know you."

"You know me *now*. You didn't know me back when I was angry and drinking."

"What happened?" Thinking maybe it was just a fight and no one really died. And anyway, a person could get killed a lot of ways. That didn't make it murder.

"I was out with some guys. We'd been drinking. We came back to Jed's house and we heard screaming. The street door was open. We all ran in and there was a guy raping his sister, or trying to, on the floor in front of the TV. Had her down on the floor, her panties round her ankles, wrestling to get himself between her legs while she fought him. We just all laid into him at the same time. Didn't have to think about it. Jed hit him with a chair and he rolled off the sister and then we . . . we kinda stomped him to death. It was a frenzy thing. Just . . . legs everywhere. I know I stamped on his throat 'cause I saw his eyes bulge when I did it. I kicked him in the head four, five times with my steel toecap boots on – from the demolition job, you know. I felt the skull crunch. And then we all stood over him, breathing heavy. He was lying totally still face-up, his eyes open and kinda staring, and Jed's girlfriend said something like, "You've killed him!" And Jed said – I remember it exactly – "Cover yourself, Charlene," 'cause one of her tits was almost out of her dress."

Sally looked at him, holding back her questions.

"None of us was gonna call the police. There'd been a crime, a rape, and we'd stopped it. That was all. We put the body in some plastic sheeting and we waited until about 3am. and we drove out to a place over the ocean and threw it down the cliff."

"When was this?"

"Almost ten years ago. We were just kids."

"Did they find the body?"

"About a month later. It'd come out of the sheeting and was pretty rotten. The seabirds had been at it. Ants, wasps, you know. They chalked it up to suicide or a fall. Something like that. An accident."

"Well," said Sally, "he *was* a rapist, Joe. And you don't know for sure it was you who killed him. It was a group thing. Maybe one of the other guys . . ."

"It was me. I know it. I'm a murderer, Sal."

"You saved a girl from being raped, just like you'd save me. It was an accident."

"You don't hate me?"

"You didn't want to do it. Things just got out of hand. Murderers do it 'cause they want to, or 'cause they enjoy it. I don't know. What you did . . . it's like running someone down with your car. You don't want it. You don't expect it and you feel bad after."

"I do feel bad."

"That shows you're a good person."

"I see guys in the paper or on the TV – killers, you know – and I think . . . I'm the same as them."

"You're not the same, Joe. I don't think less of you. It was ten years ago. It's like a dream you had once. Hush now and try to get some sleep. Come over on my side. Put your arms around me."

And she lay there thinking she was in the arms of a murderer. The world had not ended. He was the same guy. He'd done what any man would've done. What other option did they have, those boys? Call 911 and wait for the car to come while they watched the rapist finish? Sometimes you had to act. Accidents happened. But Joe *was* a murderer. Better that he'd used his feet. It'd be different to hold his hands or feel them on her and imagine that they'd strangled or stabbed, or something worse. Funny how easily it could be explained away. Like she said: a dream. A nightmare you can wake up from.

Joe hadn't mentioned the voice to her. It'd spoken soon after he woke up in the hospital – his own voice, kind of, but from a different, deeper place. *"You'll die if you drive again,"* and, *"Don't ever drive again."*

It wasn't a thought. It was a voice from outside. He *heard* it. Still in darkness then, he'd actually replied to it. "Who's that?" Thinking someone was in the room with him. "Who's there?"

It didn't speak again right after that, but he knew he hadn't dreamed it. Maybe it'd been a doctor or one of the paramedics who'd brought him in, except it didn't sound as if it'd come from inside the room. He'd been raised a Catholic and he wondered in his blindness, in the waves of pain and numbness, if an angel had been speaking to him.

It'd soon have much more to say. More things he wouldn't want to share with Sally.

FIVE

I hadn't yet killed a woman. The urge hadn't entered my conscious will. But I'd stopped picking up male hitchhikers and was choosing exclusively young girls and women, learning my type.

The guys down at Atascadero had talked about their types. Brunettes, blonds, redheads. Petite. Big-boned. Was I a tit man, a leg man or an ass man? I didn't know. All I knew was that I had six years of hormones backed up.

I picked them all up at first and worked on a catalogue of types. The outright hippie girls, as I said, were feral and exuded a vulgar, animal sexuality. They wore no bras and often no undergarments (I could see the pubic hair coming out of the crotch of their shorts or as their miniskirts rode up on the car seat). In truth, they frightened me. The man should be dominant.

I liked the more modest girls who wore feminine clothes: dresses, blouses, skirts to the knee or even form-fitting pants that showed a little hip and thigh. *Demure,* you might say. When they smiled, it was a genuine smile – not the lurid, promiscuous leer of the hippy.

I was learning to talk to them in a way that they wouldn't see my desperation to know them and have them like me. The problem was, they were wary. There'd been a few sexual assaults and some rapes of coeds who'd accepted lifts from guys. But there were still a lot of girls hitching. You'd pass dozens strung out along the street and you just had to choose. It was like a drive-thru.

I learned tricks. I made myself look unthreatening and older in thick-framed glasses. I spoke to them casually through the rolled-down window, like I didn't care if I picked them up or not, looking at my watch and frowning. "Well, it's out of my way, but . . ." It was easier if they were holding a homemade sign with their destination on it.

Of course, a lot of them would only hitch in pairs. That gave them confidence and it made things more difficult for me. I'd have to try and form some connection with both of them and they'd sometimes be exchanging looks between them, one of them in the back, like, "Get a load of this guy trying to hit on us!" Or rolling their eyes. When that happened, I'd get this crazy impulse to accelerate and accelerate – the girls screaming, "What are you doing, mister?" – head-on into a tree and kill us all, using my last breath of life to turn to her in the passenger seat, her neck broken, windshield shards in her face, coughing blood maybe, and say, "*Now* roll your eyes!" But I didn't want to die.

They were more confident than I was – so at ease with themselves. It was their world and I was just a recent arrival in it. They were happy and carefree. But they were also dismissive and privileged. I'd stopped for them and made time to take them where they needed to be, but they treated me like a taxi driver when they found out I wasn't one of them. I wasn't studying at the university. I didn't know who Jefferson Airplane was.

"So what do you do, Sonny?"

"I work at the Arco on Dyer and Sloat."

"Like, pumping gas?"

"Yeah. That's a part of it. I also do wax jobs and fit spark plugs, fan belts. . . oil changes. You know."

"Uh huh."

And that was it: invisible. They'd talk to each other like I wasn't there, about what John Lennon said, or something Vonnegut had written. Newscasts from another planet. I was just a gas monkey – no better than the Mexican who cut their father's lawn. I'd appreciate the value of this later. Only later.

I was learning, slowly, that my type was the intelligent, well-dressed, well-spoken girl. Respectful, but entirely superficially so. Confident. Worldly. A bright future ahead of her. Trusting. The kinda girl I'd like to murder and then have sex with. Because, clearly, there was no possibility of anything happening between us if she was conscious or breathing.

I started to feel a sense of power just having them in the car with me. The Galaxie – more than the house I shared with my rummy mother – was my home and my world. As soon as the door closed, they were mine. They'd ceased to walk upon the earth. Their existence had changed so subtly that they didn't notice, but so powerfully that they'd relinquished their destinies to my control. I could take them anywhere I wanted to. Stepping into my car was stepping through a portal. Nobody knew where they were – not their parents, not their friends. They could vanish.

One Sunday, I'd been down on the boardwalk, strolling in the sun and having a few beers on the terraces, and I came upon a couple very pretty young ladies. I was wearing my heeled boots and a fringed buckskin jacket and new Levis (I'd got a good sales bonus that month) and I was feeling pretty spiffy. I saw them looking at me as I walked past and I offered to buy some drinks. They were my type, flirting with me, asking if I had a girlfriend. Really, they were playing with me, gently mocking me. There was no intention, no interest. But they *were* my type and finally I offered to drive them home, wherever that may be, not caring too much if I had to drive to Berkeley or Santa Cruz or wherever just to spend some more time with them.

Well, they lived in the nice part of Buena Vista, in the northern hills, and I pulled up alongside the mailbox. The family name was right there: Schumer.

"Is that *Lieutenant* Schumer?" I said, almost kinda to myself. "Sheriff's Department?" Amber mentioned him sometimes and I'd seen his name in the papers.

"My dad," she said. "You'd better get along in case he's home. He hates me hitching."

I wasn't angry at being dismissed like that. I drove home thinking that I'd had a detective's daughter in my car. I'd had her life in my hands and there's nothing he could have done. He didn't even know. I could have abducted her. She could have ended up buried in the forest. That was power. Who would have known? I mean, sure, I would've had to kill the other girl as well.

These thoughts were purely abstract – like a game I was playing with myself. Thoughts, like fantasies and dreams, can be anything in the darkness of the mind. Nobody can see them. Nobody knows. They're not real. I learned that, too, at Atascadero.

Detective Schumer had been investigating a local case in which a coed's car had been found empty up in the state park and the girl herself was missing. Some pretty outlandish theories had been thrown around: that she'd stopped for a toilet break, gone off into the woods and been taken by a mountain lion. There *were* lions about, but no trace of an attack was found near the car where she would've gone to pee. One thing was clear: she'd stopped, or been stopped, by someone who must have had a car. I couldn't see a woman stopping to help at a breakdown (I'd seen how clueless the female Arco customers were about engines). Nobody had said it so far, but it could've been a California Highway Patrol car.

I'll come clean right now and say I've always respected the police. I never missed an episode of *Police Story*. I didn't hold any grudges that they'd put me away for killing my grandparents. I deserved it. I'd committed a crime. Even at Atascadero, all of the guys would watch the cop shows. It was kinda like a distance-learning course for them: how not to leave evidence, how to create a good alibi, how to get through an interrogation. How never to tell *anyone* what you'd done. We talked a lot about all of that. Police shows and cartoons were pretty much the only time you'd get respectful silence in the TV room.

I guess that's why I applied to the CHP soon after I got out. I'd spoken to my parole officer about employment and we'd decided together that the things I liked were: order, guns and driving. The CHP turned me down, of course. Even though my criminal record was supposed to be sealed, I'm sure they got access to it. What could I expect? A teenaged double-murderer and subsequent mental patient in a CHP uniform? I could kinda see their point.

Maybe that's why I started going to the Holding Cell, the downtown bar where most of the cops used to hang out. At first, I'd just drink at the bar and listen to them, imagining I was in an episode of *Police Story*. One of the guys. They'd sometimes talk about active cases, looking around to make sure nobody was listening. I'd pretend I was reading the paper. They got to know me from the Arco station because Tom had a deal with the county and I'd see them often as they were going out to interview a witness or visit a crime scene. A few times, they'd come through with someone cuffed in the back and their manner was all professional – no joking with me like they usually did.

When they found out that Amber was my sister, it was like I became almost part of the police family. They'd say stuff like, "Hey, Sonny – you got any outstanding parking tickets? Get me a date with your sister and I'll see that they're wiped!" or, "How'd Amber get all the good looks in your family?" and someone else'd say, "She sure got all the ass!" and we'd laugh, men together.

It was different for me in the Holding Cell after I picked up the Schumer girl and dropped her off safely. Previously, I'd been in awe of the guys and allowed myself to feel less than them. But who really had the power? I'd had Lieutenant Schumer's daughter in my passenger seat and he had no idea. I'd had her life in my hands. His badge and his gun had no authority over what he couldn't know. He lived in a different world from me.

I imagined being in the bar if his daughter had gone missing, buying him a beer and saying, all casual, something like, "Any news, Ed? We're all pulling for you." Or maybe, "Say, Ed – wasn't she wearing those cute suede boots on the day she disappeared?"

"How'd you know that, Sonny?"

"Nothing. I just saw her down on the boardwalk that morning."

"You see her get into anyone's car?"

"No, sir. I was just having a beer in the sun."

They would never have suspected me: dumb Sonny the gas monkey who dreamed of being a cop. A murderer was supposed to be a wild-eyed lunatic who made people cross the street. You'd know a killer as soon as you looked him in the eye. That's how people thought back then.

I thought a lot about buying a gun. Not to kill – just to have one. I could go out to the forest and shoot animals, or maybe keep it at the station for the night-shift cats and dogs. But I didn't know how it'd work with the paperwork. I'd have to make a declaration that I wasn't a convicted felon and didn't have any history of mental illness. I mean, the record was sealed, but look what had happened with my CHP application. I didn't want to buy a gun and be turned down, or – worse – have the police sniffing around, knocking on my door. I had nothing to hide, but my mother would never let it go. I could hear her: "What you need a gun for? Planning to kill me as well, huh? Have I got to put a lock on my door? Maybe I need a gun, too, to protect me from my murderer son."

Instead, I bought a knife from a thrift store. I don't know why I did that rather than buy a new one. It sure wasn't over the few bucks I saved. I wondered later if it was a case of traceability. I'd be able to argue in court that it was a used knife and that any previous owner could've . . . Knives were never really my thing. Sure, I had one as a kid. Everyone had one. It was practically a toy back then. We'd use them for carving names in trees, whittling sticks, acting tough. Every American boy had a knife.

And, sure, I'd stabbed my grandmother after shooting her in the head, but that was just curiosity – to see how it felt. The blade bent the fourth time, so I knew I now needed something with a hefty blade. I ended up buying a Bowie-type thing almost as big as a machete. It had a drop-point, hollow-ground blade, a blood groove and part of the back of it was serrated. Pretty mean looking. It came with a smart leather sheath and I'd wear it on my belt if I went into the state park – even if I didn't get out of the car.

Obviously, I didn't take it with me when I went to see the psychiatric social workers as part of my parole conditions. We'd talk about my job and what kind of dreams I was having – the same sort of deal as at Atascadero. I knew the script. I knew what to tell them. I knew the red flags and what sane was supposed to look like.

My Achilles heel was always going to be personal relationships and intimacy. They asked me if I had a girlfriend and I said I was trying.

"What kind of girl are you looking for, Sonny?" (Expecting me to describe some variant of my mother.)

"Well, you know . . . a pretty girl. A modest girl. Someone to go steady with, who'd be faithful."

"And if she wasn't faithful?" (Warning!)

"I guess it happens. I mean, I wouldn't be the only guy who'd been cheated on, right? It'd hurt. Sure."

A smile. "Would you give her a piece of your mind?"

"Like, raise my voice to her? Raise a hand? What'd be the point? Any girl who cheated on me wouldn't be the right one. Why waste the energy? I'd just be sad."

It was that easy. All I had to do was say the reasonable thing. Only a genuine lunatic would come out and say something like, "Well, doc, I'd cave her head in with a rock and fuck her one last time."

"And how are you getting on with your mother, Sonny?" (Warning!)

"I'm not gonna lie. There's some . . . friction sometimes."

Pen poised over his yellow legal pad. "Friction?"

"I'll tell you what it is. The last time she saw me, I was fifteen years old. I was a kid. I sometimes think I'm still that kid in her mind. She'll tell me to brush my teeth, for example, or ask me if I've changed my shorts – that kinda thing. But I'm a man now. You know my history. I was among men all that time at the hospital. They treated me like an adult and I learned to look after myself."

"How do you handle that? The teeth-brushing. The friction."

"Well, one of us has to be an adult, right?" A smile. "I try to understand it from her perspective. It can't be easy for her, getting her son back after six years – her son who, let's be honest, killed his grandparents. Maybe I'm an embarrassment to her. Maybe that's the real source of her anger – not my teeth or my shorts."

The pen scribbles away. "I think you have a very healthy attitude, Sonny."

Sure I did. It was exactly what they wanted to hear.

I came away from that session understanding a couple very important things. First, I needed a girlfriend. Not just sex. Not *even* sex. A girlfriend would be my badge of normality. A steady job. A few beers down the Holding Cell with the guys. A sweetheart and maybe an engagement ring further down the line. The American Dream. Get those things established and you could kill as many as you liked without anyone asking questions.

That, and the fact that my mother would have to die.

SIX

Dwight was back at home with his parents and taking chlorpromazine for the undifferentiated schizophrenia they'd diagnosed in Frisco. Or maybe it was just all the LSD he'd been taking; the symptoms were virtually identical. He'd have to stop taking the acid to be completely sure, but he was dropping it more consistently than the schizo drug because it calmed him. You could get it about as easily as tobacco in Buena Vista at that time.

More concerning for the docs in the city had been his uncontrolled homosexual tendencies and the penis-burning business. Was he a sexual deviant? The days of Dr. Walter Freeman's ice-pick lobotomies had not completely passed among the psychiatric community. The newer thing was aversion therapy. Dwight would have been shown gay pornography and fed emetics at the same time, so he vomited on himself as staff verbally abused him. Then he'd be shown 'healthy' hetero porn (the shameful objectification and humiliation of women being more acceptable) with no punishment. Maybe they also fed him laxatives and left him to wallow in his own filth for a few days, restrained in his bed and screaming. More likely, given the burning behavior, they would've used the penile plethysmograph, its electrodes administering scarring shocks when he responded to the wrong stimuli. I'd seen or heard it all before. The wonders of psychiatry. The price of normality.

His parents gave him things to occupy him, but also to get him out of the house – at a safe distance. He spent a whole afternoon meticulously cutting the lawn with the petrol mower, then on his hands and knees with his mother's dressmaking shears.

"What's that, Dwight?" said his father, looking at the swirling design in the grass.

"Yin and yang," said Dwight. "The eternal equilibrium."

After that, they sent him further afield: into town for groceries, or up into the state park to gather firewood. It was up there he got arrested the first time.

A forest ranger found him sitting in a yoga position, stripped to the waist and oblivious. His torso was covered in homemade tattoos: blue-black scrawls depicting animals or astrological signs. 'Acid,' said his left pectoral. 'Mary J,' said his right bicep. He had a hunting knife in a sheath beside him.

"Sir – could you show me some ID?" No response. "Sir? Are you under the influence of any intoxicating substances?"

Dwight's hand moved slowly toward the knife as if in a dream, his eyes still closed.

"Okay. Put your hands up," said the ranger.

His father picked him up from the cells downtown. There'd be no charges because he'd not broken any laws this time and because he was clearly loco. They rode back mostly in silence, the father's mouth fixed, knowing any attempt at conversation would be a losing battle. He'd lost his real son three years before to lysergic acid diethylamide. The kid in the passenger seat was Dwight Paulson only in name and appearance – a *Twilight Zone* version, a *Body Snatchers* copy grown in a hallucinogenic pod. Was it bad to wish he'd never come back from the city?

The docs had said they should try to be as normal as possible with him and establish patterns. One of the first weekends after he returned, they asked his sister and her husband round for dinner – all the family back together, candles on the table, meatloaf and chocolate chip ice cream. Strained smiles and forced conversation.

"So, Dwight . . . how is it in the big city?" asked his brother-in-law.

"It's corrupt and rotten. There's a lot of Angels selling junk."

"Junk? Like scrap metal?"

"He means heroin," said the sister, signaling with her eyes to change the subject. "Why don't you help me with the melon, Dwight? Come to the kitchen."

He stood watching her carve green-skinned red crescents.

"You wanna ball?" he said.

The knife paused, but she didn't look up at him. "I'm your sister, Dwight. Think about it."

He appeared to think about it. Was there still some part of him that recognized incest was wrong? Some vestige of normality inside that he'd find if he looked hard enough? Maybe he'd forgotten who his family was.

"What about Mark? Would he want to ball?"

"My husband? Really, Dwight? He's a man. You *do* know that, don't you?"

"Uh huh."

"Are you taking your pills?"

A giggle. "Yeah."

"I mean the chlorpromazine."

"Uh huh."

They were eating the meatloaf when they noticed Dwight was copying Mark's every movement. If he raised a fork, Dwight raised a fork. If he sipped a drink, Dwight sipped a drink. He didn't seem to be joking. He didn't even seem to be conscious he was doing it. Mark wiped his mouth. Dwight wiped his mouth. They all stopped and looked at Dwight, who was now grinning fixedly, teeth bared, eyes focused on nothing.

Dwight's mother and father looked at each other, his mother

watery-eyed. How much more of this could she take? Mental patient. Jailbird. Only God knew what else.

Dwight seemed frozen. He was sweating.

"Is it some kind of fit?" said Mark. "Like a . . . whaddya call it? A seizure?"

Father waved a hand in front of Dwight's face. No reaction. No recognition. He gestured to the kitchen and they all got up quietly from the table.

"We should call the psych ward and have him taken away," said father.

"We should wait a little and see if it passes," said sister.

"Is he dangerous?" said Mark. "I mean, that's the main thing."

They peeked around the door to look at Dwight, straight-backed and unmoving, his cutlery still grasped in his hands.

"Do you think he's in pain?" said mother.

"Is he taking his pills?" said sister. "They thought the LSD was causing a lot of it. If he's still on the acid . . . We could look in his room. Flush anything he's got."

Mark stayed in the kitchen, watching Dwight through the doorway. He'd cough if Dwight came back from wherever he was. The family went up to Dwight's room.

They looked under the bed and in the closet, checking bags and pockets. There was a stack of books from the town library: yoga, the macrobiotic diet, astrology, Mayan civilization, Einstein on peace, a biography of Michelangelo. Sister flicked the pages in search of acid blotter.

"Have you seen this?" said father, holding one of the notebooks open. Its pages were filled with tiny text so that barely a quarter inch of space showed anywhere, the words running vertically and horizontally.

"What does it say?" said mother.

"Nothing. It's just nonsense. Look."

TUESDAY 07 July, 1970, 214 Larch Street, Buena Vista (Home), California, USA. 72°F and sunny with light cloud. 03:02AM. Yin and yang in perfect balance. Need to eat more asparagus, avocado, eggplant, fennel, green peppers, plantains, potatoes, red peppers, spinach, sweet potatoes. Practiced carbon-cancel breathing for fifteen minutes . . .

"There's a pile of them like this," said father.

"Maybe it helps him," said sister.

"Is that what his mind's like?" said mother, looking at the page. "It seems so organized."

"The Nazis were organized," said father.

"That doesn't help, Pop."

A cough from the kitchen.

They left the room as they found it and went back to the dining room.

"I'm really beat," said Dwight. "Think I'll turn in."

Mother looked at the wood-framed clock. "But it's only–"

"Let him sleep if he's tired," said father.

They closed the door to finish dinner, the darkness of an insane son hanging heavy between candle flames.

"Maybe we should go to that family therapy group with him. Like they offered," said mother. "It might help."

"I'm not going to sit in a circle and sing kumbaya and tell strangers about my crazy kid," said father. "It's a private matter."

"You're ashamed," said sister.

"Who wouldn't be?" said father. "He's brought shame on this family."

They had no idea.

Joe got his eyesight back after a couple weeks like the docs said, but the light was intense and painful. He wore a pair of Sally's circular purple sunglasses she'd bought in the city. She said he looked like John Lennon.

"I'm not going back to work, Sal. I can't work with cars again."

"You're just leery, hon. It's normal after an accident. Give it time."

"I can't do it. They're instruments of death."

"Instruments of death?"

Not *his* words. The voice had told him. "Yeah. That's what they are."

"Fine. But what'll you do? My mom won't help us out forever and we can't live on my tips."

"I don't know." Maybe the voice'd tell him.

It was a week or so later when Sally's brother came from the city for a couple days. He was a corporate guy who flirted with the long-hair lifestyle like it was an alter ego. He was a pothead and took psychedelics at the weekend when it wouldn't affect his job. Peyote. Acid. Mescaline. Mushrooms.

"You gotta try it, Sal, Joe. It's like seeing the face of God."

"I don't know . . ." said Sal. "What if the effects don't wear off? What if you're, like, stuck in a trip? I've heard stories."

"You sound like one of the squares, sis! These drugs are all natural. They come from plants. If you're afraid, do it with another person to keep you steady and talk to you so you don't jump out the window."

"You said it was safe!"

"I'm joking! Almost nobody jumps out the window."

"I'm not gonna do it," said Sally. "I'm a mother. What kind of mother leaves her child sleeping while they're on drugs?"

"I've seen hippie chicks tripping while their kids were smoking pot. I've seen a five-year-old with a lid pestering his mom for acid."

"Exactly. That's not me. That's just wrong."

"Look – I'm gonna put a couple pills in this drawer here. See? It's mescaline – good stuff made in a lab up at Berkeley. If you wanna expand your universe, you know where it is. Open your mind!"

They didn't take the pills, but they didn't throw them in the trash.

Joe never went back to work. He was growing his hair and beard. He stopped washing so often and wore the purple sunglasses even inside the house. They'd once seemed funny, said

Sally, but now he was starting to look like Charles Manson. He'd stopped having the night terrors, but he was moody. Distant.

One time, she came home from work to find him sleeping in a chair. Surprised, he quickly hid a book he'd had open on his knees. She checked later between the cushions, expecting to find . . . What? Some kind of porn? It was the Bible: a small leather-bound copy with that rustly onionskin paper that seemed like it'd rip if you turned a page too quick. Joe'd never been religious, though some of his foster parents had been.

He was also spending more time outside the house. He looked like a mountain man with his plaid shirt, his hiking boots, his new beard and a knife sheath on his belt. He smelled like one, too.

"I'm gonna try that mescaline," said Joe one Friday afternoon.

Sally's friend LeeAnn had come over and they were chatting while the baby slept.

"Are you sure, hon?" said Sally. "Aren't you afraid?"

"A lotta people take it. How bad can it be?"

The voice had been telling him to take it. Occasionally at first. Just casually. *"Why not try that mescaline? Remember that mescaline in the drawer?"* Then more insistently until it was almost constant. *"Take it. Take it. Take it."*

"Why not take just a half?" said Sally. "Or a quarter? You don't know how strong it is."

"Yeah. Good idea."

Half. Joe broke the pill between dirty thumbnails and swallowed it with the beer he was drinking. A half-hour later, there seemed to be no effect.

"Maybe it got old," said Sally. "How long do they last?" Or maybe they sold her brother a dud. They probably looked at him in his hippie costume and his corporate hair and thought, yeah, this square'll buy anything if you tell him it was made by a PhD in a lab up at Berkeley."

"I'm gonna take the rest of it."

"Well, be careful, Joe. Sit down after. I'm here. We're here." Sally looked at LeeAnn like, We don't do this. We're not like that.

I'm just being a supportive woman, you know? Give him some slack while he gets back on his feet, however long that's gonna take . . .

Joe sat in his chair and waited. He blinked behind the purple lenses and closed his eyes. Stars were bursting in his brain like when you hit your head or stand up too quick, but without pain or disorientation. Millions of stars. A blizzard of stars. He was starting to melt, liquefying into the chair, oozing slowly into the spaces between the cushions. He gripped the armrests, hoping to stop the descent, but his fingers closed on warm marshmallow that flowed between them. He smiled.

"OK, Joe?"

"Uh huh."

He moved the sunglasses onto the top of his head. The room had started to swirl in magnificent color. The blank TV screen had become an ornate picture frame around a roiling, pearlescent vortex. The opposite wall was twenty thousand miles away, its clock face a glowing yolk-yellow sun. Glorious. The ceiling lifted like a box lid and liquid light poured in, white-blue and crystal, and the room was underwater but he could breathe. The rug rose and swam by him, an ultramarine manta ray. This was the firmament. This was the brilliance on the other side. It was from there the voice came to him, speaking now with the sound of many waters.

Sally was talking. "Yeah, that guy with the hunting cap! He tipped me four cents once. Four cents! I mean, I find more than that down the sofa cushions in a month . . ."

Joe stood. They looked. He had a strange, staring urgency. His body was rigid.

"Be not afraid!" he said.

"Are you okay, Joe?"

He raised his arms slowly like wings and looked up at the ceiling. "I am Ananiel, the watcher. I come to you with things that must shortly come to pass. I come to you from Pergamos, Thyatira and Leodicea."

"Joe? Why are you talking like that?"

"Hark! The time is at hand."

"Let me get you a glass of water. Maybe you should–"

"Do you want me to go?" said LeeAnn.

"I don't know . . . He's never taken anything like this before. We smoked pot a couple times last summer, but . . ."

Joe was standing with his arms out, smiling and looking around as if the room was full of people. "Name yourselves!" he said, "that you may be recorded in the Book of Life and pass unto eternity."

"It's Sally, hon." She looked nervously at her friend. "This is LeeAnn from the diner. You know her."

"Henceforth, you shall be Rebekah and Jochebed. I see rainbows luminous about you. You are chosen. Leave your earthly bodies behind. Where is the child that I might bless him?"

"He's sleeping, Joe. Best let him sleep."

"I am Ananiel! Bring me the child!"

"We shouldn't wake him . . . How about some coffee? I'll put a new pot on."

"Don't you understand? Those who aren't blessed must perish in the fire." He went toward the bedroom.

"Joe? Joe?"

The two women followed and found him standing at the drawers where he kept his .38. The top drawer was open. Sally had taken the bullets out the last time he'd been sleepwalking and put them inside a sock.

"Where are the bullets?" he said, looking into the cylinder's empty chambers.

Sally nodded to the baby in his cot and spoke quietly to her friend. "Take him to the other room."

The baby burbled and whined as LeeAnn carried him out the bedroom close to her chest.

"Where are the bullets? The trumpet has sounded. The time is upon us. I've seen the twenty-four elders in white raiment with gold crowns. I've seen the seven seals."

"Joe – you're frightening me. Why do you need the gun?"

"Abaddon cometh. The time is at hand. It's been foretold."

"Why're you talking crazy like this? This isn't you."

He found the bullets clinking in the sock and started to load them.

"Joe! I'm gonna call 911 if you don't stop this *right* now!"

He stopped. He looked at her, but didn't seem to see.

"I'll do it, Joe. I'm not joking."

He clicked the cylinder closed and turned to the cot. "Where is the child?"

"Right. That's it."

Sally went to the dining room and took the handset off the wall. She hesitated, looking at LeeAnn cradling the baby, looking back toward the bedroom door. She'd never dialed 911 before. She dialed the numerals.

"Yeah. It's my husband. He took . . . he's gone crazy and he's got a gun and he's looking for our baby and I'm scared. Yeah. It's 102 Durero . . ."

Joe went past her. He had the .38 in his hand and his hunting rifle on his shoulder. His brown leather jacket was over his arm. He went right out the door.

"Joe. Joe! Yes, yes, I'm still on the line . . ."

SEVEN

Finding a girlfriend was easier than I expected. A friend of Tom's sister came to the station about two days after I'd seen the psychiatrist and brought her daughter along. The two women left the girl alone in the office when they went out for drinks, saying, "Don't let *him* talk to her."

She was young – in her final year of high school – and innocent looking. Her family lived in a kinda private community up along the coast at Merluza and she seemed in awe of the downtown, the noise, the constant flow of traffic through the intersection. Tom got her a milkshake and she sat in the back waiting for her mother. Seeing her like that – shy, out of her element, formally polite – I knew she was perfect for me. She wore clean Levis and a white blouse. Her straw-colored hair was clean and held back with a blue-black Alice band. A virgin, I was sure.

"Hi. I'm Sonny."

"I saw you out front. You fill the cars, right?"

"Yup. Wash the windshields, check the oil, fill the radiators . . . It's a full service here at Arco." It was somehow easier to talk to her while I was at work and wearing the uniform. I was playing a role – the same way I did with all of the customers.

She laughed. "You talk like an ad."

"I *am* an ad. Look at this uniform. Do you like it?"

"It's okay." A little smile – not vulgar and leering like that whoreish bitch my mother set me up with. Like she was saying I was handsome in my uniform, but not reducing it to sex.

There was a calendar on the wall over Tom's desk: one of those cheesecake ones with a big-breasted bikini'd woman offering herself to a black column of tires. I felt like I should apologize for it.

"Say," I said. "I wonder if you'd like to go for a coffee or an ice-cream or something sometime? I've got a car. I could pick you up wherever and drop you back at home by nine or whatever."

"How old do you think I am, Sonny?"

"I don't know . . . Did I say the wrong thing?"

"I'm almost eighteen. And, sure, we could go out. I'd like that."

"Great." I'm sure I was blushing. "Well, I guess I should get back to the pumps."

"Aren't you going to ask me my name?"

"Uh . . . right! What's your name?"

"Promise you won't laugh?"

"Why would I? My parents were so imaginative that they called me Sonny."

"I'm Dulcimer."

"Huh?"

"Dulcimer. It's a musical instrument. Like a zither. A psaltery? I can see you have no idea what I'm talking about."

"I don't really know instruments . . ."

She shrugged. "My dad teaches music. He thought it'd be funny if everyone I ever meet greets me with a 'Huh?'"

"I like it. It sounds Spanish. *Dulce* means sweet, right?"

"You know Spanish?"

"Not really. I knew a Spanish guy once." Rodrigo the rapist murderer.

"Sonny!" called Tom. "There're people waiting out front!"

"Gotta go," I said to her.

"Here," she said, writing in ballpoint on the back of a carbon order pad. "This is my number."

I'd pretty much decided I was going to kill one of the girls I was now picking up almost daily in the car. The realization seems inevitable looking back, but it came slowly, an accumulation of thoughts and fantasies as I drove, their bodies just inches away from my hand.

The scenarios'd play out in my mind as they chattered away about whatever. I'd work on variations of a script, imagining both sides of the conversation.

"I have to tell you that we're not going to the campus."

Pause. The sound of the engine. Tires on asphalt.

"Huh? What'd you say?"

"You won't be going to the campus. I'm taking you somewhere else."

"But I gotta get to class. I'll be late."

"Well, you'll be late. Sorry about that."

"Are you that rapist? The one from the paper?"

They'd probably assume this. There'd been a lot about it in the press. There was a general awareness.

"I'm not a rapist. I'm not going to hurt you. We're just gonna get to know each other a little and then I'll take you where you wanna go . . ."

You had to control the situation. That's what the guys at Atascadero taught me. You can't come right out with it. That provokes instant panic. The threat has to be implicit. They might start screaming. You have to give them a glimmer of hope that they're gonna get out of it. Let them rationalize it to themselves: I might get away with jerking this guy off in the forest and then *definitely* no more hitching from here on in. Worse things happen at parties. Besides, this guy seems okay. He's polite. Doesn't seem like a rapist . . .

But I really needed a gun. Not necessarily to use, but to underline who was in control. You just have to show the gun initially to get their attention, but then you put it away, so they don't get fixated on it. You can even say something like, "I'm gonna put this away. I don't need this, do I?"

I went to Scott's Sporting Goods for the gun. I'd been looking at the Ruger for a long time, first in a magazine ad and then in the company catalogue I ordered by post. I would've ordered the gun itself by post, but Oswald had ordered his Kennedy-killing rifle mail order, so they'd banned that in '68. Mine was the rimfire semi-auto .22 with the six-inch barrel. It looked a little like a German Luger, a little like Napoleon Solo's spy gun, a little like a kid's ray gun. It had rubber grips and a blued finish. It's the gun I would've bought as a fifteen-year-old.

I didn't realize back then that it was a bad gun for my needs – for close-quarters, tactical use. The front sights were prominent so it could catch on a pocket lining in a quick draw. The two-stage trigger would later cause me problems and the rear bolt mechanism could jam. Meanwhile, the cartridges were ejected and could fly anywhere, leaving evidence. It was basically a target-practice gun. A revolver would've been a much better choice for me. One would fall unexpectedly into my hands later on.

I had to fill in a Record of Sale form at Scott's. By law, he couldn't sell firearms to fugitives, those under criminal investigation, those adjudged mentally ill or those who'd been committed to a mental institution. Well, I'd been released from a mental hospital as sane and my record had been sealed as a juvenile criminal. I was an adult now with a clean start. I didn't mention any of this and Scott told me to come back in two weeks to collect the gun, assuming no flags had been raised by the Sheriff's Department.

Two weeks never passed slower. Without even thinking about

THR3E

why, I bought a hatchet at Webster's. I didn't need a hatchet. I didn't do any gardening to speak of. Something was waking in me. I just saw it hanging there on its peg and it appealed to some aesthetic sense. I liked the shape. It was almost like a piece of art. I went into Frisco and bought a Polaroid camera, too.

Maybe I was getting ideas from the news. A lot of bad stuff was happening. More cars were being found with their female drivers missing. No bodies had yet been found. And there was this in the paper:

> BUENA VISTA POLICE HUNTING FOR RAPIST – Buena Vista police are searching for a rapist who has been assaulting female hitchhikers in the area for the last three or fourth months. Lt. Schumer said that seven young women were reportedly raped after accepting a ride from a young black man. Although different vehicles were used, said Lt. Schumer, it appears that the rapist was the same man, described as black, 20-30 years old, with a bushy – but not afro – hairstyle. The rapist's practice is to take victims to a secluded place and then return them to town after.

The guy was clearly an amateur. Not every rapist wants to kill, but he wasn't even wearing a disguise or a mask. Changing vehicle each time might've looked smart, but it probably suggested he worked with cars – detailing them, repairing them, scrapping them, driving them for a living. The cops'd be onto that already. They almost certainly had a composite sketch of him. It was also possible he was stealing the cars. Sometimes, the police kept details back from the press to root out all the loonies who wanted to take credit or get their brother-in-law thrown in jail or whatever. There are some pretty messed-up people out there.

I went on my first date with Dulcimer the day I collected the Ruger. We went for a meal down on the boardwalk and I had the sense I was almost divine as we drove down the coast from Merluza. Not just because she was there beside me, hair blowing through the open window, a picture of normality.

Whenever we passed people, I imagined what they were thinking. Stuff like: look at that guy out for a drive with his sweetheart. He's a lucky guy. Look at her hair blowing like that, carefree. A young couple with the world in front of them.

Also, I had the gun under my seat. It was talismanic. It made me taller. It made me omnipotent just knowing it was there. I didn't show Dulcie because not many girls are interested in guns. Also, she might have been frightened. There was no way I was gonna screw it all up just by showing off.

"There sure are a lot of hitchhikers," she said as we got closer to Buena Vista's downtown.

"Well, you know. There's the campus and the college. Around this time of week, they start thinking about going to visit their friends in the city, up at Berkeley. They have big parties."

"Do you pick them up?"

"Sometimes."

She turned to look at me, serious. "Girls?"

"Well, yeah, sometimes . . . but not like that. They usually travel in pairs and they don't talk to me. They talk to each other. I'm like a taxi driver for them. I only do it if I'm not in a hurry, or if it's raining, you know. I can stop picking them up if you don't like it . . . I mean, I don't have to do it."

"I'm joking! I think it's chivalrous stopping to help people in the rain. And there's that horrible rapist going round as well. Can you imagine? Some young girl wanting to get to class or whatever and then . . ." She shuddered.

"It's horrible. But they'll get him soon. He's leaving too much evidence."

"Yeah? Do you know about that stuff?"

"I watch all the cop shows. *Police Story*?"

"We don't have a TV. Dad says it poisons the brain."

"So, what do you do? In the evenings, I mean."

"We read. Play card games. I have to study as well, so, you know..."

"Sure."

"Did you go to college?

Six years in Atascadero was a rare education. I'm sure I learned more about the human mind and its telescoping corridors, its goblin chambers, its shadows than any psych major at UCBV.

"I wanted to," I said. "But my dad needed my help with the family business. This was when we lived in LA."

"What business?

Adultery? Divorce? Recrimination? Each of them trying to get rid of the kids rather than fighting for custody?

"Gas station," I lied. "I was born to pump gas, I guess."

"There's still time."

"Sure there is, Dulcie. Sorry... can I call you Dulcie?"

"People do."

We went to the Mexican place on the edge of the boardwalk and drank wine. I gave her my fringed buckskin jacket when the wind picked up off the sea. There was nothing vulgar in her. She'd never smoked a joint or dropped acid or peyote. She was afraid of such things, as she was afraid of crowds or noise or traffic. She saw danger everywhere.

I took a few pictures of her with the Polaroid, mostly to familiarize myself with how it worked. I remember the pale gold of the afternoon sun on her hair, the red collar angles of her shirt and the white frame of the print like I was looking at the image through a window.

"You don't mind that I'm a gas monkey?" I said.

"It's a steady job and you help people."

"Right. But you're from a family of artists. Wouldn't they, you know, look down on me with my oil rag and my gasoline shoes?"

"They're not *artists*, Sonny. My dad just teaches music. And

I'm not a snob. It's more important that a guy is kind and thoughtful."

There was no kiss, no 'parking,' on the way back to Merluza. I wanted to be a gentleman. Besides, we saw the curtain twitching at her parents' window when we pulled up.

"There's a movie showing Friday if you'd like to go," I said. "The reviews are good. I mean, if you're interested in going out with me again."

"I don't often go to the movies. But I'd like to see you again."

"I'll pick you up. About six?"

"Sure!"

I picked up a mini-skirted hitchhiker on the way home. She was standing there with her hip flung out, knowing that her long, tanned thighs would stop traffic. As she chattered away braless, I held the Ruger heavy by my thigh, feeling the rubber grip in my palm. It was cocked and ready to fire. I was aroused. All I had to do was pull it out and say my line. "You're not going to Buena Vista," or, "Listen – there's been a change of plan. . ." Or just hold the gun on her, inches from her head, until she turned then pull the trigger at the exact moment she saw it, staring, mouth opening to say something.

But I dropped her off and watched her rolling her ass in her miniskirt as she walked up into the campus. Would she ever know how close she'd been to beheading and dismemberment? She might read about it in the papers and squint at my face and wonder – going through the numberless catalogue of lifts – if I'd been one of the drivers who'd picked her up.

I stopped off at the Holding Cell after. I didn't particularly want a drink, but I wanted to be there among the cops and the detectives after I'd left that girl unmurdered, joshing with them, playing the fool. A couple weeks back, I'd bought some police-issue handcuffs at Webster's and the guys gave me a lot of shit about that. I think they secretly knew I'd been rejected by CHP and they saw me as a wannabe.

"Okay, Officer Boden," they'd say. "You got me! Take me in."

And they'd hold their hands out, like in the movies or on TV, though I knew the correct way was behind the back. I'd seen it done.

"What do you need cuffs for, Sonny?" they'd say. "Your girl got a thing for cops? Bring her down to the Sheriff's office and we'll give her a cavity search."

I laughed with them, imagining them on their knees begging for their lives.

My sister Amber came over to the house infrequently to make sure me and my mother weren't fighting and that Mom's alcoholism was within practical limits. Unconscious on a weeknight was cause for concern.

Amber gave us gossip from the Sheriff's office: the kinda stuff the detectives were usually too careful to drop at the Holding Cell, or which the press were withholding because it was a live lead. It was often better than *Police Story*.

"You know those cases where they find the woman's car but no driver?" she said.

"Uh huh." I'd been following every word in the papers.

"Well, they've found one of them. She was covered with logs and leaves down a ravine south of Hudd Canyon in the state park."

"It's not been in the paper," said my mother.

"It will be, but there are some details they won't release. The woman had been hit on the back of the head and strangled with a wire. The wire was still around her neck when they found her."

"Was she raped?" I said.

"What a question!" said my mother.

"It's important for the MO," I said. "I mean, is he killing them to rape them, or is he just killing them to kill them?"

"What's the difference?" said my mother. "He's a monster

either way." She turned to Amber. "Do they know what car he drives? Is it a Ford Galaxie?"

"Mom . . ." I said.

"Well, you *are* a murderer! I wouldn't be surprised if we had cops up here every week checking whether corpses were connected to you."

I didn't rise to the bait. I'd explained too many times already about the record being sealed, about it being a juvenile crime and how no sexual deviance had been involved. I just looked at Amber like, See what I have to tolerate?

"You know he's put a lock on his door?" said my mother. "Why does a young man need a lock on his door if he hasn't got anything to hide?"

"You've got a lock on *your* door, Mom," said Amber.

"To keep the murderer out!"

I didn't mention that she was usually too trashed to lock or even close her door when she went to bed. Her drunken snoring kept me awake.

"He'll be masturbating in there," said my mother.

I got up. "I'm not listening to any more of this shit."

"Watch your language in my fucking house!"

Amber followed me to the kitchen.

"Why don't you find your own place, Sonny? You have a job. You're old enough to manage on your own."

"It's the parole conditions. I can't get around them."

It wasn't that. It was destiny.

"Mom says you've met a girl."

"Yeah. She's the daughter of Tom's sister's friend. She lives up at Merluza with her family. Here – I've got a Polaroid."

She looked at the photo and then at me.

"What?" I said.

"How's it going?"

"We've only had one date. I'm taking her to see *Zabriskie Point* on Friday."

"That's a sexy movie."

"Is it?"

"Is she old enough to see it?"

"She's eighteen, Amber."

"Well. Be careful."

"What's that supposed to mean?"

"You know."

"I really don't."

"Take it slow."

"You gonna treat me like Mom does? Like I'm still fifteen?"

"Ask him if he's masturbating!" called my mother from the other room.

"Right. I'm going out."

"Where?"

"For a drive."

It was going to happen this time. I was sure. I was going to kill.

EIGHT

Dwight stood at the end of an aisle in Scott's Sporting Goods, pretending to look at knives in a cabinet, but really watching the customer buying a gun at the counter. The customer seemed to know a lot about the .22 Ruger, talking to Scott about ammunition and whether he wanted a holster. There was a form to fill out and questions to answer.

The customer didn't notice Dwight as he left. Dwight watched him get into a Ford Galaxie he'd parked just outside and drive off. He'd been wearing an Arco forecourt uniform. A gas monkey.

"Yes, sir," said Scott, putting the previous customer's documents in a drawer and smiling at Dwight. "How can I help?"

"There's a knife I like in that cabinet."

"Sure. Let me get the key. Will it be for hunting, skinning, general utility?"

"For stabbing."

Scott looked at him. "For self-defense?"

"Uh-huh."

They went to the cabinet and Dwight pointed through the glass.

"Well, sir, I'd say the Bowie model is more of a hunting or outdoors knife if you want my advice. Doesn't lend itself particularly well to self-defense. It's difficult to conceal. Could be awkward to draw or use at close quarters. I'd recommend the smaller drop-point—

"I want the big one."

Scott nodded and opened the cabinet. He knew his customers. This one wanted a Big Knife. Probably'd never use it. "It's a strong blade," he said. "And long. You could clear ground with it in a pinch. Like a machete."

Dwight weighed it in his hand.

"Well balanced, eh?" encouraged Scott.

"Yeah. And I'm looking for a gun. I heard the other guy just now. The Ruger sounds like what I want."

"It's simple and reliable. Do you do much target shooting or pest control?"

"Uh huh. A sport gun." Dwight had heard the previous customer calling it that.

"Well, let's get your details. You know there's a two-week wait period until the documents are processed?"

"Sure." Dwight handled the knife in its sheath, smelling the leather.

Scott observed him for a moment and took out the forms. "Here's a pen."

Dwight omitted his arrest record and his time in the psych ward.

"Enjoy your knife!" said Scott. "See you again in two weeks." Thinking, No way that one's gonna clear.

The bell above the door jangled tinnily as it had when the Arco gas monkey left.

He drove through Buena Vista with the previous day's acid still working in his brain. Traffic signals left snaking trails. Cloud edges pulsed purple. A couple in a billboard ad turned to watch his car go by while a stop sign winked. As he waited at an intersection, a stone lion on a gatepost said, "Why don't you go and visit Father MacLeish?"

Dwight pulled out into traffic, horns blaring, and drove to

where Father MacLeish used to live when Dwight was attending church with his family. Streetlamps bent to the road like drinking giraffes and he laughed as he approached the priest's house.

"Dwight Paulson! Is that you? How long's it been? I heard you were living up in San Francisco. But listen to me rambling on. Come in, come in. Tell me your news."

Father MacLeish looked older. His eyebrows were caterpillars moving about his forehead. His sofa and armchair were upholstered in red: large mouths open. They drank coffee.

"You look just the same, Dwight. Maybe a little taller. You know, we've missed you in church. Oh, I know a young man has to find his way in the world and choose his own path. Doubt is a part of that. There are questions to answer. But many come back when they see what the world looks like. I suppose you saw a lot in the city. Am I right? Drugs and promiscuity. There are terrible temptations. Violence, too, I expect."

Dwight nodded. "Some Angels beat me half to death."

"Angels . . .? Ah, you mean those bikers. Well, you're home again now. I'm in touch with your parents, of course. I know a little about your . . . your recent problems. We could pray if you like. If it would help. There's no challenge too great for God."

"I was thinking about that camping trip we did," said Dwight.

"Ah, yes. Wonderful. Wonderful. The majesty of nature. I have fond memories of it. Nothing better for a young man's spirit than the great outdoors."

"You came into my tent at night and ejaculated on me."

Father MacLeish slowly put his cup on the table. "No, Dwight. That didn't happen. Why would you say such a thing?"

"I wasn't asleep. You thought I was."

"That's a very serious . . . I would *never* do anything like that. You must have dreamed it, Dwight. Your memory is unreliable with all those drugs you've taken. It's a shame. A whole generation is–"

"I remember it perfectly. I heard the zip on the tent and I saw your silhouette. You – not one of the other boys. I didn't know what it was, the sticky stuff." Dwight shifted in his seat and Father MacLeish saw the knife tucked into his waistband.

"I'm sorry that you're saying this, Dwight. I'm sorry that you're confused."

"I'm not confused."

Father MacLeish looked at the wall clock. "I have somebody coming round in a few minutes, Dwight. Dwight?"

Dwight was grinning fixedly. Some variety of catatonic episode? Father MacLeish did pastoral work at Buena Vista hospital and he'd seen epileptics, schizophrenics, the paranoid and the psychotic. He knew the signs.

"Nobody's coming round," said Dwight.

"I can assure you that Sergeant DeLallio is coming round to discuss the charity event–"

"Nobody's coming." Dwight grinned.

The knife was out of its sheath and glinting. It was an ugly blade, designed to cause harm. The important thing with the insane and the addicted was to humor them. No sudden movements or challenges. No excitement. They could often be distracted.

"I have some delicious chocolate cake. It'd go wonderfully with the coffee. Or perhaps you need a refill?"

Dwight seemed to have lapsed into a distracted state again. Father MacLeish stood slowly and backed away toward the kitchen. He closed the frosted glass door and went to the phone.

"Hi, Don. Father MacLeish here. Yes. Uh huh. Look – no reason to be alarmed, but 've got a local boy here. He's had some trouble with drugs . . . The Paulson boy . . . that's it. Well, he's here with a knife and I believe he may be under the influence of something. If you could send somebody round. No sirens . . . Yes. I'll be here."

He replaced the receiver silently and went to the kitchen door. There was no sound from the other room. He opened the door a fraction and peered at the red-upholstered armchair.

Dwight was gone. He'd left the street door open.

Two weeks later, Dwight returned to Scott's Sporting Goods to collect his Ruger. The purchase had not been flagged by the Sheriff's Department and Scott let it go. A sale was a sale. He showed Dwight how to use the gun: its simple bolt mechanism, loading bullets in the magazine, the two-stage trigger that seemed to fascinate Dwight. Two boxes of hollow-point .22 rifle rounds were added to the purchase and a happy customer left the store.

Out on the street, he saw the Galaxie that'd been outside the sporting goods store a fortnight previously. Same license plate. The gas monkey must have come back for his gun, too. Dwight walked over to the car and stood by it, looking at the deep red of the tail light that seemed to be communicating something. He stared at it, seeing his own silhouette small like an insect. He took the knife from inside his jacket, unsheathed it and stabbed it into the light. Red plastic fragments clattered to the road and he nodded, satisfied.

Gun and knife in his jacket, he called into a barber shop on Main Street and took the seat.

"Just a trim?" said the barber, tying off the cape round Dwight's neck.

"Cut it all off, my good man," he said in a British accent.

"You sure, buddy? Full buzzcut?"

"All of it, my fine fellow! I'd hate to be taken for one of those bloody long-hairs!"

"You got it, fella."

Joe was up on the water tower above El Bosque, watching the town and its people through the telescopic sights of his rifle. All were deep in sin. The time was upon them. Their bodies would lie in the street where they fell and not be suffered to put into graves.

Up there, he could lie on the mesh parapet and listen to the wind breathing its instructions. Sounds came to him distant and muted from below. Scraps of voices. Engines. A dog ceaselessly barking the same rough note. He spoke to the dog: be not afraid. The reaping does not concern you. But the dog wouldn't listen. Barbarous beast. He fixed the cross hairs on it, shot it. Nobody came to see.

Sanity came and went like weather, Sally the sun. Later, he stood outside the house in darkness, watching domestic light through purple lenses. The voice told him, No. That is not your fate. You have left that world.

He went to see Jackson, who he'd worked with at the garage. The voice told him, *Hide your majesty. Do not let them see your wings.*

"Hey, Joe," said Jackson. "We miss you at the garage. Feeling better? Gonna come back?"

My name is Ananiel. "I remember you had a shack up in the state park."

"Yeah, right. Up near Cascade. Not been there in a long time. You thinking of doing some camping?" He looked at the rifle over Joe's shoulder, the .38 in a holster and the knife. "You know there's no hunting in the park, right?"

"I need a place awhile. You know, to get away."

"Having problems with Sal? I know it can be tough with a little one. Just give her some time. She'll come round."

"The shack?"

"Are you okay, Joe? Lookin' a little . . .You wanna come in? I'll have Alice make some coffee. You can call Sal if you like."

"I just need some time . . . I need a place."

"Well, okay. The shack's nothin' special. It's no hotel. You'll need to air it out. Might be damp. Light the stove – that'd be my advice. There's firewood under a tarp 'less someone stole it. Wait a minute – I'll get you the key. Sure you won't come in?"

"I'm fine. I'll wait."

Voices from inside: "It's not our business, Al. Just give him some time and they'll be back together. Don't meddle so."

Jackson emerged with the key and a string bag. "Here's somethin' for tonight. Some bread, some fruit, a jar of Alice's soup. A couple beers. There might be some tinned stuff up there if you look, but check the labels. I don't wanna come up there and find you've killed yourself eating some expired corned beef."

"Thanks, Jackson."

"Hope you come back, Joe. We miss you."

Later, the voice told him which private house to enter – a big place up near the state park where Buena Vista's wealthy lived. Canyon View Road. He'd watched it for a few days first, standing within the forest cover with his binoculars, learning when the owners left and returned. No dog, but a cat. He broke a rear window with the .38 butt, clearing glass from the frame with the barrel.

It smelled of family: shampoo and deodorant, the previous night's dinner and that morning's coffee. Drapes, carpets and furniture had absorbed their presence, the cushions shaped by familiar weights. He sat on the sofa, the .38 resting on his thigh, and looked at himself, warped miniature in the TV's gray eye. The cat, a sleek black thing with emerald eyes, emerged from its sleeping spot elsewhere and paused on the room's threshold, one paw slightly raised.

I am not your foe, said Ananiel. *What is your name?* The cat said nothing. "I asked you a question," said Joe, pointing the revolver.

It watched him and approached, rubbing its head on his lower leg, purring.

Joe went to each bedroom and lay on the beds, looking up at the light fittings and leaving the impression of his head on pillows that smelled of man or woman. He opened the drawers and riffled through small garments. The wardrobe clothes exhaled scents. He ran the faucets in the bathroom and watched water swirl in a coral pink basin.

The garage had tools pegged to a board, stacked pots of paint, packing boxes and a child's bicycle. Its oil smell reminded him of the garage where he'd worked before he was Ananiel.

In the nursery, he stood looking at the crib and thought of Sally and the baby. The cerebral weather changed. Sun. He seemed to wake and looked around, seeing his muddy footprints on the carpet. The cat watched him, blinking, front paws folded, from the warm spot Joe'd left on the sofa.

He needed to go home.

"Joe. I've been worried," said Sally.

He stood on the stoop, his clothes dark from the rain, his hair sleek on his skull.

"Come in," she said. "Sit at the table. I'll bring you something."

He ate quickly, hardly pausing to chew.

"Where've you been?" said Sally. "Was it because I called the police? I was worried. You were acting crazy, talking like the Bible. Do you remember any of it? Are you okay now?"

"I've got to do some things, Sal. I need to be alone."

"But are you coming back? Are you better now?"

"I'll be away awhile. It's better if you don't see me and don't know."

"I don't understand. I was just worried. Look at you all wet. You've got a real beard. Take some time off and get well again. Maybe you need to go back to the hospital. One of the customers at the diner was saying there can be complications after a serious concussion. You might have an injury nobody knows about. Or maybe it was the mescaline. There's no more. I won't let my brother bring anything like that into the house ever again . . . Don't you want to come home?"

"I can't, Sal. I have to do some important things."

"What important things, Joe?"

"I might be gone awhile."

"Where are you living? Is there . . . Is there another woman?"

"It's nothing like that. You know I wouldn't . . . I'm staying at Jackson's shack. Jackson from the garage."

"I don't know *what's* going on with you, Joe. Why don't you change out of those wet clothes?"

"I can't stay."

"Don't do this, Joe. We were doing so well . . . We've got through worse. I'll get you some dry clothes and some coffee. You look frozen."

She went to the bedroom, opening drawers and the wardrobe. He was sick. He still had something wrong with his brain after that crash. Two weeks blind – that wasn't normal. That was a serious injury. Maybe something was bleeding still. More tests'd show what it was. She went back to the living room.

"Here, put these on and I'll . . ."

He was gone.

Next day, the police were investigating the break-in on Canyon View Road, surprised, perhaps, that nothing had been taken. It looked like the perpetrator had spent time in each room, looking through drawers and lying on beds, which was somehow worse. He hadn't robbed the place; he'd *occupied* it. He'd spent time in it. Doing what? Sexual things? What had he been thinking? Was his energy still there?

It was unnerving to be in a house that had been occupied like that – to sleep in the same bed the intruder had lain on. To wear clothes he might've touched. They'd have to wash everything.

Strangest of all: the cat must have seen him, possibly interacting with him. He may have stroked it or spoken to it. The cat, mute witness, knew his face and his voice.

Joe watched the squad cars leave. He saw it all from his position within the trees, pine needles soft underfoot and the scent of resin in the air. There was nothing left for them to investigate – not yet. The police had two theories. Either it had been some acid-blasted kid who'd broken in thinking it was his own home or Shangri-La, or God-knows-what. Or it had been some kind of reconnaissance mission and the perpetrator would return later with accomplices. The homeowners should be vigilant.

Vigilant! That meant worrying that someone was in their home when they were away. It meant worrying when they were at home that someone was watching or about to enter. Or was already inside.

Joe waited until after nightfall, until everyone had left.

He approached along a road that glistened damply, his hooded shadow shortening and lengthening between the streetlights' misted cones. A dog snuffled unseen under a fence, but didn't bark. He walked up the driveway to where he knew the phone line descended from the pole to the side of the house, passing down wood cladding to travel along a window ledge. He cut it with the heel of his knife, leaving a bright copper eye in the black-rubber insulation.

The window he'd smashed before had been replaced, putty fingerprints still about its edges. A metal grille had been bolted over it. The rear door had six beveled panes and he smashed the one closest to the handle, reaching inside to unlatch and swing it open.

The cat walked toward him and wove between his legs, almost tripping him.

"Stop that."

He sat in the same seat as before and looked at himself in the dead televisual eye. White flames burned around him. His wings flashed brilliant. He checked the six bullets in the cylinder and counted ten more back into his jacket pocket. In the other pocket was five yards of cord he'd bought from Webster's and a lock knife to cut it. The cat approached and jumped onto the chair's arm, stepping lightly onto his lap and pawing him before settling into sphinxlike comfort.

Now to wait.

NINE

Dulcie sat beside me in the movie theatre darkness. The projector's rays danced through cigarette smoke above us and I was aware of her pale face close in profile. Our legs were almost touching. I could smell perfume – a light floral scent – rising warm off her skin. But all I could think about was the girl's head at home on my bookshelf.

Murder isn't what you think. You see it in the movies and it seems so fast, so easy. The gun goes off, the knife goes in and death is instant. The body falls heavy and lies still. You don't imagine the work – the sheer physical effort – that's involved in driving the life from a person that struggles and screams. You don't anticipate the panic and the rush of adrenaline that gives killer and victim superhuman resources. You can't prepare for the primal struggle. The mutual terror. The heat of the blood on your hands and its seemingly endless quantity. The smell of it. The sounds. The ripping cloth, the dull impact thuds. Time accelerates beyond immediate focus. Everything happens in one manic blur. No possibility of reflection – only reaction. The memory of it is fractured into milliseconds of intense focus – a movie played frame by Technicolor frame. Details you missed completely in the moment become feature-length in recollection.

THR3E

You can pause the tape to examine every frozen movement. You can run it backward and forward. You've become a master of time.

Murder is a state of grace more intense than religious ecstasy, longer lasting and more nuanced than orgasm, more exhilarating than the roaring stadium adoration of the rock star. There's no greater connection, no greater *intimacy* between two people than between murderer and victim. They share sublimity. One takes and the other gives *everything*. You become truly divine in the act of murder, passing to a higher plane beyond common morality. You've broken the deepest held sacrament, the profoundest human taboo – and you've emerged into a field of light where no punishment exists. You cross the boundary between life and death and no cataclysm occurs. Nobody knows but you. The world is the same, but forever changed. You now walk among other men a higher being. Transcendent.

It was as if every event and consequence that night occurred to prove my invulnerability. I should've been caught three times. Three times, I walked into certain discovery, but passed through each situation without harm or suspicion.

The first time was immediately after the killing. I'd put the body in my trunk and I was pulling out onto Cascade from the parking spot in the state park where it'd happened. Well, a guy was standing right there in the road – a weird looking guy with all of his hair buzzed off. He didn't seem to be hitching, just standing there close enough that he must have heard the screams, must have heard the murder happening. It was still daylight.

Perhaps he'd been walking and stopped at that spot when he heard the girl. It's so quiet up there that you'd notice. Maybe he even saw something. I'd killed her inside the car and been totally oblivious to anything outside. He could have been bending at the side window, hands on his knees, looking in.

So I pulled out onto Cascade Road and he looked right at me. I was turning and there was time for him to see me clearly. He'd know me again. He'd be able to pick me out of a line-up. It seemed for a second that he was going to raise an arm and maybe say something.

I didn't stop. That's what you have to do. Don't show any guilt or hesitation. Let the witness think they're mistaken. Let them explain away the noises they heard. Let them rationalize it. I was a guy alone in a car. Maybe I'd pulled off the road to take a piss. Maybe the sounds had been the radio. Or I'd been talking to myself. Who'd leap immediately to the assumption of murder?

I drove on, looking at him in the rearview. He was standing in the middle of the road, watching me. If I had the chance again, I would have stopped and asked him something like, "Hey, buddy – you know if there's a turn-off round here for Oso Grade?" Then he would've remembered me as just some lost driver. You always think of these things later.

So I continued driving back down to Verdugo. It was twilight turning to dusk and I had the lights on. I was sticking closely to the speed limit. I didn't want to get stopped for any reason with her body in the trunk. Then I saw the CHP patrol car behind me, its lights flashing.

Panic. Hands tight on the wheel. I had the Ruger under the seat. First thought: cock the bolt and blast the cop as soon as he came to my window. Except there were two of them. I wouldn't be able to get both. After the recent mass shooting of four CHiPs, they were wary and taking no chances.

Focus. I looked at the passenger seat. It was soaked with blood. The car smelled of blood. One of her shoes lay in the footwell. I dragged my buckskin jacket from the back and dropped it casually over the passenger seat as I watched the cops approach. I kicked the shoe more out of sight into the shadow beneath the dash. It was dark under the forest canopy and they wouldn't see it unless they used flashlights. Even then, I could say it was my sister's. I'd committed no traffic violation. It had to be a routine stop. I just had to appear normal.

Then I saw my hand. I'd cut myself during the murder, a nasty slice between thumb and forefinger that I didn't remember doing.

I hadn't even registered it. But now, seeing it, I felt the pain and saw the blood. I thrust it into my mouth and sucked the blood, probably tasting some of hers, too, though I'd dried my hands with her clothes.

"Evening, officers." There was one on each side of the car.

"License and registration," said the one at my open window. The other was looking inside the car. I wondered briefly that there might be some spark of life left in the girl. A peri-mortem spasm might thump the trunk's bodywork.

"You know you've got a broken driver-side tail light?" he said, holding my documents.

I could have lied. What? Really? I've not seen that, officer. It must have happened as I was pulling out of . . . but I guessed they heard such crap all the time. They were smarter than that.

"I know it, officer. It happened in town and I've been meaning to get it fixed, but with work and all . . . It's ironic 'cause I work in the Arco station downtown and I could easily order a replacement light. What's the saying? The butcher's kids don't eat meat?"

He looked at me as I gabbled on. A fool, maybe, but not an outright dick.

"Is that Tom's station?" he said.

"Yeah! Tom and his sister own the place. I'm one of the attendants."

He looked at his partner over the roof and I missed whatever signal passed. My gun was inches from my hand.

"Where you headed, sir?"

"Verdugo. Home. I can be there in twenty."

He handed back the documents. "See that you get that tail light fixed tomorrow. Next time, it'll be a fine."

"Thanks so much, officer."

He nodded and jerked his head at his partner. They went back to the patrol car, probably saying what a loser I was.

I arrived home and parked in the courtyard. Mother wasn't back yet. The flickering blue light of a TV set showed in just one window of the two-story building.

The girl lay nakedly fetal inside the trunk, her pale skin smeared with blood. Still wet with it. I had to get her up to my room while she was still warm. I had a sleeping bag for the purpose and rolled it loosely around her, wedging the bloodied knife between her thighs and hoisting the body up to my shoulder. She wasn't heavy. I only had to get her to the end of the ground-floor corridor.

There was an almost sexual thrill to all of this. I felt her hair against me. Her bare legs dangled and her buttocks were smooth through the silky fabric of the sleeping bag. But more than the physical contact of it was the excitement of openly carrying the body of this girl I'd murdered across the parking lot and up the wooden stairs to the door. I was flouting every conceivable law of morality, civility, humanity. I seemed to pass through a corridor of light, untouchable. She was my victim. My trophy. My possession.

I was opening the door to the building when the corridor light came on and the tenant from apartment two backed out, his key in the door. I let the door go and ran back down the steps toward the car, fumbling in my jeans pocket for the key and heaving the girl back into the trunk. Her head struck the metal with a dull *thunk* and I slammed the lid.

"Oh, hi, Ken," I said, waving. "Going out to work?"

He'd paused on the steps. He was looking down at something.

The knife had dropped from between her legs as I ran and it now lay on the steps, completely filmed with blood.

"Is this yours?" said Ken.

"Uh huh." I bent and picked it up. It looked like it'd been dipped in a bucket of blood. "Yeah, I cut myself pretty bad." I showed him the slice in my hand. "That'll teach me to play with knives, right?"

He nodded and continued to his car. Would he report the incident? Any idiot could've seen that the amount of blood wasn't comparable with my injury. But why would he suspect me of anything worse? Murder is too enormous. You might suspect some stereotypical bear of a man with crazed eyes and a human limb in his hands, but I was Sonny from apartment one. I lived with my mother and worked in a gas station. I couldn't possibly belong to that other world – the world of monsters.

Three times. Three times, I passed within touching distance of discovery and capture. What kept me free, if not some destiny or divine will? It was meant to be. How else would you interpret it?

But I was angry. I'd very seriously mismanaged the first murder. I thought I'd been prepared after so many months of visualizing it. I'd made a lot of mistakes. But I could learn. I would learn. The next one would be perfect. If I'm honest, I didn't know at the time why I started, or what I wanted from the kills. I needed the first one to teach me.

That girl was waiting for me at home, the body in the closet, the head on the shelf. Meanwhile on the movie screen, two young people were walking in the element-riven monochrome badlands of Death Valley National Park. The guy was tall and handsome. The girl was just my type – the type of hitchhiker I'd pick up in a heartbeat. Long, light brown hair. Honey-colored thighs. Full mouth and wide eyes. She was wearing a mini-dress that rode up to show her ass whenever she leaned in over the engine. The kinda girl who'd never normally look at me, who came through the station and looked at her lips in the rearview as I cleaned her windshield.

Now they were kissing and rolling around in the sand, slipping off their clothes. It was very erotic. There was an electric charge among the audience of mostly young people. I saw, or sensed, hands moving between thighs. Heads joined. Beside me, Dulcie sat rigid, the sex scene reflected in unblinking eyes. The space remained empty between us. It seemed to grow wider.

I had no experience of this. I mean, I'd seen movies as a kid and as a mental hospital inmate, but never as a guy with his girl. I didn't know the rules. Was she expecting me to touch her knee or kiss her? What was the code? It was only our second date. Other girls weren't so traditional. They'd just take your hand and tell you what to do, but Dulcie was shy. What if she rejected my hand

and stood, outraged, into the undulating nicotine rays? "Get your hands off me!"

We remained in that static impotence until the end of the movie and emerged with the crowd into the street.

"What did you think?" I said.

"There wasn't much story," she said. "It was just a series of impressions. It probably makes more sense if you're high. How about you?"

"It was a little too hippie-ish for me. Very anti-police. Too pro-revolution. The photography was good, I suppose."

"The girl was pretty."

"She was okay. Perhaps a little vulgar. Do you want to go for a drink?"

"My parents are expecting me home."

"Of course. I'll take you."

I hadn't collected her from Merluza. She'd already been in town seeing a friend. We walked slowly to the car. Would either of us mention the prolonged sex scene in the movie? The nudity? Other couples were walking hand in hand, fired by the eroticism – probably going off to beds and back seats.

I'd spent the previous night engaged in frenzied, exhausting lovemaking with the girl I'd killed. Six years of suppressed libido had flooded out: every lurid thought and fantasy made real with her compliant body and uncomplaining head. The guys at Atascadero had spoken about their frustration at the inability to consummate their lusts as often and as comprehensively as their passions compelled them when with a victim. The male body has only so much capacity. But I was young and aflame with God-like potency. I was mythological. I was epic in my exertions.

I'd bought some covers for the front seats and Dulcie noticed them immediately.

"Yeah, I spilled some wine yesterday," I said. "Must've hit the bottle on the door frame and didn't notice 'til it was too late. The covers are just until I can get the seats cleaned."

"Did you buy some meat, too?" she said when we'd been driving a few minutes.

"You can smell meat?"

"I don't know. Something like that."

"Right. Yeah. I bought some steaks. Don't worry. I'm gonna take a couple days off to see about my hand and I'll clean the car. You won't smell anything again."

"Your poor hand." She looked at the bandaged palm. "You should really get a professional gardener for that kind of thing."

"It was just a couple branches, you know. Tapping on my window. I'm a klutz."

It was true I needed to take some time off work to get rid of the body. I had to cut it up and leave the parts in different places. No witnesses. No evidence. No connection to you – that's what the guys at Atascadero had taught me. If there's no obvious motive and you've cleared up those other things, nobody can touch you.

At the same time, I didn't want to let the girl go just yet. She'd been in full rigor that morning and less pliable, but she'd be ready and waiting when I got home. I'd finally found someone and she was pretty foxy. A real looker. I wasn't afraid that my mother would try to go in the room. The lock I'd fitted was maximum security. It'd be easier to smash the door in.

"Why do you stare at the hitchhikers like that?" said Dulcie.

"I do?"

"We've passed three girls now and you've stared right at them. You even looked in the mirrors after we passed. A girl could get jealous, you know."

"I'm sorry. I didn't realize. I was just thinking how vulnerable they are. You know, with that rapist going about. They stand out here alone and get in strangers' cars and they don't know who they might meet. The county should really make more buses available."

"You're right. But the girls should be more careful, too. They know the danger."

"I guess."

We arrived in Merluza, getting closer to Dulcie's home.

"There's something happening on the boardwalk next week if you'd like to go," I said.

"Call me," she said. "Let me know which day."

We sat in the car, the engine running. A silhouetted figure appeared in a ground floor window of the house.

"Thanks for the movie," she said.

I watched her walk to the door and wave from the doorway. I turned the car around and drove back along the coast to Verdugo.

"Been out whoring?" said my mother, the minute I stepped into the house. She was drunk.

I put my head around the living room door. "On your second bottle, I see."

"What mother *wouldn't* drink, with a son like you?'

"Night, Mom."

"That's right – you go into your locked room and do your filthy business."

"I'm going to sleep, Mom. You might think about it, too. You've got work tomorrow."

"Ha! Lectures on responsibility from the *murderer*. I'll do what I goddamn please."

I locked my door behind me and lifted the girl out of the closet. I unwrapped her from the sleeping bag on the bed. All of the rigor had gone, but the livor mortis, the pooling of blood at the body's lowest points, had discolored her flesh with patches of burgundy and the fingers were bluish purple. This would have to be our last night together, a decision confirmed by the slightly higher temperature inside her. Heavy bacterial action. The decomp had started. I couldn't afford for there to be any smells. Tomorrow: the hatchet and the tub.

But tonight she was all mine. We lay on the bed, her arm

across my chest, my hand on her ass, and I looked at her head on the shelf, eyes closed like she was sleeping or pretending to.

"The girl in the movie was hot, but nothing compared to you," I told her. "I wouldn't even look at her in the street if you were on my arm. Sure, you can smile! But it's true. You want me to prove my affection, babe? Okay, but you'd better be ready."

She was.

TEN

"No, no, no! I've had fish *twice* this week, Mom. You should be cooking something with whole grains and fresh produce today, with green and red capsicums. Didn't you read the book I gave you?"

"I'm sorry, Dwight, honey. I've not had time. You've always liked fish and I thought–"

"*And* you're using a metal spatula! I told you: glass or wood."

"Who ever heard of a glass spatula, honey? It'd break right away."

"How can I balance my essence if you're not feeding me macrobiotically?"

"What's going on here?" said father, entering the kitchen.

"Dwight doesn't want his fish."

"He'll eat his fish."

"I will *not*."

"Are you taking your pills, Dwight?" said father. "You know they said you'd have to go back if–"

"Pills pills pills pills! Gimme a goddamn break!"

Mother and father looked at each other.

"Listen, Dwight," said father. "We've been talking to Father MacLeish."

"Oh yeah? The pedophile MacLeish who beats his meat over sleeping adolescents?"

"Dwight!" said mother.

"Father MacLeish has experience of these things over at the county hospital," said father, grimly, "and he thinks you should be admitted."

"Sure he does."

"He's spoken to the doctors there and we think – your mother and I, and Father MacLeish – that it would be best if you were to go voluntarily. Admit yourself." Dwight stared at the fried fish on the plate as if waiting for it to speak. "Of course, there are alternatives – legal avenues we can take," said father, "but it'd be easier if you just went there and told them, well, that you need some time."

"You mean *you* need some time."

"Yeah, Dwight. We need some time, too. These damn drugs have rotted your brain. You look like some delinquent with all your hair cut off like that."

"This is how they have it in the *Marines*."

"You're not a marine, Dwight. You'll never be a marine."

"Don't say that," said mother. "Who knows what he could be?"

Father stared, incredulous. "He has a criminal record. He's a mental case, for God's sake!" Mother shuddered out a sob. "Now look what you've done to your mother."

"I've done nothing. *You're* the one shouting at her."

"Why don't you go and get some firewood? Maybe you can buy some of that hippie yoga shit you want to eat while you're out."

Dwight took the car keys off the peg by the door and left, not breaking stride on the stoop as he grabbed the baseball bat he'd used as a kid.

He drove north toward the state park, the suburbs dwindling along Highway 9 until he was rising in switchbacks into thick forest growth. He turned off onto Cascade Road, cracked the car window and let the nature smells enter: leaf mulch, wet bark, moss. The acid tab he'd taken the previous night was still in his system, making trunks wave like soft spaghetti and the engine sing like a sperm whale from Pacific depths. "Call me Ishmael!" God, he'd hated that book in high school. *Moby Dick*. But now he kinda had an urge to try it again. The author must have been an acid head, the weird, trippy things he wrote.

A man was walking by the side of the road up ahead. He carried a rucksack, wore hiking boots and used a long walking pole of the type they called an alpenstock. Dwight fixed on the man, who was speaking directly into his mind. "Kill me, Dwight. I don't mind. I've been waiting for you to kill me. I'm weak and old – no use to society anymore. You'd be doing me a favor, really. I'd appreciate it."

Dwight drove by and watched as the man waved in the rearview. It was a message. Dwight had come to realize that he'd been chosen as an agent of humanity's perfectibility. People were corrupt, diseased, weak, acquisitive. The future of the Earth depended on rooting out this contamination. Clean living and good health were paramount to purifying the oceanic consciousness. Macrobiotic diets for all and meditation daily. Excellent personal hygiene. Old age was a cancer. Such people had given their best and were now a weight, a hindrance to humanity's development.

He slowed and pulled over onto a verge of loose soil and pine needles. He got out of the car and raised the hood, bending over the engine's hot petrochemical odor until the old man came alongside.

"Engine trouble, son? Need a hand?"

"I don't know what's wrong," said Dwight. "It just kinda cut out."

The old man leaned in under the hood. "It all looks okay. Start 'er up and let's see what we got."

Dwight sat in the driver's seat and started the car. He took the bat from the rear and came round to the front with it beside his leg.

"All seems fine now," said the man, still peering into the engine.

Dwight raised the bat and swung it down on the back of the man's head.

"Shit! The hood!" said the man, reaching above him.

Dwight laughed. He thinks the hood closed on him! He struck again, harder, and the old man's knees buckled as he fell inside the engine compartment, still groping above him for the hood that hadn't fallen. And again. This time the old man slumped to the road. He began to spasm and Dwight hit him again until he stopped. Blood was running freely from the crushed skull.

Birds sang. A squirrel's claws scratched unseen up a trunk. Dwight took a deep breath of healthy air and laid the bat on the old man's body. The rucksack had nothing interesting in it: a sandwich and a bottle of beer, a wallet with ID and fifty dollars, and a delivery slip to an address up on Oban Drive. Dwight took the beer, the sandwich and the delivery slip.

He peered into the forest. It looked like there was a shack about 100 yards into the trees. He grabbed the old man's feet, dragged the body about seven yards distant from the road and lit a joint.

"Thanks, Dwight," said the old man. "You really did me a favor. Now the world's a better place."

"My pleasure. Glad I could help."

He lowered the hood and sat on it, smoking the weed and listening to the forest. Tranquility. Maybe he could meditate.

He folded his legs up on the hood, looped his fingers and closed his eyes.

A muffled shout. A thump. A clang of something striking metal.

The sounds were faint, but sounded close. Contained inside a car, maybe.

He slipped off the hood and walked along the road toward the sounds. There was a turn-off up ahead.

A scream, deadened by closed windows.

He stopped and listened. A car door opened. A trunk slammed. The door closed and an engine started. A Ford Galaxie emerged from the trees and came toward him. It was the same Galaxie. The guy who'd bought the Ruger at Scott's.

Dwight stared at the driver. The man's face was intense: eyes wet, large and dark. He seemed somehow to glow. "I'm the same as you, Dwight!" the driver said directly into his mind. "We have the same mission."

Dwight started to raise his hand, but the Galaxie went by without stopping. Dwight turned and saw that the driver's side tail light was still out. It was a sign. It was meant to be. He thought about running to his car and following the Galaxie to flag him down and tell him, "Hey, we're on the same mission!" But destiny didn't work that way. Everything was already planned. They would meet soon.

The delivery slip he'd taken from the rucksack rustled in his pocket as he reached for his keys. The address was Oban Drive. It was close. Maybe the old man had been walking there. Maybe it was his house or a cabin. He wouldn't need it now. He'd gifted it to Dwight.

"Take my cabin, Dwight. You deserve it. Get away from the negativity of your parents for a while if you need to. Up here in the forest."

Dwight drove a few minutes to the intersection with Oban and guessed that the house numbers increased the further away they got from downtown. He turned right and drove slowly, looking at mailboxes until he found the right number.

It looked like a small wooden cabin rather than a house. He drove into the trees and along a rutted drive, fallen twigs cracking under the tires. The place seemed abandoned, the roof and the stoop thick with leaves and pine needles. He went up the bowed steps and looked through a window, opaque with dust and spider's webs. The inside was very simple: timber furniture, a wood stove, a bunk. It was a place for a single man. Maybe it'd been built before the state park had opened. A hunting cabin or a bootlegger hideout.

The doors were locked, but he remembered that the rucksack had a ring of keys in it. He'd stop on the way back down and get the keys. But first he had to get some firewood.

THURSDAY 09 July, 1970, 214 Larch Street, Buena Vista (Home), California, USA. 68°F with sunny spells. 11:42 PM. I've seen another. This was the second time. We have the same gun. We have the same mission. We're connected in the cosmic scheme. We'll meet soon and do remarkable things together . . .

Joe waited with the cat asleep on his lap. A clock ticked hollowly, somewhere unseen. He saw himself brilliant in the TV reflection, a white aura burning around him.

A car approached and parked in the driveway. Its door banged once. He heard the jangle of keys outside the door and saw a figure indistinct through the narrow opaque window. He stood and the cat dropped to the floor with a trill of annoyance.

Joe stood to one side so that the homeowner wouldn't see him until they entered the room. The .38 was pointed casually at waist level. He heard the keys fall into a ceramic bowl. He heard the rustle of a jacket being removed. He heard the faucet run in the kitchen and the clink of glasses in a cupboard. A shadow approached down the hallway and a woman in a dark pantsuit walked three steps into the room before seeing him.

"Oh!" She saw the gun. "Oh! Who . . . Who are you? What do you want?"

"I am Ananiel."

"How did you get in? Are you one of Jed's friends? This isn't funny."

"I don't know Jed. I am Ananiel."

She looked at him. She seemed to fold a little. "Are you the one who broke in before?"

He nodded.

"Look. You don't need the gun. Just take whatever you want."

"Who else lives here?"

"Why?"

He pulled back the hammer on the .38.

"My husband and our daughter."

"There's a baby, too," he said.

She touched her belly before she realized she was doing it.

So.

"When will they be back?" said Ananiel.

My husband picks up Sarah at three after her tennis class, but sometimes they go for a milkshake."

"We'll wait. Lie face down on the floor here."

"Please." Her voice quavered. "Just take whatever–"

"On the floor."

He tied her hands behind her back and her ankles to each other. "You can scoot over there and rest your back on the edge of the sofa if you like," he said.

"What are you going to do?"

"Do you believe in the power of Christ?"

"We're . . . We're Jewish. But, I mean . . . Yes, sure."

"Of the tribe of Issacher were sealed twelve thousand. Of the tribe of Zabulon, a great multitude which no man could number, of all nations and kindreds and peoples and tongues."

"I don't know what that means."

"There's a Book of Life. The seals have been opened."

"Uh huh . . ." She was looking at the phone.

They waited. Ananiel sat again in the armchair. The cat went over to the woman and rubbed its head against her thigh where she sat on the floor. The woman whimpered slightly.

"You might have to wait a long time," said the woman. "It might be better if you take whatever you want and just go. We don't deserve this. We've not done anything to hurt anyone. We're just a hardworking family."

Ananiel said nothing.

Another car arrived in the drive. Two doors opened and closed.

"No," said the woman. "Please."

"I'll have to shoot you if you make any noise," said Ananiel.

The door to the house opened and two people entered in mid-conversation.

"I should've won that second set. I know it."

"I know you do, honey. It's all a learning experience."

"Run! Run away!" shouted the woman.

Ananiel stood with a sigh as the father and daughter entered the room. They saw the woman. They saw the gun.

"What's going on here?" said the man. "Get out of my house!"

"Call the police!" said the woman, her voice taut and high.

"I will," said the man, walking to the phone on the wall even as the gun followed him. "I'll not have some long-hair punk come into my house and threaten my family with a gun."

He picked up the receiver and started to dial before realizing there was no tone.

"Lie on the floor face-down, or I'll shoot your wife first and then your daughter," said Ananiel.

"Do what he says! Please!" said the woman.

The man looked at Dwight, measuring the distance, wondering whether he'd really shoot if he rushed him. But the intruder didn't look afraid. He seemed totally relaxed. The gun was steady in his hand. He'd not raised his voice once.

"Are you the burglar from before?" said the man. "Look – just take whatever you want and go. You don't need to do any of this. You don't need the gun."

"On the floor. Both of you."

"Please!" said the woman, a keening plea.

He tied the father and daughter as he'd tied the woman and

allowed them all to lean their backs against the sofa. He took his seat again to address them.

"Do you acknowledge the power of Christ?" said Ananiel.

"Whatever you like," said the man. "Yes. Yes, we do."

"Answer individually." He pointed at the girl with the .38.

"Daddy?"

"Tell him that you acknowledge the power of Christ."

"Yes I do," she said, eyes downcast.

"Me, too," said the man. "Christ is very powerful."

The .38 moved.

"Christ is powerful," whispered the woman, nodding.

"Then you are ready to die," said Ananiel.

"Wait! Nobody has to die," said the man. "This is nonsense. This is crazy."

Ananiel shot the girl in the chest. Her body jerked with the impact.

"Sarah!" screamed the woman.

"You fucker! You fucker!" shouted the husband, struggling to stand.

Ananiel shot him in the chest and he fell back onto the floor.

The girl was gasping, her eyes wide, unbelieving.

"Sarah! Sarah!" screamed the woman, trying to shuffle closer.

"I'm gonna kill you!" said the man.

Ananiel shot him twice more and he lay still.

The woman made a noise like an animal – a strangulated wail.

Ananiel shot her twice in the chest.

The cylinder was empty. Ananiel opened it and tipped the shells into his lap, feeling their heat through his pants. He reached into his pocket and took six more, loading them one by one.

The girl was still moving lethargically. He shot her twice more.

Gunsmoke hazed gray in the air. His ears rang with the shots.

He went out to the garage and found the length of rubber tubing he'd seen last time, using it to siphon gas from both cars into a khaki-colored jerry can. He poured it all around the ground floor of the house, going back until no gas was left in the cars.

THR3E

The flames flickered at the windows as he was walking down the street. He stopped momentarily to watch. *A fire infolding itself, a brightness about it, and out of the midst thereof, the color of amber, out of that midst of the fire shone the glory of heaven.*

It was night when Joe returned to Jackson's shack, his breath steaming in the cold forest air. He cut off the road and into the soft loam, hands deep in his pockets, beard low in the coat's fur-lined collar. That's when he saw the body.

He almost fell over it in the darkness. He felt for his flashlight and shone it on the figure. It was an older man dressed for hiking: boots, rucksack, waterproof jacket. The head looked like it had been smashed in and it now glistened with writhing insects. Ants and shiny-backed beetles.

He looked around for a sign, some significance. This could be no coincidence. But Ananiel was silent, for now. Joe stood amid his floating breath and looked up at tree-fractured stars. He'd probably have to bury it.

ELEVEN

I woke to the sound of hammering on the bedroom door and instinctively pulled the sheet over the girl's head on the pillow beside mine.

"You're late for work!" said my mother.

"I'm not going in today, Mom. I told you. Because of my hand."

"You're gonna lose that job. And I don't appreciate talking to you through a locked door in my own house. You're not in jail anymore."

"Could've fooled me."

"What did you say? I don't have to let you stay here, you know. Goddamn ingrate. I should've had my tubes tied after Amber. But no, I had to let myself get knocked up again . . ."

Her voice faded as she walked away. The front door slammed and I listened to her drive away.

I pulled back the sheet and looked at the girl's face. I'd have to dispose of the body today. It wasn't really in a great condition. To tell the truth, it never had been.

I was very disappointed with this first kill – very dissatisfied with every part of it. I'd wanted a girl, a beautiful young lady to take home, and instead I ended up with a face and a body covered with stab and slash marks. Even the hands and knees were ruined with scuffs and grazes. Sure, I'd cleaned her up, washed the blood off and combed her hair, but there was no hiding the damage. Such beautiful skin, so horribly marked. I almost left her in the forest when I saw what a mess she was, but I also wanted to get her home as soon as possible.

Nothing went as I'd planned it. Nothing. All those weeks of preparation and playing it out in my mind. All those lines rehearsed. The three times I almost got caught. The only thing I did right was the first part: pulling out the gun.

"I'm sorry, but we're not going to Berkeley." She'd looked at it, serious but apparently unafraid. She didn't say anything. "But I'll put this away," I said. "I don't need it. We can just talk."

"You gonna try and fuck me now?"

Her language offended me slightly. I'd expected a little more respect for a man who'd picked her up and who had a gun. At the same time, it was odd her first assumption was rape. None of them assumed murder right away. Perhaps it was because so many of them were being assaulted by drivers at that time. Almost like they expected it.

"I thought we could just drive a little and go back to my place."

"Your place?" Sneering. Sarcastic.

"Sure."

"Why?"

"Well, it'd be more comfortable. I could open a bottle of wine. Do you like wine?"

"Your place. Like a *date*?" Her tone was distinctly mocking, now.

"Yes. Like a date. I'm not some kinda monster."

"A glass of wine before the rape. *That's* a new one."

This girl really had an attitude problem. I should've been the one in control, but it felt like she was. I put my hand on the gun again. I thought about shooting her just to end the awkwardness.

"Look," she said. "You seem like a nice guy. Maybe you're

doing this for the first time. If you want some advice, just drop me off. You don't need to do this. Go to a bar in town and you'll find plenty of women to fuck you. Won't cost you more than a few drinks."

"Could you stop using that word?"

"What – 'fuck?' Are you for real?"

"Listen – it's not been easy for me. I've missed out. All these things that are so natural for you are much more . . . It's like a language I've not learned, you know? I just want a nice girl and romance. Love. Intimacy. Physical love. But I don't know how. I say the wrong words and . . . Well, my experience . . ."

I started to hate myself just listening to me. So pathetic. I hadn't meant to say any of this.

She looked at me with pity. I guess that's what made the difference.

"We're gonna stop," I said.

We were up in the forest. There was a turn-off I knew and I pulled the car away from the road so we were out of sight. I knew that this was the moment when she might try and bolt, but I was prepared.

I'd practiced dropping a length of wooden dowel into the door-release mechanism on the passenger side. Sleight-of-hand stuff, but real simple. When she'd got in, I just leaned over her, saying something like, "It's a little cranky, this door," closing it again and dropping the dowel into the slot.

But she didn't try to run. She felt she'd already got the upper hand. She felt she knew me.

"I want you to put this canvas bag over your head," I said.

She looked at the sand-colored bag. "I won't be able to breathe."

"Sure you will. It has little holes."

"Why don't we just get in the back seat and get it over with?"

That pissed me off. "Put the bag on your head."

She sighed and put the bag on. I gently pulled the drawstring around her neck.

"Now hold your hands out in front of you. I'm going to cuff you."

"Won't that make it more difficult?"

It turned out she was right about that, but I was giving the orders. I cuffed her. She was starting to become mine. I looked at her flawless legs and her breasts, braless, under the blouse.

"What now?" she said, like I was giving her a driving lesson.

I reached under my seat for the knife and took it out of the sheath. This was the moment. This is what I'd dreamed about. She was totally within my control, or soon would be. I felt like an Olympic athlete out ahead of the pack, just about to cross the finishing line with a new world record.

"I don't see how it's going to work like this," she said, holding her cuffed hands up. "You really haven't thought this through, have you?"

That was the final provocation.

I stabbed at her, not really thinking where I was stabbing. The knifepoint went into the seatbelt crossing her upper chest, barely penetrating the textile. She must've felt it more like a punch. I didn't realize it at the time, but the unexpected jerk caused my hand to slip off the handle and over the blade. I cut myself pretty badly.

"The fuck are you *doing*, man?" said the canvas bag.

"I told you not to use that word!"

I stabbed again and the knife went in. She felt that one.

"*Fuck*!" She started to scream. "Help! Help! Help!"

I don't really remember any details after that. I just kept stabbing and stabbing, her cuffed hands flailing blindly, the bagged head jerking as she screamed. People are supposed to die when you stab them, but her energy was limitless. I didn't want to stab at her heart because I didn't want to damage the breasts and so I sliced away, hitting her forearms, her elbows, her shoulder, even her legs when she deflected my downward thrust.

I finally waited until her arms were down and swiped

ferociously at her throat, releasing a wave of blood down her front. That's when she finally settled and stopped moving.

I slumped back into my seat and sat on the Ruger. The gun! Why hadn't I just used the gun? I'd completely forgotten it existed.

She seemed to be dead, but there was a wet gurgling in her throat. I learned later that this was due to blood flowing down the windpipe, but it unnerved me. I was about to shoot her in the forehead just to finally get it over with, but she stopped making the noise.

Time vanished. I'd done the thing I'd dreamed of. I'd accomplished it. I was briefly without gravity, without weight. All was light.

I should say that the killing itself – the actual stabbing, the shooting, or whatever – is only a small and even insignificant part of it. The most disagreeable part, frankly. More important is the taking of the life – *having taken* the life. If I could've done it with a click of my fingers, I would have preferred it that way. I just wanted to own the girl. Maybe it's like a big-game hunter. The actual rifle shot is just a second of time. Then you have your lion, your rhino. You don't want the animal to suffer – just to die. It's your kill.

But I'd completed only the first step. I needed to act quickly while she was still warm. Also, it wasn't yet dusk and anyone could pass at any moment.

I lifted her under the arms and carried her round to the trunk, realizing too late that I should've opened the lid. I had to leave her on the ground while I got the keys to open it. I stripped off her clothes and laid her gently inside, using her blouse to wipe my hands.

I cut her head off in the trunk in our building's parking lot before I carried her body up to the apartment. I hadn't planned that part. I suppose I'd expected to do it inside, but when I opened the trunk and looked down at her, I felt such immense satisfaction at what I'd achieved. I almost wanted to blow the horn and get everyone around the car so I could say, "Look what I've done! Look at my girl!"

I looked up at the windows around me and imagined all the residents were watching me. I was standing there openly with a dead girl in my trunk and it occurred to me that cutting her head off right there in the parking lot would somehow be ceremonial – like cutting a wedding cake, or the inaugural ribbon for some new civic structure. I imagined applause as I did it.

You shouldn't imagine that cutting a head off is easy, even putting the anatomy of it to one side. The muscles at the sides and back are very thick. You really need a fine-edged blade to get through the fibers and between the vertebrae, but I'd bought some big macho knife for showing off. I did a pretty ragged job of it. But I got it off. I'd learned a lot of lessons for the next time.

First thing I did after getting her inside and cleaning her up was to take Polaroids. I posed the body on my bed – erotic stuff. Positions. Hers were the first adult woman's breasts I'd seen in reality and they were beautiful. I'd been right not to stab them. I also took pictures of the head – eyes opened and closed. The eyes would be the first to start deteriorating and I wanted to capture her face as perfectly as in life. The pictures really did her justice. She looked genuinely alive.

I must've taken fifteen Polaroids. I knew that the body wouldn't last long – three days max – and I wanted to be sure of the memories. I kept them in an envelope under a floorboard and wrote the date on each one. I'm not sure why I did that. To fix it in time, maybe, and remind myself that it had happened in reality. It was a dangerous thing to do. I was going to dispose of the body to get rid of all evidence connecting her to me, so the photos were a significant risk. I knew that.

Anyway, now she was used up. I could smell the decomp and if I could smell it, others would, too. My plan was to dismember her in the tub. I'd made preparations. I had oceans of bleach and Drano. I even dismantled the shower screen and its aluminum rails so that no blood could hide in crevices.

I won't go into details except to say that it was disagreeable work. There's a lot of mess and smells. Removing the teeth with a hammer was just plain irritating. But necessary. I'd have to dispose of the head and the hands carefully. They'd be discovered in the end and possibly she'd have fingerprints if any existed on record – but absolutely nothing to connect her to me. I wasn't sure if they were able to get a blood type from semen, so I rinsed her out with detergent using my mother's douche, which I didn't clean afterwards.

Disposal, like dismemberment, is a lengthy and boring process. I would have loved to have just thrown the body off a cliff into the sea, but I had to be careful. I had the torso in one refuse liner, the limbs in four others, the hands in two more and the head in an eighth. The car's trunk also had other bags of garbage in it, so if anyone stopped me I could happily open it up and say I was going to the county landfill. The smell would put any cop off looking closer.

I didn't think too hard about the locations. I'd throw a bag into a ravine, off a cliff or a canyon precipice by the side of the road – anywhere with no hiking paths or roads. The kinds of places, generally, where nobody could possibly walk because it was too steep. Birds and animals would scavenge there and the plastic would accelerate putrefaction. Even if someone found the parts, they'd be virtually unidentifiable.

I did wonder about discovery. I imagined someone – a municipal worker, a forest ranger – coming through the forest and seeing one of the bags. What's this? What's that smell? Often, I couldn't see where I was throwing the limbs – just into a mass of trees. What if there was a clearing down there and a family was having lunch and suddenly this arm appeared out of nowhere and landed smack on the picnic blanket? No kid would forget that. It'd be a story they told at school and for the rest of their lives, never knowing who'd thrown it or who it'd belonged to.

Nor could the girl herself have imagined when she left home that she'd wind up in pieces in a tub in Verdugo. That's the power of the killer. Murder is destiny. It changes life stories, frustrates expectations, cuts threads. You go out to catch the bus or buy a bottle of milk and you never come home. You're taken by a greater, irresistible force. Maybe you're found later or maybe you're never seen again.

There was always some degree of risk in the disposal. One time, I was just about to swing a bag out into the void – an arm, I believe – and I heard a car coming round the bend behind me. I quickly dropped the bag on the ground and just started to urinate, standing slightly side-on so the car would see the arc of urine. It embarrasses people. They'll stop if they see you throwing garbage into the forest, but they won't stop to speak to a guy with his dick out. Not even another man will do that.

Sometimes, I'd find litter at the side of the road where I stopped: cigarette butts, polystyrene cups, bus tickets, curled-up magazines. I'd put bits and pieces of these into the bags before I tossed them. My thinking was that it could complicate any investigation and create false trails. They'd open up the bags and look at the stuff and be like, Yeah, the perp's a coffee drinker. Yeah, he reads *Time* magazine. He's a Wrigley's man. You never know. Better to give the police too much information and slow down the process.

Anyway, I buried only the heads. It was important nobody found those until they'd rotted away. I put the first girl's head about three feet down in some forest back of Las Arenas.

Still, it was a day wasted. A day off work. As I drove around the county, I made a mental list of things I'd need to buy and do next time. It was on this occasion that I threw the hatchet I'd later recover with Lieutenant Schumer. It was very imprecise as a dismembering tool. A leg is not a branch. It needs to be taken apart carefully at the tendons and ligaments.

So after spending hours disposing of her parts, I went by Webster's with my list.

"A boning knife?" said Webster.

"Uh huh. My mother won't eat off the bone. She's picky like that."

"You should cook it slow. The bones just fall right out."

"I'm with you on that, Mister Webster, but my mother has a bee in her bonnet you wouldn't believe."

My mother never shopped at Webster's. She'd sooner buy a root beer than a hammer or a pot of paint.

"And there's a thin dagger in your cabinet," I said. "Can I look at it?"

"The stiletto style? Sure. For self-defense?"

"That's it. Not for me. My mother's terrified of all these rape stories in the paper. I told her: 'Put a dagger in your purse just in case.'"

Webster nodded. Here was a customer who knew his knives.

"I figure a fixed blade is better for stabbing," I said. "You don't want it closing on your hand."

"That's right," said Webster. "This is a full tang blade."

The dagger was beautifully weighted with a very fine, sharp point.

"It's strong if that's what you're thinking," said Webster, fingering the point. "Carbon steel. Go through a thick coat like butter."

"Perfect. I'll also need some paracord. Say, three yards."

Afterward, I went to the Holding Cell for a few drinks. The cops weren't yet off duty and the place was quiet. I had a couple beers and looked at the newspaper. On page one:

BODY OF WOMAN DISCOVERED – A body identified as that of missing Buena Vista woman Veronica Coulson was found today in a ravine about one mile south of Hudd Canyon Road. Her car was discovered last Wednesday on Oban Drive. Police had been searching the area for evidence. The undersheriff said that marks on it indicated foul play . . .

Marks. Foul play. It must have been the same case Amber had

talked about. They were withholding the details of the wire around her neck, as I expected they would. They did that to root out the crazies who later claimed credit for the crimes. Only the real killer would know it.

I felt a stab of envy. Would *my* girl feature on page one? It would be potentially risky for me if they found the parts and identified her, but I resented the killer who took women from their cars. Everyone was talking about him. Him and the black rapist. Nobody knew about me. Nobody knew my power.

It was a paradox. I was Superman. I was Spider-Man. But nobody could know. As soon as my powers became known, I'd start to lose them.

The first cops started to come into the bar, smelling of sweat and strong cologne, of cigarettes and too much coffee.

"Hey! It's Joe Friday!" said one of them (referring to the character from *Dragnet*). "Got your cuffs, Joe?"

I raised my glass in acknowledgment of their wit. Cheers! Here's to your next discovery in the ravines of Buena Vista State Park, gents!

TWELVE

Dwight returned to the area where he'd killed the old man and seen the Arco attendant driving away. The verge where the old man had fallen still showed drag marks leading into the forest. There was some blood. He paused and held his breath, waiting to see if the old man would speak. Nothing.

He stepped into the trees and followed the track of bent stems, scraped earth and blood to where he'd left the body. There was nothing. The man had gone.

Dwight looked around. Maybe the man had come round and walked to the shack Dwight had seen before through the trees, though it would have been difficult with his brains out like they were. The shack showed itself through the trunks and fronds. Pretty close.

He went carefully over mossy logs, rotten branches and spongy leaf compost to examine the shack. There was no smoke from the rusted iron chimney and no sound from within. He went to the stoop and saw that the steps had been recently swept. Stiff broom bristles had left marks in the accumulated dirt.

The door was locked. Through the window, he could see a blue sleeping bag unzipped, a single coffee cup on the table and a revolver next to it. Looked like a .38. Had the old hiker managed to crawl here?

Dwight walked around the property until he saw fresh boot prints on a muddy path leading away from the shack. Some of these old shacks had a cesspit out back from before the sewer pipes had been laid in by the county. He followed the path and came to a patch of raw earth that had been stamped down with the same boot prints. It was roughly the size and shape of a grave.

He looked around and listened. Maybe the old man would speak from under the earth. No – just forest sounds: birds, the distant hammering of a woodpecker. There was some undulation of the cosmic consciousness at work here, but he didn't know exactly what it meant.

He got back in his car and drove the few yards to the turn-off from where the gas monkey's Ford Galaxie had emerged. He saw the twin tire marks and followed them, stopping where the car must have parked.

There was blood on the ground. Quite a lot of blood concentrated in one place, as if someone had lain there awhile, or at least been bleeding heavily. He squatted and looked at the stain. Something glinted.

He pinched it between his thumb and forefinger: a small stud earring. Gold, maybe. It was almost completely coated with blood. The back of it was missing. It must have been pulled out.

A car passed on the road. Dwight looked up. It was a black and white Dodge – a CHP cruiser. It stopped a few yards down the road and he heard the engine cut out, the doors open. The two voices were clear in the forest silence.

"See that? I told you. Drag marks. Probably throwing garbage in the forest."

"Wait. There's blood. That's a lot of blood."

Dwight tried to see through the foliage. One of the patrolmen was bending to look at the ground.

"It goes into the forest. There's a blood trail."

"Uh huh."

"Come on. We need to check it out."

"In these shoes?"

"Seriously? There might be a body."

"Or maybe someone hit a deer and it dragged itself into the forest. That's what they do."

"Look – I don't wanna wear a uniform the rest of my life. You can wait here and protect your shoes. I'm gonna take a look."

"Whatever, man. Go crazy."

One of the cops went into the forest. Dwight heard him rustling about and swearing occasionally as twigs cracked. He emerged wiping dirt from his hands.

"Nothing."

"Like I said: a deer. Driver probably dragged it off the road thinking it was dead and it came round later. Probably in shock. It happens."

"Yeah."

"And you've ruined your shoes."

"You know they don't give medals for having clean shoes, right?"

"I don't wanna goddamn medal."

"No shit. Come on."

The cruiser drove off. Dwight stood rolling the ear stud between thumb and index finger, waiting for it to speak. It had nothing to say.

Joe was in the forest near the shack. He'd heard the engine then heard the man moving through the trees. He watched through his rifle's telescopic sights as the figure came around the shack and approached the place Joe'd buried the old man.

The man had all his hair buzzed off like a marine, but he didn't look like a marine. He looked kinda dorky in his collared shirt buttoned right to the neck and he moved through the undergrowth like someone who didn't know the hills. Was this the guy who'd left the body of the old hiker? Maybe he'd come looking for him. The rifle's crosshairs centered on his head.

No, said Ananiel.

Joe lowered the rifle and stood silently as the guy went back to his car and drove off, though apparently not very far because the door opened and closed again within earshot.

Another car arrived, out of sight on the road, and Joe heard indistinct voices. A lot of people in the forest today. Maybe he should go into town and get some supplies. Maybe call in on Sally and the baby.

Dwight was back home and writing in his bedroom. He'd taken an acid tab first thing that morning.

SATURDAY 10 July, 1970, 214 Larch Street, Buena Vista (Home), California, USA. 74°F and sunny with high humidity. 10:12AM. Other people can occupy your soul and you can occupy theirs. Vision becomes spherical and without boundaries. With practice, the Kriya practitioner can see into buildings, into the earth and even into people. The gaze becomes panoramic and consciousness is oceanic. Seek light wherever you may find it and conjoin with the light. It is the Universal . . .

"Dwight? Dwight!" His father's voice. "Can you come down here?"

"I'm writing."

"You'd better get down here."

Dwight closed the book and stared at the wall, trying to see through it. It undulated slightly but there was no transparency. He'd have to practice more. If only he didn't have to tolerate his family. They were really bumming him out with their killjoy authoritarianism. More than once he'd thought how cool it'd be if he went down for breakfast and found them dead on the kitchen floor. He'd just step over them – "'Scuse me" – and eat his oatmeal while looking at them. Maybe flick a spoonful at his father's face, which'd obviously be frozen in some outraged postmortem expression. He laughed.

"Dwight, goddamn it!"

He went down the stairs and found his father in the kitchen holding the baseball bat he'd used to kill the old hiker.

"What's this?" said father.

"It's my old bat."

"I mean, why is it covered with blood and hair like this on the stoop? Do you have something to tell me, Dwight? Because I'm five seconds away from calling the cops."

"There was a coon."

"What?"

"I don't mean a Negro. I wouldn't use a racial term like that, though I've heard you say it. I had colored friends in the city. No, there was a raccoon. I saw it out back. I think it might have been in the garbage. So I waited for it and hit it with the bat."

"You killed a coon with a bat?"

"Uh huh."

Father looked at the thick smears of brown coagulate and hair. "It looks like you beat it to mincemeat, Dwight. How many times did you hit it?"

A shrug. "It wouldn't die. I had to hit it a few times. To put it out its misery, you know."

He couldn't stop himself. He imagined his father's face with cold oatmeal slopping down it, frozen in this same outraged expression. Not just a spoonful of oatmeal, though. A whole bowl upended over his face. He could *see* it now, oozing in a grainy beige wave. He giggled a little. He couldn't stop it.

"You think this is funny? Does this seem normal to you? You beat an animal to death with your own hands."

"No, I used a bat. I wouldn't use my hands. A bite from a coon could be pretty nasty. Some of them carry rabies or TB."

His father looked at him, pressurized frustration giving way to anger. He was holding the bat with one hand. It wouldn't have taken much to use the bat on Dwight, his drug-addled, schizophrenic homosexual son. Sure – the doctors had told him everything. He'd never tell Dwight's mother about that part. It'd break her heart. It wasn't a subject that would ever be raised at their dining table.

"Can I go back to my writing now?"

"Your writing. Sure, go back to your writing. And take a pill."

"I took my pill." A smirk.

"If you see any more coons, tell me. I'll use the .22. It's much cleaner and more humane that way."

"Sure, Dad."

Dwight decided he might be happier if he moved up to that abandoned cabin in the state park – not the place he'd seen that morning, but the other one that belonged to the old hiker guy. He probably wouldn't be returning to it any time soon.

And he wondered about whoever had buried the old hiker guy. Had it been the Arco gas monkey? Maybe he'd returned to the turn-off and seen the body. Why bury it? Something weird was happening. Consciousness is oceanic. Those who have transcended can become as one, even if on different continents.

"Joe. God, it's you," said Sally at the door. "I saw someone standing out there on the street and I was about to call the police. You look terrible. Come in."

Joe paused, looking behind him into the street. He was wearing the exact same clothes as the last time and a plaid hunting cap with earflaps down. "Why would you call the police?" he said.

"Haven't you seen the news? A whole family was murdered and their house burned down. It was just a few miles from here. Police say it must have been some maniac. A junkie, maybe. Are you going to come in?"

Joe went in.

"I've got some hotpot if you're hungry," said Sally. "I always save something in case you come round."

He ate without taking his coat off. There were matches, a knife and bullets in the deep pockets. The .38. Hotpot dribbled into his beard.

"I'm afraid, Joe."

"You don't need to be afraid." Ananiel had promised. Their names were in the Book of Life. They'd be saved. They wouldn't have to be reaped.

"But there's some maniac going around killing families and we're alone here. We need a man at home, Joe. I'm even afraid to drive alone. Have you seen there's another one killing women? He gets them out of their cars and leaves their bodies in the forest."

He thought of the old hiker under the ground up at the shack. There were still blisters on his hands from cutting through all the roots to dig that grave. Who was the young shaven-headed guy peeping around? Was he the one who'd left the body? A message? Some kind of communication? A connection had to exist. Ananiel had said nothing, but . . .

"You don't have to go back to work if you're not ready," said Sally, "but I could really use you at home. You know I can't take the baby to work and LeeAnn sometimes has the same shifts as me."

Joe slurped at the hotpot and tore off a chunk of bread.

"One of the guys called me," said Sally. "He said you're in his shack and he's worried. He said the auto shop'd take you back tomorrow. He said it's not healthy being up in that shack at night with all the damp . . . Are you listening?"

"Yeah. But these are little things. The sea's going to give up the dead. There's gonna be a lake of fire. The fearful and the unbelieving and the abominable and whoremongers and sorcerers and idolaters and all the liars'll be in the lake of fire."

She looked at him. "Have you been taking more mescaline?"

"You don't understand, Sal."

"Then explain it to me, Joe! Jesus! You're a father. You're a husband. Why are you living out in the forest and putting drugs in your brain when your family needs you? How'd you feel if the next time you came round the house was a pile of ashes and we were dead in it?"

"It's not gonna happen."

"You don't know that."

No, said Ananiel. *Don't tell her. The mortals can't understand.*

"Look, Joe. I can't take much more of this. I've been patient. I'm not gonna wait forever for you to get your head straight. We got lives to live and bills to pay. Don't give me any shit about lakes of fire. This is the real world here."

He stood. "Sal . . . I've gotta go."

"Don't you wanna see your son? Wait. I'll fetch him."

He stood with his hands in his coat pockets. Matches. Knife. Bullets. .38.

Go, said Ananiel. *Your destiny awaits.*

Sally came in with the baby in her arms, cooing at it. "Look here! It's your daddy. Let's say hello to Daddy." Then to Joe: "Are you gonna hold him?"

Joe took the baby in his arms. The tiny face seemed to grimace.

"It's the smell," said Sally. "You stink of smoke and damp."

Do not be distracted from your purpose, said Ananiel. *The child's place in heaven is certain.*

Joe looked at the baby. His son.

Ananiel said, *And the sun will be as black as sackcloth of hair, and the moon will become as blood.*

He handed the child back to Sally. "I gotta go."

"Well, don't be surprised if I'm not here next time you come around," she said. "I can't pay rent just on tips, Joe."

He left and walked the three miles to the house he'd been watching. All of the lights were out. The driveway was empty. He cut the phone line with his knife and lifted the unlocked garage door. There was a connecting utility room: washing machine, clothes spinner, a strong detergent smell. A single red sock lay on oatmeal tiles.

Ananiel sat in a leather armchair and counted the bullets.

Now to wait.

THIRTEEN

Amber came round to the apartment Saturday, giving me a hard time. We sat drinking coffee, waiting for my mother to come home.

"I saw you two lovebirds at the movie theater the other day," she said.

"What? Spying on me? Did Mom send you?"

"Mom? What are you talking about? I was getting out of work and I just saw you leaving the movie theater. You didn't look very happy. Either of you."

"It wasn't such a good movie, to be honest."

She looked at me.

"What?" I said.

"Nothing. I just can't see you two together."

"What are you trying to say, Amber?"

"What are you doing, Sonny? I mean, really. She's not the right kind of girl for you. She's still at high school, for chrissakes."

"So what? There's only three, four years between us and she's mature for her age."

"You need some easy hippie coed who'll get you up to speed with love in the '70s."

"This is none of your business, Amber. And that's not my type at all. I prefer modesty."

"Listen to you! It sounds like you went back in time at Atascadero. We're not in the fifties anymore."

"Just butt out. You don't know her. And you don't know me."

"Sonny – I'm probably the only person who *does* know you." Serious now.

She was referring to our childhood. Things I'd never told the doctors. Things Mom didn't know. What really happened to the neighbors' cat, for example.

"Does she know about Gran and Gramps?" said Amber. "Or that you were in a mental hospital?"

"Just leave it."

"You think she's not gonna find out? That kind of thing is kind of hard to explain away once you're at the altar." She put on a mimsy voice as Dulcie: "'Say, Sonny? Why aren't your grandparents at our wedding?' Then a deeper voice: 'They couldn't come, honey, 'cause I shot 'em.'"

"That's not funny, Amber. And she doesn't talk like that. I'm gonna go if you keep on with this shit. In fact, I've got my parole psych appointment this afternoon. I wouldn't be surprised if they sign me off for good. They've been saying I'm making great progress."

"I'm sure they have."

"What's that supposed to mean?"

"You know. You're a smart guy."

I didn't want to be angry when I went into the city later. I took some deep breaths. I drank some coffee. I knew she was trying to rile me.

"I saw that story you were telling us about," I said. "The killer who strangled and buried the girls. They didn't mention the wire round her neck in the article."

"Of course not. In fact . . . no. I shouldn't tell anyone."

"There's been another one?"

"I can't say."

"We'll you've kind of said it anyway now. What's happened?"

"Okay, but you can't tell anyone. I know you go drinking at the Holding Cell."

"Do they mention me?"

"Joe Friday with his cuffs. The wannabe cop. Screw 'em. It's what they're like."

"Right."

"Well, anyway. A witness called in to give a statement. He was driving on Highway 9 and there was a car in front of him – a silver Chevy, he thinks – and he could see a girl's long blond hair hanging out the back of the trunk. Like the driver had thrown her in there and slammed the lid, not realizing. And then the CHiPs found another abandoned car belonging to a woman."

"So the police are looking for a silver Chevy."

"Yeah. But they're not going to give this to the papers, or the guy might change cars like that black rapist does."

"What cars is the rapist using?"

"A blue Corvette Stingray and a Pontiac GTO. There's another but I can't remember. A Dodge, maybe."

I'll be honest: I was kinda irritated that the police and the papers were talking about these other guys when *my* girl was missing. I'd not seen anything about her in the papers.

Amber sipped her coffee. "But a lot of the cops think it's the girls' own fault. The ones who get raped, anyway. Everyone knows hitching is dangerous, but they do it anyway. It's like prostitutes who get murdered. They're kinda asking for it when they get in a car with some guy they don't know. And anyway, most of the detectives are on this arson-murder case right now. They're getting a lot of pressure on that one because, you know, it's families. It's in the suburbs."

Amber talked all self-assured and knowledgeable like she was one of the detectives – like she was personally responsible for fighting crime in Buena Vista – when she was really just a Sheriff's Department typist who gossiped too much with the other typists. I suspected she was sleeping with one of the detectives. Anyway, she had to tell *someone* this stuff. Unlike me, she couldn't keep anything secret for long. I would've been a much better cop.

"Someone said at the gas station today there's been another arson murder," I said.

"Yeah. Last night. North of El Bosque. Family of three shot and the house burned. They say he cuts the phone line and he's probably waiting for them when they get home. Can you imagine?"

"I've read they think he's some acid head. Is he leaving evidence?"

"Why do you say that?"

"Well, a professional wouldn't leave shell cartridges or fingerprints. If they're saying he's on drugs, it probably means he's making a mess of the scene. Maybe he's, I don't know, drinking milk from a glass and leaving it on the table so they can test saliva and get prints. Sloppy."

"You watch too many cop shows, Sonny."

But her face said I was right.

I'd been thinking a lot about those family slayings. They were dramatic. A whole family shot as they sat in a line, bound, in the same room where they watched TV, or played cards, or ate a meal together. Thanksgiving. Christmas. Birthdays with tone-deaf serenades and candles. These arson murders were executions, really. Why the fire? To destroy evidence? To better erase the victims? Maybe there was some religious or ritual element that the police weren't revealing – bloody hieroglyphics on the walls, or other satanic paraphernalia.

I couldn't have killed like that. Too cold-blooded. Too impersonal. There was no human connection that I could see. The killer conceived his victims in a purely numerical sense – as though accumulating units. To every man his own choice and methodology, I guess. It's misguided to think that a killer will kill just anyone in any way, unless they're genuinely, certifiably crazy. Those people barely know that they're killing. There's no art to it. Their victims are accidental – the most pointless kind of death.

THR3E

I wouldn't have killed Dulcie. I wouldn't have killed my sister. The very idea repelled me. It's equally unlikely that the arson murderer could do what I did. His kills seemed clinical. Did he talk to them? Did he try to form a connection? Did the victims mean anything to him? How did he choose them – or did he choose the house rather than its residents? Did he take souvenirs? I didn't think so.

I'd been thinking a lot about evidence. *My* evidence. I'd disposed of the girl's body, but I'd kept some of her things: her photo ID, a stud earring, the shoe she'd left in the car's footwell. It was a bad idea. I knew it. Those things would put me in jail if someone found them in my closet. But I couldn't let her go.

We'd shared something very few people have shared – experiences that most humans never have. The intensity of our short relationship was totally fresh in my mind. I remembered everything because every moment together had been so electrically vivid. A girl like that comes along just once in a lifetime. Don't let anyone tell you any different; the first time is the most intense. Every subsequent one is measured by it. There'd be more beautiful girls and greater pleasure, but the first was like ripping a diaphanous membrane into another dimension. It could be ripped only once and its ripping was sublime.

A lot of kids my age had travelled. They'd gone cross-country in campervans. They'd gone to India in search of enlightenment or whatever and they'd had adventures, romances – the kinda things that would define them and create memories they'd commemorate in postcards and photos and keepsakes for the rest of their lives. They'd get married, have kids, grow old, but those memories of youth and excitement would remain with them always as something perfect. I'd traveled, too – but to a place few could ever reach or even imagine. I needed my souvenirs.

I also had the Polaroids in the envelope under the floorboard. They sustained me for two, three weeks after I disposed of the parts. Taking them out was almost a sacrament. I touched them only on the edges to avoid marking the images and I laid them on the bed to create scenarios. Sometimes, I added dialogue: hers and mine. My hands would tremble as I handled them, astounded at this proof of what I'd achieved. I might not have believed them if they'd been written, but photographic images are undeniable. I'd been there. I'd taken them. It was real.

The problem was I'd internalized them so completely after three weeks that I didn't need to look anymore. They were still valuable as objects, as artifacts, but the excitement had waned. I needed something new as a stimulus. Also, they were evidence more damning than the ID or the ear stud. I could hardly say I'd found them somewhere and decided to keep them out of interest.

I thought about scattering them in different places: one on the street, one in a phone booth, one in a public toilet. I imagined the reactions of the people who found them, wondering if they were real or some grisly Halloween put-up job. I mean, Hollywood has shown us the same thing. The average person wouldn't know the difference either way. Their minds would just reject the reality. It's a mannequin. It's a doll. It's not a real head.

But there were details in the photos: my bed, a piece of carpet, certain architectural shapes. Possibly enough for a smart person to join the dots. And any pathologist would see the telltale signs of livor mortis, petechia and the rest. I'd have to destroy them. That was non-debatable.

I took them in my jacket pocket when I went to see the psychiatric social worker in Frisco. We chatted about work, my dreams, my mother and Dulcie. I was the picture of non-lethal sanity. He tried to trick me at one point, but I was ready for him.

"So there's been a lot of abductions and murders down in Buena Vista recently, huh?" he said.

"Yeah? I guess."

"You don't read the papers? Watch the news?"

"I mean, I do – but I prefer not to focus on the negative, you know? I've had enough negativity in my life already. There's plenty of good things I should be concentrating on. Anyway, don't you think the news is a little obsessed with generating fear?

It's their product. That's what keeps people coming back. People like to be afraid and imagine the worst. Maybe it's the same thing that makes horror films attractive. Something vicarious. I don't know . . . I prefer a comedy."

He smiled and scribbled away in his notebook. He closed it and rested it in his lap, his hands folded over it, smiling like he'd cured me.

"Listen, Sonny – I don't think you need to keep coming to these meetings."

"Are you sure? The parole specifies–"

"I make the final decision. If I deem you safe for society, I make the call."

I thought of the photos in my pocket: the headless girl in porno poses.

"Wait outside on the sofa," he said, "and I'll write my conclusions. Grab a coffee. Ten minutes or so."

I waited in the reception area, where I'm pretty sure the girl at the desk was making eyes at me. Something had changed since the first kill. It was as if women could see the real me. They could see the power. The potency. I thought about wandering over and casually taking out the photos. "Say, do you wanna see some pics of my girl?"

But the doc came out and handed some handwritten notes to the receptionist – swirly and illegible as usual.

"Cassie will type this up and I think we're done here, Sonny." He held out his hand for a shake. "I wish you all the best. It's a new start. A new life. Make the most of it."

I sat in the car afterward, reading and re-reading his summary:

> The patient has made a full recovery from the violent split within himself that led to his adolescent crime. He appears to be functioning as a fully unified self, focusing on his work and his relationships. He understands and is able to verbalize his emotions and his motivations. There appears to be no neurotic build-up. He has responded positively and effectively

to years of treatment and I see no psychiatric reason to consider him a danger to himself or to any other member of society. I thus recommend a permanent expungement of his juvenile records and an end to the psychiatric element of his parole conditions.

Essentially, I was fully sane. I had a certificate to prove it.

Saturday, I picked up Dulcie from Merluza and we went to the boardwalk downtown. It was some kinda public holiday and the place was so crowded that she hung on to my arm, afraid of the massing humanity.

There were street musicians, people eating and drinking out on the terraces, jugglers, local craftspeople selling their pottery and paintings and beads. There were swooping screams and the rattle of the rollercoaster, the *pop-pop* and tinny clink of a shooting gallery, swirly organ music from one of the rides and a barker shouting, "Roll up! Roll up!" because that's what circus barkers are supposed to shout. I bought Dulcie a pink cloud of hot cotton candy on a stick and I got myself a bucket of buttered popcorn. It was all pretty jovial.

A crowd had gathered around a dais and we strolled to the periphery.

"A hypnotist!" said Dulcie.

I'd had some experience of that. They'd tried it on me at Atascadero.

"Who'll come on up and be hypnotized?" called the man on stage. He was dressed in an old-timey three-piece tweed suit with a bowler hat to match. A bow tie and a waxed mustache. "Don't be afraid!" he said. "There's nothing to fear but your own mind!"

"Oh, go up and do it," said Dulcie.

"It's really not my thing."

"Are you afraid?" Wheedling now.

THR3E

"It's not that . . ."

"Here! Here!" said Dulcie, her hand in the air. "Sonny'll do it!"

"We have a taker," said the man on stage. "Come on up, young man."

People clapped encouragement and cheered.

Well, I was angry. I didn't want to do hypnotism and I especially didn't want to get up in front of all those people. But it would almost have made a bigger scene if I hadn't gone.

I went up the steps and onto the dais, looking over the heads of the crowd. Dulcie waved from the back, delighted.

The hypnotist approached, looking me in the eyes, smiling, trying to form a connection. He said quietly so the audience wouldn't hear, "Don't sweat it. Just a little fun." This was to show me that he was identifying, empathizing. Then louder, for the audience: "What's your name, young man?"

"Sonny."

"Perfect! It's a lovely sunny day."

The audience laughed obediently. They were with him.

"First, I'm going to ask Sonny to do some simple things," said the hypnotist.

Right. He was seeking acquiescence and trust. If I did something simple, I'd be volunteering my will. If I suffered no harm, I'd trust him for the next step.

"Raise your left arm, Sonny."

I did it.

"Now your right arm."

I did it, feeling a little stupid standing there like that. He saw it immediately.

"Very good. Drop your arms. Better to be relaxed. Okay, now we'll proceed to the hypnotism. Are you comfortable?"

Identifying again. Reassuring me. "Yes," I said.

"Now I'd like you to close your eyes. Good. I'd like you to roll your eyes up without opening them. Very good. Listen to my voice. You're feeling very relaxed. You're forgetting all these good people here and you're in a happy place – a place where you like to go, where you truly feel yourself. Are you there?"

He was speaking smoothly to lull me and, in fact, I did think about such a place. I also faked a few of the symptoms of a hypnotized person: the rapid eye movement, a slight twitch of the hand, a slight droop of the head. I licked my lips once. "Yes," I said.

"Describe your place," he said.

I could sense the audience buying this, whispering and muttering among themselves.

"I'm on a beach, relaxing in the sun," I lied. "I have a cool beer."

"Wonderful. Can you taste that beer?"

"Uh huh." It wasn't a beer I was tasting.

"Why don't you lick that beer foam off your lips?"

I did it, but only to avoid a scene. I was getting really tired of this stuff.

"I think I hear the music of a hula band, Sonny. Can you hear it?"

Hula music started through an amplifier. The audience tittered. Some of them must have seen the show before.

"Yes."

"Why don't you show us a little hula dancing?"

I didn't move.

"Sonny? Can you hear the music?"

I opened my eyes and stared dead into his.

"I'm not gonna dance."

He caught my stare full on, his pupils rushing into black dilation. His mouth opened slightly. He jerked his hand and the hula music scratched silent on the turntable.

The audience gaped and chattered. Was this part of the show?

He was still looking at me. I knew what he was thinking. He thought I'd been under the whole time. He thought he'd had me. But he didn't look angry. He looked afraid.

He turned to the audience and put on his professional smile.

"Well, folks – not everyone can be hypnotized! It seems I've failed with young Sonny here. Thanks for having a go, young man!"

The people clapped uncertainly.

He offered his hand and we shook, but he was looking at me funny like, What's your game? Where'd *you* come from?

Dulcie was confused. "What happened? Didn't it take? We thought you were hypnotized."

"I was just messing with him."

"Why would you do that?"

"I wasn't going to stand up in front of a bunch of people and make a fool of myself for entertainment."

She looked at me. "But you *did* make a fool of yourself. It was embarrassing."

"I made a fool of *him*."

"Come on. Let's get out of here."

We went for a drink and a meal. Dulcie prattled about her studies and what school she might choose and something someone said somewhere. Amber was probably right: she wasn't the right girl for me. She was the part of me I needed to project. Anodyne. Naïve. Harmless. The relationship with her made me more invisible. She could never really be my girl because I didn't want to kill her. When we walked hand in hand, I thought of the other girl's severed hand in mine. Dulcie's hair was dry and flyaway like hay, while the other girl's hair had been heavy, dark silk through my fingers. Dulcie was entirely sexless.

I was thinking about the first girl most of the time I was with Dulcie. After dropping her back at Merluza, I drove by the address of the first girl (her address was on the ID I'd kept) and I sat watching the house, imagining her in her room combing her hair or listening to records in her underwear. I even thought about walking up to the door and asking if I could see her room to smell her perfume again. Her body. Maybe lie on her bed and look at the ceiling and imagine her doing the same.

"How do you know our daughter?" they might say. (She was still technically missing at this point.)

"She was my girlfriend. I cut her throat."

And they wouldn't be angry or sad. They'd understand how special it was. How rare. Because she'd been chosen.

Obviously, I wouldn't actually do something like that. I'm not crazy.

But something had to change. I was like a lovesick puppy. I would have to find another girl and this time do it differently.

I'd been thinking a lot about process and how to control the situation to avoid the kinda violence that happened before, which had ruined her beautiful skin.

I waited a little longer outside the girl's house. There were often more hitchhikers around dusk after class got out, so I killed time just sitting in the car and imagining who would be next in the passenger seat. I'd managed to clean it at the station, though you could still see a faint stain in daylight. Another reason to wait for dark.

Later, out in the state park, I pulled off the road and turned to the pretty blond sitting next to me.

She smiled, so innocent. "Problem with the car?" she said, not thinking of rape or murder. I took that as my cue. I hadn't even planned it, but she'd given me a scenario that was better than my own little drama.

She was lovely. I knew from the first moment I'd seen her three cars ahead that she was the next one. I almost accelerated, fearful that one of the other cars would pick her up first, but they all swerved around her as she stood with her thumb out. She was wearing a feminine flower-print dress and mischievous heeled boots that gave her legs some attitude. I'd stopped. I'd let her in and leaned over her. Excuse me . . . it's a little cranky, this door.

Up in the forest, I said, "Yeah. There might be a problem. Did you hear the rear wheel on your side? We might have a flat. I'm just gonna check it if you don't mind."

"Okay!"

I took the gun and held it out of sight along my thigh. I walked around the back and made a big show of squatting to examine the tire. The situation she'd suggested was really perfect. I opened the trunk as if I was going to get the spare and the jack.

I motioned for her to roll down her window. "Say, do you think you could hold a flashlight while I fix this? It won't take five minutes."

"Sure! No problem."

I reached to open the door from the inside so she wouldn't notice the dowel blocking the mechanism. Once she was standing next to me by the rear wheel, I showed her the gun.

"I'm sorry but you'll have to get in the trunk."

She looked at me confused, like she was unsure what getting in the trunk had to do with fixing the flat tire (that wasn't flat) or maybe that she'd misheard me.

"Get in the trunk?" she said.

"Yeah." I raised the gun. "It's just that, well, we're gonna pass my girlfriend's house and if she sees me driving with a beautiful blond in the passenger seat, she's gonna kill me, you know? It's just for a mile and I'll let you out."

She clearly didn't believe me. I didn't believe myself. Why the gun? It was a really stupid explanation. But I hadn't mentioned rape and the whole little speech kinda made me look inadequate, unthreatening.

"I could just lie down in the back seat," she said. "Then your girlfriend wouldn't see me."

I didn't have the heart to pursue the farce any further. I just pulled back the bolt and pointed the gun more threateningly. I wanted to avoid it descending into discussion like the last time.

She was uncertain but hadn't yet veered into refusal. The gun helped.

"Here, let me help you," I said as she stepped on the fender and into the trunk, looking back at me all the while. I'd laid out a blanket in there that looked like it was for comfort but was really for the blood.

"It's hard," she said, trying to find the right position.

I shot her in the back of the head, just behind her left ear, and she slumped heavily. There was a single spasm, a faint sigh and she was dead. Just like that. The bullet hadn't even exited, being a .22, and there was only a thin trickle of blood. I couldn't believe it. No cuts. No bruises. Her face and body were pristine.

I closed the trunk and looked around at the tattered darkness of the forest. I wanted to whoop. I wanted to fire off a few shots into the sky.

Instead, I drove down to the Holding Cell. I couldn't control myself in the parking lot. I had to open the trunk and look at her curled there like she was sleeping – right in front of the bar where cops were passing almost every moment. It was foolish, but I felt such immense pride and joy at what I'd done. I had a new girl and I'd be taking her home within an hour to decapitate her and lie with her in my bed.

FOURTEEN

Dwight had been doing some reasoning. The bloodstained ear stud he'd found in the forest meant that the gas monkey must have killed a woman. Possibly a hitchhiker. The nature of oceanic consciousness meant that everything was linked. Minds were intersecting ripples. It was no coincidence that Dwight had seen the gas monkey buying the gun. It was no coincidence they'd both been on that stretch of road at the same time, both with victims. These were all signs.

Dwight's task was to interpret the signs and form the right connections. The acid helped. It opened doors and made connections easier. He'd flushed that other crap down the toilet, that chlorpromazine the docs had given him. It slowed his mind and made it dull. Now he saw everything clear as day. The ear stud was a message: kill a female hitchhiker. The next step would make itself clear. He just had to continue toward the light, even if that meant first passing round the crater-pocked and unmapped dark side of the moon.

There were a *lot* of girls thumbing lifts. Which one? He drove by three or four, looking at them, waiting for a sign. Some of them stepped out into the road, smiling like girls did, but he felt no oceanic ripple.

Then up ahead he saw a flash. It seemed a flash of God: a brilliant, splintering burst that briefly blinded him and made him raise a hand to his eyes. There was a girl with a bag that seemed to be covered with mirror fragments or polished shards of silver metal. It had caught the sun as she turned. He pulled alongside.

"Where you going?" he said.

"UCBV? The campus?"

"Hop in."

She got in and he drove off west through downtown as the girl fussed with something in her bag.

"I like the mirrors," said Dwight. "They're flashy."

"Yeah? I made it myself. It's kinda heavy but it's unique, you know?"

"I thought I'd seen God."

"Huh?"

She looked at him properly: a guy with a recently buzzed head and a kinda glazed expression. Probably a pill-head.

"You high?" she said.

"Sure."

That explained it.

"Got a lid?

"I got acid."

"Okay, but I won't take it now. I got a class."

"In the glove compartment," said Dwight.

She opened it and took a pill from the amber-colored glass jar, tucking it carefully into her jacket pocket. "You got a lot. You a dealer?"

"Nope."

"Hey, man . . . You've passed the turn-off for campus."

"Shit. I'll turn around up here."

He didn't turn around or stop.

"Listen – just drop me off right here," said the girl, her tone steady. "I'll still get there if I run. Are you listening?"

Dwight stared ahead, smiling. He didn't stop the car.

THR3E

"Fucking pill-heads," muttered the girl. "Hey, man! Wake up! We're headed out of town."

Dwight didn't hear this. He heard, "It's fine if you kill me, Dwight. I was hoping somebody would. Will you help me join the universal consciousness?"

He reached down beside his seat for the big knife and slashed sidelong across her throat. Blood sprayed on the inside of the windshield, on the side window, on Dwight in hot spurts. Her hands went to her neck like maybe she could hold it together. She gasped and bubbled, eyes gaping, mouth open, rigid in her seat, then still, blood rilling over her chest with decreasing force. Her head fell against the window with a thud.

He drove to the spot where he'd found the ear stud and parked. The smell of blood was strong and its heat seemed to fill the car. He rolled down the window to inhale the forest air. A fresh breeze was coming off the Pacific, whooshing in the tops of pines and redwoods. Beautiful.

Dwight dragged the girl's body out of the car and onto her back in the soil and fallen needles. He stood looking down at her. What now?

He had the ear stud in his pocket as a talisman and now he understood why. This girl didn't have pierced ears, but he was able to push the pin through her lobe using his thumb and his knife blade as a sort of anvil. That felt right. It had symmetry. Equilibrium had been partially restored to the oceanic consciousness.

He left her where she lay and headed back into town.

I was on duty at the gas station. It was a slow morning. I'd booked in a couple wax jobs, sold a few fuel oil changes and filled a couple dozen tanks, but I was bored and distracted. I was thinking about the previous night with my new girl.

What a beauty. What grace. What skin. We'd spent the whole

night together copulating then embracing, copulating then embracing. She'd posed for a bunch of photos and I'd left her rigid in the morning on my way to work. I was hoping she'd be pliable again when I got home.

I'd cut off her head in the building's parking lot and was carrying it up the steps in her brown leather rucksack when I met the tenant from upstairs going out. He was a guy of about thirty, a kinda bachelor type, and he was leaving with his girlfriend, presumably on a date. Both were well dressed and smelled of perfume or cologne. We nodded a greeting to each other. I might've said something like, "Good evening."

And as we passed on the steps, I had the sensation that I was outside myself looking down at the situation: the young couple heading out for a romantic date and me carrying a girl's severed head in her own bag and us greeting each other like everything was totally normal.

Now, I've never been legally judged as clinically insane. I've always been aware of my actions and able to describe them if not justify them. But in that moment, I felt it, or I wondered if perhaps I was caught somewhere in a gray area between crazy and sane. I mean, I recognized the outrageous nature of the situation. I could imagine the young couple's perfectly natural reaction if I'd opened the bag and said, "Hey – look at this." I mean, I could see the horror of it. Stranger than that was the idea that they were in a loving relationship and so was I. The only difference was that my date was in two pieces.

It could've gone either way. I could have looked at them and seen myself as monstrously aberrant. Instead, I saw it as an acceptable difference. I wasn't hurting them. They weren't hurting me. We were all happy. That's when I knew I was essentially sane. I was balanced.

A car came up the ramp and onto the gas station forecourt. I checked my collar in the mirror by the till and went out to serve the customer.

"Fill her up, sir?"

THR3E

The guy looked at me kinda weird through the rolled-down window. He had a recent buzzcut and was grinning fixedly. I smelled the blood before I saw it. He was covered in it. At least half of him was sprayed with it: his sleeve, his pants leg, his face and neck. I looked inside the car and saw it thick and brown inside the windshield, on the dash. The passenger seat was pooled black and coagulant.

"Are you okay, sir? Have you had an accident?"

"I just killed a girl." He held up a big, bloody bowie knife.

I nearly lost it. My first thought: he was a cop. They were onto me. They'd rigged up this unmarked car and sprayed it with red-dyed corn syrup as a way to catch me out. They were expecting me to break down. Cry, maybe, and confess it all.

We stayed like that. Minutes seemed to pass. It wasn't corn syrup. It was blood. It smelled like death. This was real.

"I saw you the other day," said Buzzcut, smiling, over-familiar.

I looked over the car's roof to see if Tom was inside watching me. I looked to the road to see if any other cars were coming in.

"Up near Cascade Road in the park," said Buzzcut.

Him. The guy standing in the road when I took the first girl.

"What do you want?" I said.

"I found the ear stud."

"What?" I looked again into the office. No Tom.

"In the bloodstain where you were," he said. "I found it there."

It was true the first girl had only one stud when I got her home. There was no way he could have known that.

"What do you want from me?" I said.

"Nothing. I think we're connected."

"Connected how?"

"Through the oceanic consciousness."

Shit. An acid head. Tom was moving about in the office. Any moment now, he'd see I was talking, not filling. If he came out and saw the blood . . .

"What'd you do with the stud?" I said.

"I put it in the new girl's ear. The one I just killed."

Another car pulled up behind Buzzcut.

"You got her in the trunk now?" I said.

"No. I left her in the same place up there. Where I found the ear stud."

Tom was standing at the door and looking at me like, What's the hold-up?

"Listen," I said. "You've gotta get out of here. I can't be . . . You can't be seen like this. You've got blood all over yourself and your car. The evidence . . ."

"Can you fill me up?"

"No. You've gotta leave *right now*. Go home. Wash up. Clean your car."

Another car joined the line for gas.

"I've got a cabin up on Oban Drive," he said. "My name's Dwight."

"Okay. Go home, Dwight. I'm helping you. Go. Now."

Tom was approaching. I stood and banged on the car's roof. Dwight pulled straight out into traffic, almost causing a smash. Horns blared. Tires squealed.

"What's going on here, Sonny?" said Tom. "They're waiting almost out to the road."

"Sorry, Tom. Some kid on drugs. He was virtually incoherent. I couldn't get rid of him."

"What was wrong with his windshield?"

"The windshield? Yeah, he'd thrown a chocolate milkshake at it. Real mess in the car."

"Goddamn kids. He should be in Vietnam. A couple tours under heavy fire and he'd not be throwing any milkshakes around."

"I'm with you, Tom. Let me get these cars serviced."

The customers passed in a haze. I have no idea what I did or said. I could only think of Dwight, who was clearly insane. Imagine if a cop had stopped him for his terrible driving and approached the car to find him covered in his victim's blood, the murder weapon right there in the car with him. He was an idiot and he was going to get caught. And he knew about me.

I thought about that ear stud. It seemed I'd been careless and left it at the scene. Now this lunatic had found it. Was he following me? Why was he up there on Cascade Road at the same time? How did he know where I worked? I even started thinking maybe he'd been at my house and found the first girl's ID or the other stud. My mind was speeding. As soon as one o'clock came around, I went to Tom. "Hey, Tom, I need to go home over lunch. I just remembered I left the gas cooker on this morning. Don't wanna burn the house down!"

"Fine, Sonny, but don't be late."

It was a struggle to maintain the speed limit on the way back to Verdugo. I left the car parked at an angle and raced up the steps to the apartment. I could hardly get my key in the lock for trembling. I went straight to my room.

The lock had been smashed off. A claw hammer lay on the floor amid splinters and the hasp. It was the hammer I kept in the kitchen. I could feel the pulse in my throat, in my head. If this was my mother, I'd have to kill her immediately.

I pushed the door open, fighting the urge to throw up. I'd left the girl in bed under the sheets, but now she was uncovered. Her head was on the shelf where I'd left it. I checked under the floorboard. The photos of the second girl were still there. I went to the wardrobe and lifted the carpet at the bottom. The ear stud and the new girl's ID were still there, but the ID of the first girl was missing. It was *missing*.

I checked again. Had I disposed of it accidentally with her stuff? I checked the pockets in all of my clothes. Nothing.

Was this my mother? Had she taken the hammer and busted the lock and seen the body and had all of her suspicions confirmed? Had she gone looking for evidence and found the ID and taken it directly to the police? "My son's the killer. He's got a headless body in his bed right now!"

Or was it Buzzcut? Maybe he'd followed me home and knew my shifts at the gas station.

I looked at the girl lying there nude and beautiful. I'd have to get rid of the body right now. I'd have to throw it all away before I'd had time to fully enjoy it. I might have to kill my mother.

Time was passing. I needed to get back to work. I needed refuse bags. No time for dismemberment. I'd have to dispose of the body whole.

Then I noticed the gun. It was a Smith and Wesson .38 revolver just sitting there on my bedside table beside the lamp and an empty glass. I opened the drawer. My Ruger was gone.

Stop. Think. What's going on?

I looked round the rest of the apartment and found the broken window in the bathroom, glass lying on the floor inside. So. A burglar. Not my mother.

I imagined myself in the burglar's shoes, walking into the corridor, approaching the open door of my mother's room. Nothing seemed disturbed within, though my mother always made her bed before leaving and there was an indentation in the linen and in the middle of a pillow as if someone had lain on top. No drawers or wardrobe doors were open.

The living room was as I'd left it that morning. Had he sat in here, too? The seats were pretty old and worn and it was hard to tell if anyone had occupied the space.

Then he must have passed the kitchen – nothing of interest there – and arrived at my room with its metal hasp and padlock: very attractive to a house-breaker. What's this? Treasure in here!

He breaks the door down and maybe recoils at the unexpected sight of a figure in the bed. He draws his gun but there's no movement. He flicks a toe. Nothing. He pulls down the sheet and sees the ragged hole where the head should be, the full breasts, the creamy abdomen. His mind's whirring. What's going on here? What *is* this?

He sits on the edge of the bed and sees the head on the bookshelf, eyes closed as if in sleep. Maybe a shiver goes up his spine. He came here as a criminal but he's entered a whole different dimension. The body. The head.

He looks in the bedside drawer and finds the Ruger – a pretty stylish gun. Pretty accurate. He weighs it against his .38 and decides on a swap. He could have stolen it but maybe for him there's some honor or fairness among transgressors.

But why did he take the first girl's ID? Why not the girl whose head was on the shelf? Some kinda souvenir to remember the experience by? Or was I now looking at a blackmail situation?

No. Wait. There was no evidence connecting me to the first girl except that ID. I could say I'd found it by the side of the road and was intending to hand it in. A smart blackmailer would have taken the second girl's ID because he had me red-handed. My Polaroid camera was right there on the shelf next to the head. He could have snapped a few evidence pics and taken them with him. Maybe he had.

I checked the camera but it was out of film. That's right. I remembered. I'd run out and needed to get some more.

Time was ticking. I had to be back at work.

I couldn't leave the room like this with the smashed lock and the dead girl and the head. My mother'd come home from work, see it all and be on the phone to the police in two seconds flat, delighted to have finally caught me at it again. I equally didn't want to get rid of the body in a rushed manner that could leave evidence. And, God, she was beautiful, this girl. I needed another night with her.

Only one thing for it. I drove like a maniac to Webster's to buy another lock and hasp.

"Problem with the last one?" said Webster, always happy to shoot the breeze in his down-home, drawling way.

"This one's for the tool shed," I said. "Been a few burglaries recently."

"Don't I know it. Scott says he's selling more guns and knives than ever."

Which reminded me: I now needed some .38 ammunition.

I raced back home and fitted the new lock as fast as I could – a real shoddy job, but the best I could do. I swept up the splinters and tossed the old lock. I pulled the bed linen straight and fluffed the pillow in my mother's room.

The broken window! *Shit*! No possible time to repair it now.

I scribbled a note and left it in the bathroom:

> Mom. Sorry about the window. I broke it.
> I'll pick up a new pane on my way back from the station.

Would she buy that? I didn't have much choice. And nothing had actually been stolen except that ID. She wouldn't assume a burglary. Would she notice the new lock on my door? Probably not. She'd be in the brandy bottle thirty seconds after seeing the window.

Tom was waiting at the office door, looking at his watch.

"Twenty minutes late, Sonny. That's coming out of your pay."

"Yeah. Sorry, Tom. It won't happen again."

FIFTEEN

Joe sat in the shack and watched the flames in the wood-burning stove. He was taking mescaline he'd bought from a hippie selling it openly on the sidewalk over by the UCBV campus and he was melting like a wax figure into his chair.

The dingy environment was warm and cozy amid gently swirling colors. The walls were swaying velvet drapes. The floor undulated: liquid chocolate. But lit by fire-hued flickers, he kept seeing the headless body of the girl in the bed in that apartment in Verdugo.

It was a fracture in his already broken reality. A nightmare within a dream. Everything had been so normal: breaking the window, lying on the bed, browsing the kitchen, sitting on the sofa. Then the horror. The head and the body in the same room but separate, like they were connecting units that had come accidentally disconnected and might easily be joined again. It was unsettling.

Ananiel had initially been silent and Joe had wondered if perhaps the whole thing had been a hallucination. But the body was real. It smelled real. It had smelled of meat in the airless room. Freshly butchered meat. To kill a person was one thing – quickly, for their good and as part of the divine reaping. To send them to heavenly glory. But cutting them into pieces? Bringing them home to bed? The homeowner had to be some kind of . . . what?

Ananiel had spoken then, *And they had a king over them whose name is Abaddon: the beast that rises out of the bottomless pit.*

Abaddon – the king of the beasts who reaped living creatures. Right. It made sense. Here was Abaddon's lair on the earthly plain.

He took the girl's ID out of his coat pocket. Her photo smiled. Pretty girl. It was clearly a sign. Her address was right there on the ID. Abaddon had given him a sign: the next house. The next family.

Cars swooshed by, occasionally unseen on the road. It had rained overnight and the forest was heavy with moisture. It dripped on the tar-papered roof. The shack sagged, sighing.

Joe looked at the Ruger. It was fully loaded but there were more .22 cartridges in the cabin if he needed them. It was a less powerful gun than the .38. He'd have to go for headshots, but that was easy enough when they were restrained. And Abaddon meant for him to have this gun. He'd intended an exchange of weapons. It was an offering.

Ananiel had said so.

Naturally, the whole broken window thing caused a massive argument with my mother.

"Leave the window broken like that and go back to work? Are you crazy? Anyone could've got in. I could've come home from work and got raped or murdered in my own home. Haven't you been reading the papers? Whole families shot and burned. *He* breaks the window to get in. But no – you did it *for* him! Sure, *Come into this house. My mom'll be home soon and you can shoot her and burn her.* You'd love that, wouldn't you?'"

"No, Mom." Nobody else but me was gonna have that pleasure.

"And how dare you break a window in *my* apartment."

"It was an accident, Mom. Accidents happen. I fixed it all as good as new. I even put an iron grille outside for security."

"An accident? Right. Like killing your grandparents."

"I'm going to my room now."

"I could have the lock taken off, you know. It's *my* apartment."

"I need some privacy, Mom. I lived for six years with none."

"Because you killed your grandparents!"

"Why do you have to keep mentioning it?"

"Is it you? Tell me. Are you the one who's been cutting girls up and leaving their parts all over the forest?"

Yeah. It had been in the newspapers. The county had been putting in pylons for a phone line and found the first girl's torso. After all my hard work cutting her up, they'd managed to identify her from a mole on her side.

"How could you even say that, Mom?"

"I wouldn't be surprised if we had the police over here asking questions. It's only a matter of time until they come looking for the crazies."

"I'm signed off, mom. I told you. They've said I'm completely sane."

"*That's* the funniest thing I've heard all year! Who's your psychologist over there in the city? Doctor Pepper? Doctor Scholl?"

My mother thought she was a real comedian after a few sherries. I had an idea. "If you're so suspicious, come and look at my room. Come on."

"I don't want to see your filth."

"No. Come on, Mom. You're always going on about the lock like I've got something to hide."

"Let go of me."

"Come on. Satisfy your curiosity."

"You're certifiable."

I unlocked the door and pushed it open. "See?"

It was pristine. After the break-in, I'd spent one more night with the second girl then disposed of her over the weekend while mother had been in the city. I was spooked. I didn't want any evidence left in the apartment. I'd even burned the photos, which cost me a lot. There hadn't been enough time to use them or memorize them. I'd been cheated out of my prize.

"Well, this proves nothing," said my mother, looking at the order within.

"Okay, then. I'll leave you to your drinking."

"You show me some respect in my home."

I closed my door and locked it from the inside.

"Now he starts the masturbation," muttered my mother as she walked back to her glass.

That day's newspaper lay folded on the bed. I'd been studying the press a lot since I'd taken the first girl, waiting for anyone to report her missing. They didn't always. The torso was page-one news:

BODY IS IDENTITIFIED – The female torso discovered in the forest north of Three-Mile Beach Wednesday has been positively identified as missing Buena Vista coed Sharleen Miller. The twenty-year-old disappeared after telling friends she intended to hitchhike to Berkeley . . .

It didn't worry me too much. There was nothing to connect her to me. I asked Amber about it in a roundabout way in case the police were holding back any details, but all I learned was about the birthmark. The girl's family was going to have a memorial service in town. I thought about going, but I'd seen an episode of *Police Story* where the cops had a photographer at one of those things to capture unknown attendees. Murderers were known to go.

Bigger news was the body they'd found in the exact same place I'd killed Miss Miller. Buzzcut Dwight had been telling the truth. Not surprisingly, his victim had been discovered almost immediately. What the newspaper didn't say, what Amber had told me and what was setting the Sheriff's Department on fire, was how one of Miss Miller's earrings had ended up in this other girl's ear. The parents had identified the stud, a birthday present. Obvious conclusion: the same killer was responsible for both girls.

That made me angry. My crime scene was flawless apart from the blood, which could have come from anywhere and which the rain would quickly wash away. Dwight had simply dumped the body. I felt like writing a letter to the police, or at least to the paper, pointing out that the MO was clearly different. Why dismember one, but leave the other to be found? But I couldn't explain the earring, and I knew that writing letters would be a bad route to go down. At worst, they'd think I was a crank. And a handwriting sample could say a *helluva* lot. There'd been studies into it. The FBI reportedly had a department.

It also made me nervous. What evidence had Dwight left at the scene? He was such a loose cannon that they'd be on to him in no time. Get him in an interrogation room and sweat him. Where had he found the stud? It belonged to the other guy. The *other* guy? Yeah, he works at the Arco station, corner of Dyer and Sloat. The end.

What made it worse was that Dwight's victim was being held up as some kinda miracle girl. She was the sole survivor of an auto wreck that killed her whole family when she was a kid. A Mack Truck had pretty much driven over the top of the family station wagon and she'd been the only one to crawl out alive. Six months in hospital. Multiple broken bones. Organ transplants back when that was new and a big deal. If Dwight had looked under her clothes, he would have seen the patchwork of scars.

Well, as you can imagine, all of this made it a big story. MIRACLE GIRL SLAIN. What heartless monster had robbed her second chance at life? More press coverage meant more pressure on the police to find the perp: one Buzzcut Dwight, the acid head driving around in a car virtually painted with her blood. Shit!

Was Dwight the one who'd broken into my room? Maybe he'd convinced himself he was my fan and had stolen the first girl's ID. But then I thought: how did he know where I lived? It didn't add up. Also, he didn't seem to have the sense. The burglar had to be someone else. Someone who now knew that I'd had a girl's dead body in my room. Someone who might return. Someone who had the Ruger that could be matched with the bullet in the second girl's head if they ever found it.

Still, I had the .38 to thank the intruder for. It was a much better gun for my purposes: more powerful, less likely to jam, low-profile sights that wouldn't catch on anything. Better still, the cartridges didn't eject to leave evidence in unexpected places. It also looked kinda like a cop's gun, with the wooden grip and the blued finish. I liked that.

As for Dulcie, she seemed to be going a little cold on the relationship. I needed to fix that. I suggested going round to her place in Merluza for a meal with her folks, who I'd not really met. I was thinking I might even propose and set a long engagement.

I drove up there one Friday evening in a new shirt and a smart jacket. I'd polished my shoes and I brought a present for her dad: the knife I'd used to kill the first girl. It was another piece of evidence I wanted to get rid of. Of course, I cleaned it all up and there was no trace of blood on the knife itself. I'd bought a new sheath at Scott's to replace the bloodstained original and it smelled wonderfully of oiled leather – a good gift for a man from another man. He could use it if he went hunting, or in the garden, or just for everyday utility.

That day didn't go especially well. Her parents were stern, Christian folk without any sense of humor. They didn't watch TV and they didn't seem to think much of me.

"Dulcie tells us you're a gas attendant," said father, with a face like I was digging graves or cleaning sewers.

"For now, sir, yes."

"Do you have other plans for the future?"

"I'm thinking of applying to the State Police Academy."

"Don't you think he'd look so handsome in a uniform?" said Dulcie.

"Public order is about more than a uniform," said father.

"That's true," I said. "I'd also need to study some criminal law."

"Maybe you could become a lawyer," said the father, with a razor-thin smile, like there was more chance of me becoming President or an astronaut.

The food was wonderful. Dulcie's mom really knew how to fill a table – not like my mother's wretched attempts at cuisine, which usually came reconstituted from packets.

I'd brought a toothbrush with the idea that they might ask me to stay over in a guest bedroom (sleeping together would have been totally out of the question) but it seems I didn't make a good impression. I heard them talking when I was coming back from the bathroom.

Father: "He's vulgar and a boor, Dulcie. He eats like a troglodyte."

Mother: "There's something odd about him. I don't know what it is . . ."

Father: "Is it just me or is there a whiff of gasoline?"

Dulcie: "Oh, Daddy – that's ridiculous. He wears a uniform at work."

Father: "I'd prefer you to marry a man who doesn't wear a uniform.

Dulcie: Isn't a suit a kind of uniform? Or a judge's robes?

Father: You know perfectly well what I mean.

They all shut up when I coughed in the corridor and came back to the table. It clearly wasn't the right moment to propose. I just ate my dessert and Dulcie's and drove back to Verdugo, looking at hitchhikers. I was going to need another one soon.

Dulcie told me later that her father didn't like knives and

wanted to throw it out. Her mother kept it, though, and used it in the kitchen for quartering chickens, shucking corn and other rough work. That pleased me and I did imagine later what the mother must have thought when she realized how many family meals she'd prepared with a murder weapon.

Joe arrived at the address on the girl's ID: a large house on the edge of the golf course. There were no other properties around.

It seemed nobody was home. All of the windows were dark. He went around back and saw that all of the ground-floor windows had metal grilles over them. The garden was large and glistened with moisture. He could see marks where rabbits or squirrels had passed across the wet lawn. There was a small hut that probably held garden tools.

He prized the flimsy hasp away from the wooden frame with his knife and entered the hut, his flashlight beam pale through the heavy air. Inside smelled of dried grass and iron and machine oil from the mower. There was a six-foot wooden stepladder for fruit picking or tree work – or for entering the house's first floor.

He cut the phone line with his knife then used a shovel to break the frosted glass of an upper bathroom window and climb inside, leaving the ladder where it was out back. He'd be leaving by the front door.

A rich person's house. Plenty of dark-wood furniture and art. It smelled like flowers. Joe entered each room in turn, lying on the beds, sitting in the seats, opening drawers.

The girl's bedroom was neat and clean and symmetrical. An oil painting of her hung above the bed and he compared the face to the photo on the ID. A good likeness. He placed the ID in the center of the pillow, turning it so it sat just right.

Now to wait.

He sat in the dark of the living room with the Ruger on his

thigh and the .38 on the chair's arm. It was very quiet. No cars passed. A fox yelped out on the golf course.

Don't sleep! said Ananiel. *Stay alert.*

Joe pulled back the bolt on the Ruger.

Lights flashed across the room and a car crunched slowly into the driveway. Its doors opened and closed. The front door opened and he heard their voices.

A woman: "I'm going straight to bed."

A man: "Do that, honey. It's been tough."

A girl: "I still can't believe she's . . ."

The man: "Don't. You don't need to say it. I'm gonna have a drink before I turn in."

The living room light came on and the woman entered. She was dressed all in black. Her eyes were red and puffy. She saw Joe sitting in the armchair. She froze.

"Steve?" she said, her voice quavering.

A clink of bottles in another room. "Yeah, honey?"

"There's . . . There's a man . . ."

"What's that, hon?" He appeared with a glass in his hand and saw Joe.

They stayed like that for a moment. Just looking at each other.

"I've just said goodbye to my girl," said the woman. "What's left of her."

"You need to get out of this house," said the man. "Right now."

"Where's your compassion?" said the woman. "What kind of . . .?"

"You've chosen the wrong place," said the man. "Don't you read the newspapers? This family has had enough . . . enough loss."

"What's going on?" said the dark-haired girl, drawn by the tone of their voices.

"Go to your room, honey!" said the mother.

Ananiel raised the Ruger. "No. Stay."

"I just buried my baby!" screamed the woman – a hoarse, animal howl.

"I'm not standing for this," said the man, starting to turn.

Ananiel fired. First at the man, then at the girl, then at the woman, who had fallen to her knees sobbing. The problem was the .22 wasn't a stopper like the .38. The living creatures kept moving. Two of them had gone out of the room.

Ananiel strode out to the hallway. The man was running lopsided up the stairs, holding his chest. Ananiel shot him twice in the back so that he fell forward onto the stairs and lay there.

The girl was struggling to unlock the back door, rattling the keys and trembling and whimpering. Ananiel shot her in the back of the head and she fell, a dead weight, to the polished parquet floor.

The woman was crawling across the living room floor toward the phone, leaving a smeared blood trail across the wood. Ananiel shot her in the back of the head and returned to the stairway. The man was still lying there, gasping. Ananiel aimed from the bottom of the steps and shot the man twice more. Enough.

The air was sharp with gunpowder. The three bodies were silent.

Why was the man going up? said Ananiel. *He probably has a gun in his bedroom. Check.*

Joe went past the body on the stairs and into a room with a double bed. He looked in the drawers and found the gun: a .44 Magnum with a six-and-half-inch barrel. *This* was a stopper. It was the kind of gun you bought after your daughter had been abducted and dismembered. A revenge gun. Joe put it in his coat pocket and found more cartridges in the bottom of the closet.

Now to burn the house.

SIXTEEN

Three days later, Dwight was driving. He'd cleaned the inside of the car as well as he could because the gas monkey had told him to. It was still pretty smeary and the passenger seat was crusted black. Getting it completely clean would have been a *lot* of work.

He realized he was on Portola, where a friend of his lived – a high-school buddy named Nicky. Nicky had been the one who first offered Dwight a joint. Later, they'd tried acid together. Nicky was supposed to have gone with Dwight to Frisco but had changed his mind because his parents had given him a load of shit about staying in school.

Why not call in on Nicky?

Dwight walked up onto the stoop and pressed the bell. It made a kind of melodic tune inside so he pressed it again and again, humming the tune to himself. *Doo-doo-doo do-do.*

An older woman answered the door looking irritated. It wasn't Nicky's mom.

"What do you want?" said the woman. "I'm busy and I'm not buying anything." She looked him over, perhaps expecting him to have a sample bag or a parcel.

"I'm looking for Nicky."

"Nicky? There's no Nicky here. You've disturbed me for nothing. Goodbye."

Dwight blocked the door with his boot. "This is Nicky's house."

"Maybe it was, but now it's mine. Now move your foot or I'm going to call the police. You're trespassing on my property."

Dwight pressed the bell again. *Doo-doo-doo do-do.* "Hey, Nicky!" he shouted through the door crack. "It's me, Dwight from high school. Tell your dragon grandma to let me in!"

"Get off my stoop, you degenerate!" said the woman. "I told you there's no Nicky here. Quit your foot right now!"

He pressed the bell again, smiling. *Doo-doo-doo do-do. Doo-doo-doo do-do.*

"I see," said the woman, her lips thin. "You're mentally retarded. That's unfortunate, but I really haven't got the time for this nonsense."

Dwight pulled his gun from the back of his pants and shot her through the gap in the door. She fell back on the wooden floor.

"Oh!" she said. "My God! You've shot me!"

He laughed. It was so obvious what she'd said! He shot her again to see if she'd say it again, but she just lay on the floor holding her first wound and gasping.

He pushed open the door, shifting her body along with it, and closed it behind him.

"Nicky! Hey, Nicky! It's Dwight from high school."

"I'm going to die," said the woman on the floor. "Call an ambulance. Call the police."

Dwight went upstairs. The house wasn't as he remembered it. It looked and smelled like an old person's house. There was a room with an easel and tubes of paint and jars of misty water. An unfinished painting sat on the easel. A rural scene: bright yellow cornfields and a dark sky. He could smell the oils. He touched the canvas and felt the paint smear under his fingers. He swirled the colors together and stood back to look at the picture. Better. He wiped his hand on his pants and continued the search for Nicky.

Nicky wasn't there. Was it possible this wasn't Nicky's house after all? Hadn't Nicky actually lived over on Valencia? Yeah, that was it. Valencia. Couple streets over. They all looked the same in this part of El Bosque.

Dwight went down the steps. The old woman had crawled away from the front door to an adjoining room and was lying on the floor, holding the phone receiver. "I've been shot," she was saying.

Dwight shot her in the head and she slumped flat.

He stopped on the stoop to press the bell again. *Doo-doo-doo do-do.* He thought about taking it and installing it in the cabin, but he wasn't really an electrician. There were wires. Pity.

He went to the drive-thru burger place downtown and sat in his car, eating fries with a hand that smelled nitric with gunpowder and had pigment in its finger swirls. He thought about dropping by the gas station to see the gas monkey and he drove over there, but the old man in the office said the gas monkey – Sonny. *Sunny:* the origin of all light. He wasn't on shift 'til three so Dwight decided to get some groceries and drive back up to the cabin.

THURSDAY 16 July, 1970, Oban Drive cabin, Buena Vista State Park, Buena Vista, California, USA. 76°F and dark. 10:14PM. I've been practicing with panoramic, all-seeing vision. I can now see the sap rising in the trees. Today at the gas station, I was concentrating on communicating a message to the old man telepathically and I think he got it, but he was confused and he didn't want to admit he was receiving. The universal consciousness can be frightening . . .

Couple days after, Joe was walking by the side of the road. He sometimes wished he could drive again, but Ananiel said no. No more driving. It was lethal. Being a passenger was okay, though. He could hitchhike if it was strictly necessary.

There was a light drizzle and his feet were killing him. He

stuck out his thumb as he walked, not hoping for much with his long hair, his beard, his John Deere cap and clothes he'd not changed for a few weeks. But a car pulled alongside him and he bent to look in the open window.

"Where you going?" said the guy with the buzzcut.

Joe recognized him as the one who'd been snooping round the cabin that time, looking at where the old hiker was buried. He waited to see if Ananiel would say anything, but nothing came through.

"Oakwood," said Joe. "Round there."

"Hop in."

Joe got in and Buzzcut swerved out into the traffic without looking in his mirrors. Horns blared. Driving was lethal.

The inside of the car was dirty and smeary. It smelled of blood. Joe realized the dried brown stuff *was* blood.

"What happened here?" he said.

"Accident," said Buzzcut.

"You should clean it up. It smells."

"Yeah. Someone else told me that. You smell of smoke."

Joe sniffed the inside of his arm. "Yeah. Guess so. I got a wood fire in the shack. Maybe need to sweep the flue."

Buzzcut went through a red light. Tires squealed.

"I recognize you," said Joe. "I've seen you before."

Buzzcut turned to him. "Yeah?"

"You were looking round my shack up on Cascade Road in the park."

"Yeah?" Dwight drove one-handed, the other hand on the unsheathed knife down the side of his seat. "I have a cabin up on Oban."

Joe had a hand on the Ruger in his coat pocket. "Were you looking for something up there? Lose something, maybe?"

"Matter of fact, I did."

"An old guy? Hiker? Head smashed in?"

"Yeah. Was it you who buried him?"

"Yep." Joe was looking at Dwight. "You have a scar on your forehead."

"Uh huh. Car wreck when I was sixteen. Went right through the windshield. Out cold for three days."

"Me, too. Look." Joe held his hair aside.

Dwight saw a bigger, jagged scar on Joe's forehead. It looked newer.

"If any man worship the beast and his image, and receive his mark in his forehead, or in his hand," said Joe/Ananiel, "the same shall drink of the wine of the wrath of God, which is poured out without mixture into the cup of his indignation, and he shall be tormented with fire and brimstone."

"Is that the Bible?"

"It's the end of times. The reaping."

Dwight drove, nodding. "I used to go to mass, but now I practice meditation. I observe a macrobiotic diet to balance the yin and yang."

They went on in silence, both still holding their weapons.

"You drop acid?" said Buzzcut.

"Mesc sometimes. I've heard it's the same effect, like peyote or mushrooms."

"In the glove compartment. Help yourself."

Joe held the bottle between his knees and unscrewed the cap with one hand, the other always on the gun. He shook one pill out onto his lap and screwed the bottle closed.

"You got a gun in your pocket?" said Buzzcut.

"Yeah."

"What kind?"

"Ruger .22 long barrel. Rifle shell."

"Me, too. In the trunk, anyway. You know, there's another one of us. He has a Ruger, too. It was him who told me to clean the car."

"Yeah?"

"Yeah. Works at the Arco station, corner of Dyer and Sloat. Sonny's his name. You ever read any Paramahansa Yogananda?"

"No. You can drop me off here."

Dwight swerved to the kerb, causing the car behind to go by with flashing headlamps and an outraged horn.

"See you around," said Buzzcut.

"Guess so," said Joe.

"Joe," said Sally. "God, you look like a hobo. You're wearing the same clothes as last time. And you smell like an ash heap." Her face was puffy and her eyes bloodshot.

"What's wrong, Sal? What happened?"

She started crying. "Oh, Joe . . . It's horrible."

"What? Is it the baby?"

Sally's brother appeared behind Sally at the door. His face was solemn. "You'd better come in," he said. "You might wanna sit down."

"Will someone tell me what's going on?" said Joe, still standing.

"Someone murdered Mom!" said Sally, erupting again into tears.

"Why don't you go and lie down, sis. I'll tell him. Go on. Take one of the pills the doc gave you. Go on."

Sally went to the bedroom.

"Is this for real?" said Joe.

The brother nodded. "Mom was at home doing one of her paintings. The police think she must've answered the door to someone because there were no signs of a break-in. Whoever it was shot her a few times. They found cartridges in two places. It was a .22." Joe stared. "The sickest thing," said the brother, "was that the killer messed up her last painting. Like, rubbing his fingers in the oil and swirling it all up. Like it was all a big joke. The police say he might be a drug addict, but they say that about almost all crimes now. They probably think he's black, too."

Joe hadn't much liked the old woman. She had a temper on her. But still . . .

"Anyway," said the brother. "The police wanna talk to you."

"Me?"

"They just wanna talk to all of the family, you know. If Mom had any enemies. All that shit. But we didn't know where you're living at the moment. Something about a workmate's shack? Sal couldn't remember whose it was. It's been hard for her. You know: girls and their moms."

"You got anything to eat?" said Joe.

"Is that all you have to say, Joe? Your wife's lost a mother. Your kid's lost a grandmother. Don't you think it's time to give up all this 'mountain man' bullshit and come down from the hills? You've got a family here, man. There's a maniac out there burning houses and killing people and Sal's here all alone, scared half to death."

"I gotta go."

"What? Are you serious? Can't you hear her crying? What's wrong with you? Look – if you need help, I can call some people. If you need medication for your head?"

"It's the reaping."

"The what? Are you high? I wish I'd never left you that mesc, Joe. It just doesn't work right with some people. I've seen bad reactions. I mean, it's rare, but . . ."

Joe was walking to the door. "I gotta go."

"Where are you staying, Joe? It's better if you talk to the police or it'll look like you have something to hide. Whose shack is it? Joe?"

Joe was walking down the path and out into the street. He didn't stop or even turn around. He didn't notice that Dwight was still parked where he'd stopped, watching the whole scene, grinning and humming to himself.

Doo-doo-doo do-do.

I was pretty nervous by this point. I'd been feverishly reading the papers and Amber had been round again with police gossip. A lot was happening and I didn't have much control over any of it.

The big news was that the arson murderer had killed the first girl's family on the same day as their memorial service – the same week they'd buried the torso in a full-size casket. The press was going crazy over it. The horror! The inhumanity! They were saying what a lot of people were thinking: that it must have been the girl's killer. Coincidences like that just didn't happen.

According to Amber, the police hadn't released all the details. They were thinking maybe it was the arson killer, but the MO was a little off. He'd used a .22 instead of a .38 this time. He also hadn't bound the victims like he had the first two times. These details and the weird coincidence were making the detectives think maybe it was a copycat thing, or that there was a family connection.

Turned out the girl's brother in Monterey was heavily into dealing acid, mescaline and peyote. The rumor was that he'd cheated his suppliers and they'd killed his family as a warning, trying to cover it up by burning the house. It was a theory. I couldn't stop thinking about those .22 rifle shells they'd found and why the killer had suddenly switched from a .38.

The black rapist was still at work. Two more girls had been assaulted and then dropped off in town to report all the details to the police. God knows how he wasn't yet in custody. They'd all seen his face. The artists' impressions were pretty consistent. The police started with checkpoints on all routes leading into the park, but they were only stopping black drivers and there was a lot of fuss about that. Why weren't they stopping the white drivers for the arson murders? It was a fair argument, because there was no evidence either way about *that* killer's race. In the end, they quietly stopped the checkpoints.

The guy who lured women out of their cars had also been busy. Another girl had disappeared, her car left abandoned. There was currently no trace of her. I was still going with the theory that

THR3E

he was a cop. A woman wouldn't get out of her car unless she had a good reason to. There were no signs of struggle at the abandoned cars.

More directly relevant to me: the police had found some more pieces of my two girls. It wasn't clear to them who they were, but I knew from the locations. There'd been an arm from the first girl and the second's legs. All the bits had been quite badly decomposed and scavengers had been at them. No positive identifications. I'd buried both of the heads pretty deep and I didn't think anyone would find them.

I was theoretically in a position where I could stop if I wanted to. There was no more evidence in my room and nothing to tie me to the two girls. Nobody knew anything. Nobody except Buzzcut Dwight or whoever had broken into the apartment. Tom'd said Dwight had come around the station asking for me a couple days previously. I had to do something about that. Anyone could see he was out of his mind. Who knew what he might say?

I had another reason to worry when something very uncomfortable happened that Saturday. I was out on the street in front of the apartment block. Tom had let me take a tub of auto wax that'd been damaged – he'd claim it on the insurance – and I was treating the Galaxie to a glossy shine. It was a sunny day and I wasn't meeting Dulcie because she had a music exam. Flute, I think.

Anyway, I was buffing the hood with a chamois leather when an unmarked car drew up and two plain-clothes guys got out. Creased slacks. Oversized jackets. Detectives. I knew them from the Holding Cell, though I'd not spoken with them before. Something in their demeanor told me this was a professional call. They'd finally come for me.

The .38 was in the trunk. My first thought: open it, wait for them to approach and shoot them both. Then shoot my mother, who was inside watching TV. Then myself because there was no way out of that chaos.

But shooting a cop was a step too far. That wasn't me. The

only man I'd ever killed was my grandpa and that was purely because I didn't want to break it to him that I'd killed his wife of fifty years. It was more compassionate to shoot him than have him live with the terrible news. He didn't feel a thing. Didn't even see me.

So these two cops are standing there looking around because the numbering on our street was confusing. They kinda hadn't noticed me working on my car – just a neighborhood guy doing his Saturday chores.

"Can I help you, gents?" I said.

"Sure. You know if Sonny Boden lives round here?"

"You've found him."

"Hey . . . You're the guy from the Holding Cell, right? The one with the cuffs. Joe Friday."

"Guilty as charged!" I held my hands out to be cuffed.

They laughed, relaxing. I was no danger to anyone.

"Listen, Sonny," said the taller one. "Funny thing. You bought a gun a while back – a Ruger .22 at Scott's Sporting Goods downtown. Is that right?"

He knew it was right. No good lying. "Sure. Nice little gun. Good target shooter."

"Well, the purchase got flagged. Should've happened before but we've just heard about it now."

"What do you mean 'flagged?'"

"We got an alert saying you can't own it. It's odd 'cause there's no reason given – just that you've been flagged."

I could have told them that my record had been fully expunged and that it probably hadn't gone through the system yet, even though I'd bought the gun before that. But I didn't want the cops knowing about my grandparents and Atascadero and all that. I mean, they could have found it out if they really wanted to, but they didn't know anything. If they knew my history, they might come knocking for any number of other things.

"So what happens now?" I said.

"It's not really clear," said the shorter one. "So we're just gonna confiscate the gun for now. We'll give you a receipt for it and return it if you or anyone else can figure out what the red flag's for. Maybe a lawyer could look into it for you."

"But I wouldn't hold your breath," said the tall one. "You probably won't get it back."

"Where's the gun at?" said the short one.

The gun that'd been stolen from my room by the burglar who'd seen a dead girl in my bed?

"It's at work," I said. "In my locker. I work at the Arco station down on–"

"Why's it at work?" said the tall one.

"Well, it'd jammed a couple times and I was planning on taking it back to Scott's so he could look at it. You know, it's still under warranty. But, anyway, I had to work late and Scott's closed so I thought I'd just leave it there and take it another time."

The detectives looked at each other.

"Where've you been firing it?" said the short one.

"Up in the park."

"You know it's illegal to shoot wildlife up there. It's all protected."

"Sure. No. I bought some paper targets and I pin 'em to trees. I'm getting pretty good at it. But I would never hurt an animal."

I knew I looked pathetic to them: the clown from the Holding Cell who lived with his mother and shot at paper targets in the forest instead of joining a range and firing .38s or .44s like a real man. I could see them mentally debating whether we should all drive down to the station to get the gun that wasn't in my locker.

"Listen, Sonny," said the short one. "You need to bring that gun to the Sheriff's office and hand it in."

"Sure."

"We wouldn't do this for anyone else, you understand. But we know where to find you. Your sister Amber's a typist at the office, right?"

"Yeah, that's her."

"She got all the looks in the family."

"That's what I always say!"

They laughed and went back to their car.

"Don't forget," said the tall one, pointing.

"Joe Friday never forgets!" I said.

They laughed and drove off, probably talking me down.

Shit. Where was I gonna get a replacement Ruger?

My mother appeared at the main door, leaning heavily against the frame with a glass in her hand.

"Was that the police?" she said, just shouting it across the parking lot for everyone to hear. "I told you they'd come rooting out the crazies!"

Her time above ground was limited.

SEVENTEEN

Part of the general anxiety I was feeling came from . . . well, I guess you'd call it an internal struggle. I was still picking up girls and dropping them off. I told myself it was a test of my resolve, like an alcoholic going into a bar and ordering an orange juice, or whatever. If I could take them where they wanted to go, I was protecting them. There were at least two other guys out there who wanted to kill them or rape them or both. I was one of the good ones.

I gloried in the power of not killing. The gun was right there on one side and the boning knife on the other. We'd shoot the breeze, flirt a little, talk about the other girls who'd been taken and discuss what the killer might look like.

It was never someone who looked like me. The man they described was some form of dark sexual fantasy. He was hypermasculine. He had an angular, stubbly jaw and hard eyes. He had big hands that could crush the life out of a slender throat. I actually saw a few of them wriggling in the seat as they imagined him.

But I was also thinking that another girl wouldn't be such a bad thing. I mean, I'd killed two without anybody knowing anything. Sure, the police had found a few body parts, but they were still basically clueless. And I'd refined a process that worked. Would it be so bad if I did one more?

I know, I know – I sound like an addict. But you can't imagine the kinda high I'd experienced. I've never actually taken anything stronger than a beer, but I know how drugs work. They artificially stimulate different parts of the brain, but those same parts can be stimulated by experience. We've all felt euphoria or ecstasy without the need for drugs. So, imagine the euphoria that comes from pure omnipotence.

Or I'd call it love. I'm basically a romantic. There's a girl; she doesn't know me; she's never seen me before. Then I kill her and she's mine. She's my everything. Imagine all of the emotions of a love affair, but condensed into the febrile moments of decapitation in the trunk of a car. Then lovemaking with no boundary but time, no taboo but the outer reaches of what lust can conceive. Until you've felt that, you don't know the lure, the compulsion. Wine? Cocaine? Heroin? They're austere, chemical experiences in comparison.

I've been good at only two things in my life: lying and killing. Picking up girls combined both talents. It was really just a question of time before I went back. It was my destiny, always.

In the meantime, Buzzcut Dwight came to the station again.

Tom had gone across the road to get some coffee. I'd just filled up a station wagon and Dwight's was the next car through. I recognized it straight away, now mostly cleaned up.

"Hi, Sonny," he said like we were friends. No blood on him this time.

"Did you break into my house and take my gun the other day? That day you came here covered in blood?"

"No. I don't know where you live."

I believed him. "Was that you who killed the girl's grieving family over by the golf course? Are you the arson murderer?"

"Nope. That's not me, either."

A thought. "What about the old woman killed in her house? The oil painting thing?" He seemed crazy enough for that. One of the newspapers wanted to call him the Van Gogh Killer because of the swirls made in the wet paint.

A smile. "Yeah! That was me. Say, what gun was stolen from your house?"

"Why?"

"Was it your Ruger?"

I felt acid hot in my throat. Another car was now waiting behind Dwight's. I decided to put ten dollars in his tank even if I had to pay for it myself.

"What do you know about my Ruger?" I said, going to the pump.

He leaned out the window. "I was in Scott's when you bought it. I got one, too. Look!"

He took it from the glove compartment and waved it out the window. The exact same gun.

"Keep it in the car, Dwight." Jesus! "Actually, listen – you could help me out."

"Yeah?"

The car behind hit the horn and I waved to him. Just a minute!

"Could I borrow your Ruger?" I said, screwing down his tank plug. Dwight looked doubtful. "I'll swap you," I said. "I've got a .38 revolver. A Smith and Wesson police issue. It's a good gun – a more powerful gun – but, you know, I really miss the Ruger."

"Have you got it here?" said Dwight.

"It's in my car. Pull around the back and wait for me. If Tom asks, say you're waiting for a wax job."

"Who's Tom?"

"Say that if *anyone* asks you."

He drove round back and I cleared the customers. When Tom came back with the coffees, I told him I was going to do a wax job and that bought me thirty, forty minutes when he'd have to manage the forecourt.

Dwight was waiting for me. He was sitting on the hood of his car, his heels on the fender, playing with the gun – spinning it round his finger with the trigger guard like a cowboy. I had a vision of him shooting himself or me and then laughing about it as one or both of us bled out.

I got the .38 from my trunk (emptying the shells first) and went over to him. "Get in the car, Dwight."

He got in. I got in, seeing the passenger seat blotched black but dry.

"It's a nice gun," I said. I span the cylinder and popped it open for him. I let him hold it and he aimed it out of the windshield, squinting his eyes and making a childish *pow-pow* sound.

"What do you say, Dwight? We got a deal?"

"Sure." He handed me the Ruger. "Say, you wanna go get a doughnut or a beer?"

"I'm working, Dwight."

"We could be friends. You ever read any Paramahansa Yogananda? Yin and yang? Panoramic vision? Circular breathing?"

"No, Dwight."

"I'll get you a book. But you gotta eat macrobiotically."

"That's interesting, Dwight. It really is, but I need to get back to work. Listen – you're up on Oban Drive, right? I could stop by sometime. But don't come here again. Okay?"

"Why not?"

"It'd mess up the yin and the yang."

He thought about that for a moment and nodded. "If I'm not home, just wait on the stoop."

"Great. I'll see you around, Dwight. Take care."

His eyes filled up and I was sure he was gonna start bawling right there in the car, so I gave him a thumbs-up and got out.

I watched him swerve dangerously into traffic and my first thought was: Great, now I need to pay for ten dollars of gas and a wax job out of my own pocket. But I had the gun. It wasn't my gun, but it was identical apart from the serial number. Would the cops check that? It wasn't a weapon of interest in a crime – it was just a guy returning a gun he'd bought. It wasn't really credible that I'd have two identical Rugers at home with different serial numbers. In fact, if Dwight had bought his gun immediately after mine, there was a good chance the serial numbers were very similar. Any small difference could be written off as human error in the documentation.

Another problem: Dwight had almost certainly used the gun to kill. He'd probably left cartridges all over the crime scene and bullets in the corpses. Ballistics would show that the gun I'd handed in was a murder weapon. But why would they check it? I wasn't a person of interest in any investigation. They'd probably put my Ruger in a locker and forget about it.

Just in case, I'd rough up the barrel at home. If I jammed some screwdrivers in there and scratched up the rifling enough, any ballistics tests would be inconclusive. The gun'd probably be ruined, but I wasn't gonna get it back anyway. Getting the cops off my case was more important.

But destiny was knocking at my door again. I'd have to hand in the Ruger within the next day or two if I didn't want the detectives coming back. I had to take advantage of the gun while I had it. The decision was made: another girl.

I'd do it after work.

She was a dark beauty with long, blue-black hair and eyes that seemed completely black in the dusk. Could have had some Mexican or Indian blood in her. I wouldn't normally have chosen that type. I've thought a lot since about why I chose her.

Could it be that something had changed in me? Does personality affect erotic preference? Might a sunny, happy kinda guy choose blonds? Might a serious, thoughtful guy choose brunettes? If so, what had happened to me that, out of nowhere, I chose this midnight voluptuary with larger hips and breasts than I'd normally like? I was drawn to her in the opposite way a moth is lured to a flame. I was seeking darkness. To hide? Or because it was home?

She said nothing when I showed her the gun and told her we'd be making a diversion. That was fine with me. There'd been altogether too much talking with the first two girls and I'd allowed them to find weaknesses. They were expecting a dominant attacker and that was the part I intended to play.

I'd been working on a new idea for how I might obtain a body completely without mess and without physical impairment. We drove to a turn-off I knew on Redwood Creek Road, climbing ever higher into the park. She sat silently all the while in the passenger seat. Thinking what? What went through their minds?

Did they consider death? Did they plan their retaliation and escape? Or were they simply in shock – numb with the terror of the gun and the accumulated horror stories of the press that they'd now, incredibly, become a part of? Did they imagine themselves as headlines, their names and ages in smudgy print on page one? Were they urgently noting details to recount to the police afterward? What make of car was this? A Ford? All cars looked pretty much the same apart from the color. And the guy? How to describe *him*? White. Glasses. Kinda handsome, but not in a classical way – not dark and dangerous like a killer should be.

It was misty and dark under the trees up at Redwood Creek.

"There's some duct tape in the glove compartment," I said. "Would you get it out?"

She took it out and an astrological-design glass from the station fell into the footwell.

"Sorry," she said, reaching down to grope for the glass as she handed me the tape.

"Don't worry about it," I said. "You can have it if you like. Know any Capricorns?"

"Uh huh. My dad."

"Great. Well, it's yours."

"Thanks."

"Don't mention it. I get 'em free."

I tore off a piece of tape. "Okay. I'm going to put this over your mouth. Close your lips like this." I pursed them tightly. "Good. I don't want it to pull on the sensitive skin."

I pressed the tape gently to her face and pushed it flat with my hand. "Now try to blow as hard as you can with your mouth. Does it come off? No? Okay. Good. Can you breathe fine through your nose? No sniffles? Great. Now, I'd like you to get into the back seat facedown. Wait, I'll come around to your door and help you."

I helped her into the back seat and taped her wrists behind her back. It was difficult to see anything inside the car, even with the overhead lights on. I should've brought a flashlight. Always some small detail. I bound her ankles. Everything was going perfectly. She was completely compliant.

Now for the part of my plan that I'd thought a lot about. I didn't need the gun. I didn't need the knife. With her face down in the back, I just needed to reach around and pinch her nose closed. She'd asphyxiate and the body would be totally flawless. Not even a bullet hole.

That was the plan. She didn't react at first, perhaps because she thought I was re-checking the tape and I'd touched her nose by accident. She went crazy when she realized what was happening.

She tried to scream through the tape and bucked wildly, almost throwing me out the open door. I lost my grip on her nose and had to grab for it again, but now she was writhing and twisting so I couldn't get hold of it. Every time I lost the nose, I'd have to start again with the whole suffocation and I knew it'd take forever.

I tried to kneel on her back to pin her down and control her, groping for her face in the dim yellow light of the car. She butted me full in the face with the back of her head. She knew exactly what she was doing. Damn near broke my nose. The pain flashed white and red. My eyes were watering. I wiped my face with the back of my hand and saw the dark smear shine.

"Hold still!" I said, but I could kinda understand why she

wouldn't want to. It was like fighting a cougar or a mountain lion, but I didn't want to hurt it. I just wanted to kill it quick.

Well, I finally got the palm of my hand over her nose and her taped mouth and it occurred to me that a sharp backward jerk would probably break her neck. Better with both hands. I pulled as hard as I could and there was a crunch somewhere inside. She lay totally still, but gurgling and moaning deep in her throat.

I'll be honest: the experience had excited me sexually in a way that the other girls hadn't. Maybe it was the proximity, or the smell of her – her heat, her presence under me – but I'd become physically aroused during the fight and I realized that I was on the brink of climax.

I crawled backward out of the car and dragged her toward me so that her knees were on the ground but her torso still on the seat. I lifted her dress, dragged down her panties and entered her from behind right there in the forest. I just couldn't wait. It was over in seconds. I believe I may have been ejaculating even before I got inside her.

She kept on with that strange gurgling and moaning. I guess she might still have been alive, but she was incapacitated. Something important had broken in her spine. I rolled her dress back down over her bottom and carried her round to the trunk on my shoulder, opening it with the hand that wasn't round her thighs.

I looked at her, folded fetal in the trunk. What a catch! What a beauty! But she kept on moaning and breathing like maybe she was trying to speak without control of her vocal cords, which, in retrospect, I might've torn when I pulled her head back. Easily now, I reached into the trunk and pinched her nose closed until the noises stopped.

With all of this excitement, I'd completely lost track of time. I was supposed to meet Dulcie downtown, have a drink and take her home to Merluza. She didn't want to hitch, what with all the stuff in the news, and the buses along Highway 1 weren't as regular as you might think. Basically, I'd have to go directly to the date with the new girl in the trunk. No time to drop her off in Verdugo and get a change of clothes.

Just a couple problems. First, I was bleeding quite badly from my nose. I could stop that easily enough with a handkerchief and some pressure, but my shirt was ruined with the blood and I could see in the rearview that there was some swelling already. I'd need to think of a good explanation.

Then there was the presence of the girl. She was in the trunk, fine, but the car smelled of her darkly exotic perfume. There were bound to be long, black hairs all about. Dulcie was pretty perceptive about these things. I didn't want to face a difficult conversation about hitchhikers all the way back to Merluza.

I drove into town with all the windows open. It was freezing, but a good way to air out the car and also to chill the flesh around my nose. If Dulcie found a hair, I could just say I'd given Tom's sister a lift.

I was about to pull out onto Highway 9 off Oban when I heard the moaning again. Still? I had to deal with that before getting into town, so I stopped at a Shell station to fill the tires with air and opened the trunk to look at her. She hadn't moved, but there was still that strange, whispering sighing. I really didn't want to shoot her, though I knew a single headshot would solve everything. The only thing to do was strangle her with my hands, squeezing until the noises stopped as traffic hissed by on the highway (it had started to rain a little as they'd predicted earlier that morning). She had such soft, smooth skin! And still warm. I put the blanket over her when I'd finished.

"What happened to your face?" said Dulcie, the second she saw me.

"A deer jumped out in front of the car up in the forest. I hit my nose on the wheel."

"Did you kill the deer?"

"No, but I nearly went off the edge into the canyon."

"You poor thing. Your shirt's all ruined."

"I know, but I didn't want to let you down. I don't want you taking any risks on the road."

"My hero."

We went for milkshakes because she couldn't go home smelling of alcohol – she *was* technically underage – and she didn't want me driving under the influence. Most of the other customers in that fluorescent, brightly colored place were kids her age wearing numbered team jackets or hippie-style clothes – all urgently expressing who they thought they were or might be. It was a glimpse of the childhood I'd spent in a maximum-security mental hospital sharing tables with violent psychopaths. Milkshakes had been popular at Atascadero, too. Who doesn't like a milkshake?

She would have liked to stay longer, but I told her I needed to do an early shift at the station the next day, so I drove her home. I thought I saw her smelling the interior at one point, so I opened the window and she started telling me about her flute exam and how she'd messed up one piece but something something something.

I was thinking about the warm body in the trunk.

What a night we had, me and the Mexican-looking girl – like a honeymoon couple! We talked, she posed for photos and she was insatiable in bed. I barely slept more than an hour.

I was asleep at around eight the next morning when my mother banged on my door.

"What is it, Mom?" I said, groggy, pulling the sheet up over the naked girl, looking urgently at her head on the bookshelf.

"There's someone here to see you."

"Who?'

"A man."

"What man?"

"How should *I* know? Maybe it's the police again."

"Can you tell him to come back? Tell him I'm sleeping?"

"He can hear me shouting at you through this locked door. And since when did I become your social secretary? You get up out of bed and come talk to your guest."

The Ruger was still in the car.

Shit. *Shit*!

EIGHTEEN

Dwight ate cold beans from a can with a fork. He'd been on an intense acid trip and it wasn't clear how much time had passed. It couldn't have been more than twenty-four hours. Some of the beans were giggling at him like little orange babies. After-effects. He really ought to tidy the place up if Sonny was going to visit.

He swung the .38 around a finger. It wasn't as cool or as pretty as the Ruger. It was a gun with a bad aura about it. Dwight tried to see through the aura to its truth, but metal was harder to see through than trees or people. And he wasn't maintaining his macrobiotic diet as well as he'd like, which affected consciousness.

A car was approaching the cabin. He went to the window to look. It was a beaten-up truck driven by an old man. The man got out and looked at Dwight's car in the drive. He looked at the cabin.

"Lyle! You up here, Lyle?" said the man.

Dwight giggled. He thinks I'm called Lyle!

"Hey, Lyle! I'm coming up."

The old man approached the shack. He had a rifle over his shoulder on a strap. Dwight heard boots thudding on the stoop and moved to where he couldn't be seen from the windows. The door rattled. It was locked.

Dwight heard the jangle of keys and the scratch of the lock. The door opened and a bar of light entered across the floor.

"You in here, Lyle?"

Dwight stepped out.

The man jerked back. "Wha? Who are you?"

"I'm Dwight."

"What're you doing here, son? This is Lyle's cabin."

"He said I could stay a few days."

"You've seen him? When?"

"Few days ago. He was walking in the forest and I gave him a lift. He was grateful and said I could stay here."

The old man looked round the shack. It was littered with half-eaten cans, fast food packaging and smoked-out roaches. His hand rose slowly to the rifle.

"Where's Lyle now?" he said.

Dwight shrugged. "The forest. He went out to get firewood."

"When was this?"

Dwight giggled. "Few days ago?"

"He went out for firewood a few days ago?"

"That's it."

"You're lyin' to me, son. Lyle wouldn't let you stay in his cabin like this. What you done to him?"

Dwight looked at the table. The .38 was on it.

The old man unslung his rifle. "You're coming to town with me, sonny."

"I'm not Sonny. Sonny works at the Arco, corner of Dyer and Sloat."

"Okay, boy. I don't know what you're smoking, but something's wrong here and you're gonna answer some questions down at the Sheriff's Department."

Dwight fought the smile that was twisting at his lips. "I know where Lyle is."

"Where?"

"He's buried in the forest. Someone beat his brains out with a bat."

The old man looked at him. He drew back the bolt on his rifle and raised it. You're coming with me. You're gonna show me the place and then we're going to town."

"Okay!"

"Where's he buried?"

"There's a shack off Cascade Road. It's real close. We could walk."

"Jackson's place?"

"I don't know any Jackson except seventh president Andrew Jackson. And the Jackson 5. You know that song?"

The old man stared blankly at the shuffling dance moves. "Let's go."

He wouldn't let Dwight go to the table to get the .38 and he didn't want to walk. He made Dwight climb into the truck bed and cuffed him to the roll bar. Why did he have cuffs?

They drove a minute or two to the cabin and the old man slowed, calling back to Dwight out the window. "This the place?"

"Uh huh."

The old man unlocked him. "You walk in front. Show me where. And don't try anything. I'll shoot you where you stand. Okay?"

"Got it!"

They walked around the side of the shack, the old man covering Dwight with the rifle all the time. The ground was very uneven: looped roots, slippery branches and mud.

"Fuck!"

Dwight turned around and saw the old man face down on the forest floor. He'd caught his foot in a root and tossed the rifle toward Dwight as he fell.

"Don't you touch that!" said the man.

Dwight picked it up and shot the man in the top of the head as he was struggling to get up. The sound was absorbed into the trees. Some birds took flight, with squawks and creaking wings.

THR3E

It was a nice rifle. Dwight worked the bolt to eject the cartridge and fired again into the still body. A very nice rifle.

He left the body where it lay and walked the short distance back to his cabin to finish the tin of baked beans. They'd stopped laughing now. He thought again about cleaning the place up for when Sonny came to visit.

Who was this 'visitor' waiting to see me?

I pulled on some jeans and looked for a shirt that didn't have blood on it. My room was full of evidence: the girl, her head, her bag, her clothes. I had to get to the car and the Ruger. If this was the police, I wasn't going to let them take me. I wouldn't give my mother that satisfaction. I'd kill the cop and her and then myself rather than hear her crowing about how she'd been right all along.

I unlocked the door and fastened it from the outside. They'd need a warrant to get inside a locked room and that might buy me time. I went to the living room, where a guy was sitting on the sofa. My mother was standing in the doorway to the kitchen and looking at him disapprovingly.

The guy looked like a hobo: long, dirty hair, a full beard and mountain-man clothes. He smelled of smoke and body odor. Not a cop.

"Do I know you?" I said.

"I was here the other day," he said, looking sidelong at my mother. "In your room."

Him! The burglar.

"Is this a friend of yours, Sonny?" said my mother.

"Let's go to my room," I said, gesturing for him to follow.

"But you just said you didn't know him," said my mother.

"He's a friend, Mom."

"But you said–"

"Leave it, Mom! We're going to my room."

"Don't you shout at me in front of guests in my own house."

I unlocked the padlock and beckoned the guy in, locking it from the inside.

"If you're dealing drugs, I'll call the police!" said my mother. "Don't think I won't!"

Hobo Guy looked around. He saw the head on the shelf. He saw the shape in the bed.

"Is it a different girl?" he said.

I nodded and motioned for him to keep his voice down. My mother would be listening in the hallway.

"What do you want?" I said. "Why are you here?"

He gestured to the sheet-covered body. "Can I look?"

"No. She's naked."

He looked at the head on the shelf. "Did you do that?"

"Yes."

"Why? I mean, why not keep 'em together?"

"It's what I do."

Well, it was uncomfortable discussing such things with a stranger. They were personal. I hadn't fully examined my own reasons for removing the heads. It had been a fantasy for as long as I could remember. Where do such things come from? Why do some men prefer tits to asses, blonds to brunettes, skinny women to larger girls? Do we actively make such choices or are they imposed on us from influences beyond our comprehension? I might equally have asked him about his favorite sexual position with his wife or girlfriend. It was pretty inappropriate behavior.

"You took my gun," I said. "My Ruger."

"I gave you the .38. It was an offering. An exchange."

"What do you mean?"

"I think we're on the same mission. I think you're Abaddon."

Right. Another *loco*. I knew how to handle them.

I sat on the edge of the bed. "Uh huh. Tell me about it."

"You rule over the locust warriors who look like horses prepared for battle, with hair like women and lion's teeth. It's written."

Sounded like a Biblical nut-job. I'd known a few at Atascadero.

"And what if I am this Abba Doon?"

"Abaddon. You have the mark. On your forehead."

I touched it. A childhood injury. I'd been chasing Amber and run headlong into an overhanging roof beam. Out cold for a few seconds and a nasty gash down to the bone.

"The end times are here," said Hobo Guy. "The reaping has begun."

Something about him made me ask. The smell of smoke, maybe. "Are you the one killing families and burning houses?"

A nod. "I am the angel Ananiel."

"You killed the parents of the girl who died."

"You gave me the address. It was a sign."

A knock on the door. A rattle of a spoon in the good sugar bowl. My mother.

"Sonny – I've brought coffee for you and your friend."

"We're fine, Mom!"

"You can't invite a guest and offer them nothing. Don't you know that?"

"We don't want coffee, Mom!"

"I wouldn't mind some coffee," said Hobo Guy.

"See?" said my mother, through the door. She must've had her ear literally against the wood. "You're a terrible host."

I felt like crying. I really did. If Hobo Guy hadn't been there, I would've opened the door and sliced her head off right there in the hallway and poured all that coffee into her gaping mouth so it ran out of her neck.

"Well, I'll leave it here by your door," she said, walking away. "But I feel sorry for your guest. If I went to someone's apartment and they denied me a simple coffee, I'd be . . ."

I turned to Hobo Guy. "How'd you know where I live?"

"I didn't. I was looking for the next house. I came in and I saw the body and I knew you were Abaddon. It is written. You're doing the same work. Now we can do it together."

"You know that now the police are looking for the same killer for the girl and the family?"

"Yeah? I don't know anything about that."

"Have you still got the Ruger you took from me?"

Hobo Guy started to take a gun out of a coat pocket, but then reached for the other pocket.

"Wait," I said. "What was that one?"

He took out a huge revolver with a long barrel and a blued finish, handing it to me.

"Is this a .44 Magnum?" I said.

"Uh huh."

I weighed it in my hand. Devastating power – twice the caliber of the Ruger. It emanated a brutal, masculine authority.

"You want it?" said Hobo Guy.

I did want it. I was imagining pulling it out in the car and seeing the girl's face. It was a barrel you didn't argue with. There'd be no cracking wise with this gun. It demanded respect. Subservience was guaranteed.

But no – it wouldn't work. A shot from the Magnum at close range would blow the head all apart. The bullet would embed itself somewhere as evidence and the recoil might even break my wrist if I tried to fire it awkwardly in a confined space.

"It's a lovely gun, but I prefer my Ruger."

He gave me the Ruger.

"Did you use this to kill the girl's family?" I said.

"Uh huh."

Wonderful. My Ruger could be matched to a mass killing and Dwight's was probably also a murder weapon. I'd have to decide which one I was going to return to the police. On the upside, the .38 Dwight was using had probably been used by Hobo Guy on those other families. The detectives were gonna go crazy unpicking all of this ballistics evidence.

Hobo Guy was just sitting there looking around. I wondered if he'd come with any intention or plan. His eyes kept returning to the head on the bookshelf.

"Looks like she's sleeping," he said. "She's pretty."

"She's my girl. You got a girl . . .? Sorry – didn't get your name."

"Joe. That's my living creature name. I'm married."

"Cool. You live together?"

He looked uncomfortable. "We have a house in Oakwood. On Durero. Do you know it?"

"No. I'm not really from around here."

Long pause. It's not always easy talking to the insane. The retarded catatonics just sit and drool, twitch or mumble. The manic psychotics, meanwhile, won't stop talking at you for hours. The solution is kinda like talking to anyone: ask them about themselves.

"So tell me about Ananiel."

"He's an angel. At least, I'm him. He talks to me and tells me what to do."

"Like an angel from heaven?"

"From the other place. He's fallen. Like Lucifer."

"And what's this reaping?"

"The end of times. The wrath of the Lamb. Death comes on a pale horse and followed by Hell, given power over one fourth of the earth to kill with sword and hunger and death and the beasts of the earth."

Yep. Standard apocalyptic psychosis. "And I'm Abaddon, you say?"

"Uh huh. The king – an angel, too, of the Bottomless Pit."

"And my job is . . .?"

"The reaping of the multitudes. I was thinking we could work together. There's another one. He has the mark on his forehead."

"Does he have his hair buzzed short?"

"You know him?"

"Yeah. His name's Dwight. We've met."

My mother shouted from the hallway: "You've not drunk your coffee."

"Thanks, Mom!"

I looked at my watch.

"My mother-in-law was killed," said Hobo Joe.

"Yeah? That's too bad."

He shrugged. "I didn't like her much."

I stood. "Well, Joe . . . I need to start getting ready for work. I'm glad you came round. It'd help me if you left quickly and didn't talk to my mother."

He stood and nodded. He offered a hand and we shook. I let him out of the room and I heard him say bye to my mother before the apartment door closed.

Of course, she was immediately out of the living room and in my face.

"Who's he? He looks like a drunk or a drug dealer."

"Someone from work."

"Well, he stinks. And he didn't even say goodbye to me."

"I *heard* him say goodbye, Mom."

"He wasn't looking at me when he said it. Next time you want to invite friends round at this time in the morning, make sure you're awake. And you ask my permission. It's *my* house, remember."

"How could I forget?"

"What'd you say? Don't get smart with me, mister. I'm going to work. Open a window. Air out the place a little. That guy smells like a skunk!"

"Don't die in an auto wreck," I muttered as she slammed the door behind her.

Well, I was angry. What attracted these people to me? First Dwight and now this guy Joe, who'd seen two different bodies in my room. Both were murderers. Both felt some connection with me.

Joe had left without defining what he thought I was going to do for him. The homicidally insane aren't typically noted for their organizational skills. But he'd be back. That was one thing you could say about them: once they had an itch, they'd keep on scratching until there was blood. Neither of them seemed to have considered the possibility of getting caught.

I was angry, too, because now I had to get rid of the third girl – my favorite so far. We'd had only one night together and there could've been more, but now Joe had seen her. He might get picked up by a police patrol in the next ten minutes and tell them that he'd just come from Abaddon's pit or whatever. I couldn't take that risk. I'd have to call in sick and spend the day cutting her up in the tub and distributing her around the county.

I went to the phone and dialed the station. No tone. I tapped the receiver cradle. Nothing. I had a bad feeling.

I went outside and around the back of the building where the wires came down from the pole. Somebody had cut right through our phone line with a knife, leaving a slice mark in the wood.

NINETEEN

Dwight was in the forest meditating on an acid comedown. The silence was almost total. He was a giant redwood. He'd been sitting there 1,000 years or more with his roots deep in the earth and his upper branches stroking the sky. The consciousness of the world came to him. He was the center of everything.

Then a spatter of shots, some metallic pings and some whooping that echoed through the trees. Sounded like a .22 rifle. Probably kids running loose in the woods. Dwight stood, brushed leaves from his pants and walked toward the sounds.

A group of four boys had put together a shabby tent structure in a clearing using a blue tarp, sticks and cords. A campfire smoked. Dwight crouched and watched them from within the trees as they took turns firing a .22 rifle at a dented hubcap tied to a trunk. They all had bottles of beer, which they'd stick in their jeans pockets before shooting.

Dwight had done the same kind of thing at their age. Shooting guns, racing cars. But then he got into pot and acid and somehow his youth slipped between his fingers and he became an unemployed burden on his parents. Next thing, he was being stomped half to death by Hells Angels in Golden Gate Park, in a holding cell, then strapped to a bed with wires attached to his dick. There was a big gap in the middle.

One of the boys saw him through the branches and muttered to the others. Now they were all turned and looking.

"Hey, man!" said one of them, waving. It was half greeting, half challenge.

Dwight stepped out of the woods. His .38 was in his back pocket. He waved hello.

"You hiking?" said one of the others.

"Uh huh."

The boys exchanged glances. This guy didn't look like any hiker – no rucksack and he was wearing dirty sneakers. He looked like he'd escaped from one of those free-love hippie communes, except his hair was too short.

"Wanna beer?" said another of the boys, holding up a bottle.

"Sure!" Dwight approached.

"We don't got no ice,' said the same kid, taking a bottle from a cooler and handing it over. "You live round here?"

Dwight drank. "Got a cabin back that way. Heard the shots."

"Sorry, man. We thought there was nothin' round here. Just lettin' off steam, you know?"

"Uh huh." Dwight sniffed. "You got pot?"

The boys laughed. A pressure valve had been released.

"Sure! Wanna lid? Come in the tent. We do it like that so we don't waste any smoke, you know?"

'Sure. Used to do it like that in the city."

"You were in SF? On Haight?"

"Yep. Spent a lot of time there. Happenings, love-ins."

"Shit, man! You gotta tell us. We been talking about getting a camper van and going up to the city."

Dwight crouched to follow them into the makeshift tent. The light inside was blue from the tarp. Like being under the sea. There were inflatable mattresses and zipped-open sleeping bags. Takeaway food boxes and tins were everywhere. They had ready-rolled joints in a tin box and passed one to him.

"This is good shit, man," said one of the boys. "Howie's cousin grows it on his farm up at Quarry Park. No chemicals. Just pure weed."

They fired up and the tent filled with pot smoke.

"So tell us about SF, man."

"It's pretty bogue if you wanna know," said Dwight, remembering the lingo. "I mean, they talk about enlightenment and love and how nothing belongs to anyone, but the chicks don't really wanna ball. They're just interested in the leaders. It's all a power trip."

"I heard they have rooms, like, just for fucking," said one of the boys. "Like, just mattresses and everyone's screwing in the same place like in *Zabriskie Point* in the desert."

"That's true," said Dwight. But what was *Zabriskie Point*?

The boys whooped. "Yeah! Bring it on!"

"But you gotta remember," said Dwight, "that those mattresses see hundreds of couples on 'em every month and nobody cleans anything, like, never. There's no sheets or whatever. It's not a hotel. It gets pretty rancid in there when the weather's hot."

The boys looked doubtful. They'd not heard that part.

"But the girls are hot, right?" said one.

"Sure, there're hot girls."

More whooping and backslapping.

"But most of 'em have VD," said Dwight. "I got it myself."

The boys looked at each other through the smoke. This guy was kind of a downer, putting the bummer on their plans.

Dwight leaned back on the inflatable bed and put his hand on the thigh of the nearest boy.

Smoke drifted. Silence.

"What you doin', man?" said the boy with the hand on his thigh.

Dwight smiled and kept his hand there.

"We're not fags, man," said another. "It's fine if you are and all, but we're not down with that. It's not our bag."

The boy next to Dwight jerked his leg away.

Dwight started to unfasten his jeans.

"Did you hear me, man? We're not into it."

Dwight pulled down his underwear and burned himself with the end of the joint. His face was frozen in a weird rictus.

"The *fuck*?"

"He's crazy!"

"Jesus!"

"You need to go, man. This shit isn't for us."

"You listening, man?"

Dwight stared at the black ash burn.

The boys were looking at each other urgently.

A scream came through the forest – a girl.

Dwight pulled out his .38.

"Whoa, man! Take whatever you want. We don't want no trouble."

Another female scream.

"Stay here," said Dwight, pulling his jeans up. "I'm gonna see what's happening. Don't make any noise. Don't follow me."

"Sure, man. Whatever you say."

Dwight went out of the tent and listened. There was a road about 100 yards south of the clearing and he could hear voices coming from there. He started through the trees with the .38 in his hand.

The sun glinted off glass and metal through the branches. A blue Corvette Stingray was parked in a turn-off. Dwight could hear indistinct voices: the gruff tones of a man, then a woman whimpering or pleading. He moved closer, approaching from the front of the car.

A skinny black man was raping a woman he'd bent forward over the trunk. She was crying, her hair all over her face. She saw Dwight emerging from the forest through the rear window and shouted. "Help! Help! I'm being raped!"

The black man looked up and saw Dwight approaching. He saw the gun, but didn't stop.

"This ain't none of yo bidnis, man! You fuck off, now. Dig?"

"Help me!" said the girl, her dress pulled up and lying creased on her lower back.

"Shut yo mouf! I tryna concentrate here!"

Dwight came closer and stood watching the rape, the gun held loosely down by his thigh.

"The fuck you doin', man? You crazy? This ain't no *show*. Get the fuck outta here! You ruinin' the moment."

The girl's face was twisted with shock and shame and incomprehension, crying, "Why don't you *help* me?"

"Didn' I tell you to shut up, bitch?"

Dwight shot the rapist in the chest.

The black man staggered away from the girl, his pants round his ankles, his naked penis erect. He fell to the ground and sat, astounded at the blood on his chest. He looked up at Dwight, incredulous.

"You motherf–"

Dwight shot him again, catching him in the neck this time.

"Oh, thank you thank you thank you," said the girl, pulling the panties up from her feet and dropping her dress. She saw herself in the rear window and started sobbing harder.

The black man was writhing on the ground holding his throat. Dwight aimed and shot him in the head. He was still after that.

"Can you . . . ?" said the girl. "Can you take me . . . ? I'm late for class. I'm . . ."

Dwight shot her in the chest and she sat down on the ground, too.

"What?" she said.

He shot her in the face and she fell over backward. Now she was still.

He stood looking at the scene and reloaded the .38, tipping the used shells to clink onto the ground. It reminded him of the bells people wore round their necks or on their sandals on Haight.

He left the bodies where they lay and walked back toward the clearing, where the boys were packing away the tarp tent and folding up their air mattresses. They saw him coming out of the woods, the .38 in his hand.

"Hey, man. What happened? We heard shots."

"It was a rapist," said Dwight.

"He shot at you?"

"No. I shot him. And the girl."

The oceanic consciousness was chiming like a bell, voices coming to Dwight like that doorbell. *Doo-doo-doo do-do.* Dwight was able to translate the music: kill us all. Let's go to the other side together!

The boys looked at each other. They looked at his revolver. Their .22 rifle was leaning against a tree about ten feet away.

"You killed them?" said a boy.

"I guess," said Dwight.

Doo-doo-doo do-do. Kill us, Dwight. You'd really be doing us a big favor.

"But . . . why kill the girl?"

"I don't know!" A giggle.

"Well, man," said one of the boys, his voice kinda high and tight. "We need to get home. It's been cool meeting you and all, but we gotta go." He started walking slowly to where the rifle was.

Dwight shot him and he fell.

The others froze, just standing in a line. Dwight shot one and then the next. The last one charged at him holding a bottle and Dwight shot him, too. The first one was still crawling toward the rifle so Dwight walked over and shot him in the head. It was a nice rifle so he slung it over his shoulder.

The others were still alive so he reloaded the .38 and went round shooting each one in the head.

"What did we do to *you*, man?" said the last one, lying on the ground, blood seeping between his fingers from the wound in his side.

"Nothing!"

He shot the boy and walked back to the road where the blue

Stingray was. A pretty cool car. He got the keys from the dead rapist's jeans pocket and drove onto the road. He was in the mood for a drink.

He was passing through the suburbs when he saw a female hitchhiker by the side of the road. He slowed and rolled down the window.

"Where you going?" he said.

"The campus?"

"Hop in!"

He swerved back onto the road, smiling, his arm resting on the windowsill beside him.

"I don't normally hitch," said the girl. "You know, with all the rapes there've been. But they say it's a black guy, so . . ."

"Yeah, there won't be any more of those rapes," said Dwight.

"No? Have the police got him? I've not seen the papers."

"He's dead. Somebody shot him."

"Well, I'm sorry but I'm glad. Someone like that doesn't deserve to live. Maybe it's not Christian to say it, but . . . you know."

"Yep," said Dwight. "The rapist's gone. It's the murderers you have to worry about."

TWENTY

HEAD FOUND IN STATE PARK – Buena Vista police investigators went to Hudd Canyon Road Thursday afternoon following the discovery of a head in the remote canyon near Las Gambas. Buena Vista investigator Lt. Edward Schumer said the head has been identified as that of missing coed Carole Litski, last seen July 12 when hitchhiking to class at the UCBV campus. Lt. Schumer said that the head was found about 30 feet down an embankment at the side of a road. He added that a .22 bullet recovered from the head had been sent for ballistics testing.

NO SUSPECT IN SLAYINGS – City police and Sheriff's investigators met Tuesday to review all aspects of the mass killing in the Buena Vista State Park. Lawmen are still without a suspect or a motive for the six related slayings of four boys, a young woman and the rapist identified by previous victims as Wendell Holmes. Sheriff John Douglas announced that the same gun, a .38, was used to kill all victims.

INVESTIGATOR HIRED TO FIND COED KILLER – Students at UCBV have raised funds to engage a private detective to seek the murderer of miracle girl Lena Cuneo. Investigator George Donahue said that the 24-year-old, whose body was found in the Buena Vista State Park in early July, had almost certainly been picked up while hitchhiking and that her killer was likely still offering lifts. The university has restated that students should take the bus or share cars only with friends.

Well, a lot was happening. I was kinda angry that they'd identified my second girl's head so easily when I'd gone to all that trouble removing her teeth. They'd dug my .22 bullet out of her head, but I wasn't too worried. There was nothing to tie her to me.

The mood in Buena Vista had changed. One morning, I saw a line outside Scott's Sporting Goods – people waiting to buy guns. Webster was selling more locks and iron grilles for ground-floor windows. Maybe New York and Chicago had more murders, but they also had much bigger populations. People were worried.

I'd been spending a lot of time at the Holding Cell trying to pick up breadcrumbs of information from the off-duty cops. They were somber and under a lot of pressure from the press and community groups. More than 100 girls had been raped or sexually assaulted while hitching in the last twelve months. Whole families were being killed. Even the perpetrators were being murdered, in the case of the rapist Wendell Holmes.

But the cops were proud. What really got them pissed was this private investigator hired by UCBV students. Why pay some tubby retired cop to find the killer when the real police were already working on it twenty-four hours a day? Sure, they knew and respected the guy, Donahue. He'd been a detective in San Jose for most of his career and had a reputation as a straight arrow. But he was treading on toes and he knew it. Some cops just couldn't retire in peace and build matchstick models in their garage with the grandkids.

And the worst thing: this Donahue had a crazy plan. He was going to arm attractive young women with concealed automatic pistols and use them as bait. The idea was that these girls would stand around waiting for a ride, get in cars and if the killer made a move, they'd effect a citizen's arrest. That was the best-case scenario. At the very least, they'd be able to defend themselves, escape alive and identify both murderer and vehicle.

There was a lot of discussion in the Holding Cell about how practical or legal this was. Californian law back then prevented the carrying of loaded weapons, but there was a kinda gray area about what 'loaded' meant. The law apparently specified 'unloaded' as no live cartridge in the chamber, but an automatic could still have bullets in the mag. All you'd have to do to fire was rack the slide (or pull the bolt, in the case of my Ruger). You'd need a specific license to carry the gun concealed, but Donahue had friends and he'd managed to secure a few short-term concealed-carry permits for his female agents.

"More people are gonna die," said the cops in the Holding Cell.

"It makes no sense," they said.

"How's it gonna work? The chick'll be digging around in her bra for the auto and then have to rack it. *"Ooh, it's too stiff. Ooh, I broke a nail!"* Meanwhile, he's filled her full of bullets."

"Or his dick."

"Or she'll shoot herself by accident."

"Or she'll go home and shoot her no-good boyfriend with it."

"Or her handsy step-father."

"Or the killer'll take the gun off her and use it to kill more girls."

"It's a dumb idea all round."

It might have been a deterrent. But mostly it was a matter of pride among the Buena Vista cops. Donahue was playing to the crowd while the real cops were doing all the grunt work behind the scenes, following leads and running tests. It was slow work and undramatic.

I tried to get as much as I could from Amber when she came round. It seemed there was a lot of confusion about the recent slaughter in the forest: the four kids, the rapist *and* his victim – all with the same gun.

We were standing in the kitchen drinking coffee.

"There's just no motive," said Amber. "Nothing was stolen. The kids and the rapist still had money in their wallets. If it was revenge, why kill the girl?"

"I thought the car was missing," I said. "The Stingray or the Pontiac, or whatever he was driving."

"Sure, but was auto theft a motive? It had nothing to do with the boys. They were in a totally different place."

"Wasn't there any evidence at the scenes?"

"You really do wish you were a cop, don't you?"

"The cops didn't want him!" said my mother from the living room.

"I've been following it in the papers," I said, "but you know they never report all the details."

"He reloaded so there were .38 shells all around the place," said Amber. "There are some boot prints, too, but they could belong to anyone. A lot of people go up there walking and it was a cleared area for camping."

"Were there boot prints at other sites? I'm thinking of that girl found up off Cascade. They could compare pattern and size."

"I don't know, Sonny. Why don't you ask your buddies in the Holding Cell? I'm not supposed to tell anyone about this stuff. And I'll be honest: it's kinda creepy that you have so much interest."

"It's in the papers, Amber. It's on page one. *Everyone*'s interested."

"You wanna be careful. With *your* history, I mean . . ."

"What? Has anybody said anything?"

"Of course not. But you know what I'm saying. If I were you,

I'd keep my head down and not go round asking too many questions about murders."

"I resent that, Amber. Do you actually think I'm involved in any of this?"

"Not really. It's not your MO."

"What does *that* mean?"

"It means you only kill grandparents!" called my mother from the other room.

"You're not a part of this conversation, Mom!" I said.

"I'm a part of every conversation in *my* house."

I looked at the claw hammer on its hook above the garbage pail.

I had to turn the Ruger in to the Sheriff's Department – something that was even more urgent now that there were so many victims turning up with .22s in them. The next step might be crosschecking purchases of that caliber gun and calling on owners. Having mine in a police locker looked like a pretty sound alibi.

Question was: which one should I turn in? My gun could be matched to the girl's head found in Hudd Canyon and the family Joe had killed. Sure, I could scratch up the rifling inside the barrel to ruin any ballistics test, but they'd also be able to see clear as day that I'd done that. The tool marks would be obvious. The alternative: hand in Dwight's Ruger, which actually did have a very similar serial number. Just a couple different digits. That one could be matched to whatever crimes he'd committed – probably more than I had. Plus, he left evidence everywhere he went and was gonna get caught soon.

I decided to hand in Dwight's gun. I figured that the last place they'd look for his weapon was in an evidence locker under my name. Besides, I had a personal connection with my Ruger. I'd used it on the second girl and it had memories for me. It was a part of the story.

So I took it down to the office and went to the front desk and waited in line with people paying fines or disputing tickets or whatever. Petty criminals.

"Hi. I have to hand this gun in."

The uniformed clerk looked at it on the counter. "Why, sir? What does it pertain to?"

"Well, it's a pretty long story. I bought it a while back and two of your detectives came to my apartment and told me the purchase was flagged but they didn't know why, so I should bring it in until they can get to the bottom of it. Some administrative glitch, they said."

He looked at me, thinking, Look at this jabbering idiot. "You got any paperwork?"

"What kind of paperwork?"

"Receipt? Record of Sale?"

"No. They didn't say . . . I could go back home and look for them, but I think I threw them out. Do you want me to bring the gun back another day when I've found the paperwork?"

He clenched his jaw and reached for a pad without taking his eyes off me. "Put your name, address and phone number here. Do you know which detectives visited you?"

"I didn't catch their names. I've been busy at work and . . ."

Another jaw clench. "Is the weapon loaded?"

"No, I emptied it."

He checked, handling the Ruger professionally. I think he was impressed. "Okay. Leave it with me and I'll see it gets to the right place."

"Thank you, officer. Should I call back later to see if it's all been resolved?"

"We'll call you." He put the gun under the counter with the loose leaf of paper I'd written on. He looked at the person in line behind me. Dismissed.

There was a good chance they'd just lose the gun in some

evidence locker. It wasn't a priority. It'd been handed in by some dummy who'd messed up his purchase, probably putting the wrong details on the form. They had better things to do with their time, what with all these rapes and murders.

I've never been what you might call an addict. Pot and acid and the rest never really appealed to me. I was put away when I was too young to be into all of that. At Atascadero, you learned to avoid the pills they gave you unless you wanted to spend twenty years drooling in a twilight consciousness. I needed to be present and aware if I was gonna get out of there without an icepick lobotomy or electrodes on my genitals.

But I did like a beer or two. I tried not to drink more than that because I'd seen what my mother got like. People said too much when they were drunk. Parts of their personality came out that they'd normally want to keep hidden. I was drinking a little more than usual those days after the head was discovered and when I had to hand the gun in. Plus, there were two crazies running about who knew too much about me. They weren't being careful.

One night, I was round at Dulcie's place in Merluza. Her parents were out at a concert in the city and we had the place to ourselves. She'd been telling me that her dad had some special aged scotch and she wanted me to try it. I don't know why. Maybe she thought it was something men liked. Maybe she was trying to loosen me up.

Well, I got chatty after a couple glasses of that firewater. It was like my mouth was saying things before I'd had a chance to think about them. I remember concentrating more than usual on what I said before I said it. All it needed was one casual reference to the mental hospital or some mention of my grandparents for Dulcie to let loose a blizzard of questions. It was a real effort, I can tell you. Some emotions started to come out.

"You're a good person, Sonny. You really are."

I laughed. "If only you knew."

"What's there to know? You're so patient, picking me up and dropping me off."

"Everyone has secrets."

"Of course they do, but that doesn't mean–"

"No. I have horrible secrets, Dulcie," my voice said. "I'm a horrible person."

"Sonny. I know you . . . You're not like other men. You're sweet. You're courteous. You don't even curse!"

No, but I stab girls and shoot them and cut off their heads and take porno Polaroids of them. I cut them up in a tub, wrap them in black plastic and fling their parts into the forest.

"Are you crying?" said Dulcie. "Oh, Sonny. What's wrong?"

"You shouldn't be with me. I'm like a black hole. I'm quicksand."

I don't know why I told her those things. Maybe the alcohol had awakened something in me – relaxed or impeded part of my usually iron will. The pressure of not telling anyone anything was intense. Sometimes it felt like a pressure building intolerably. I wanted somebody to know.

"You're just too tough on yourself," she said. "You're sensitive! That's what I like about you."

I knocked their teeth out with a hammer and cut their hands off to make them unidentifiable. The only time I've ever felt truly alive and happy was while killing and then loving these girls.

"Maybe you should sleep it off," said Dulcie. "Scotch is strong if you're not used to it. And Dad might notice if you drink any more. Here, lie down. Let me plump your cushion. That's it. Close your eyes."

I slept, her cool hand on my forehead. Dulcie. Perhaps she really loved me. The only person who ever had. But only because she didn't know me. The truth would crush her. They'd knock on her door and show their badges and say, "What can you tell us about the Decapitation Necrophile Sonny Boden?"

No – there'd be a catchier name than that. The State Park

Stalker. The Buena Vista Butcher. The Head Collector. And Dulcie would say, "No. No. He wouldn't hurt a fly. Polaroids? Head severing? Tub dismemberment? No. You've got the wrong person. He didn't even curse."

I thought I wasn't an addict, but I needed another girl. The last two had been taken from me prematurely after Hobo Joe visited. I knew I had to stop, but I couldn't. The mistake was to start. Once you start, stopping becomes the issue. And when you work out a process that keeps you free of suspicion, you've written yourself a license to continue. I told myself: just one more. The last one. The perfect girl. Then I'd have the memories. Perhaps I'd be able to lead a normal life and have children and leave all of this behind me as youthful frivolity.

The problem was this private detective Donahue and his coven of concealed-weapon coeds. I'd pull my Ruger and I'd be looking down the barrel of a .45 Colt or a Beretta twice my caliber. What if they were carrying knives as well?

I still had the stiletto dagger I'd bought at Scott's – a beautiful knife. It hadn't been necessary or favorable to use it on the last two girls, but I'd been doing some thinking about faster ways to kill without mess or fuss. A shot to the head had proved the fastest method so far, but it did mark the body. I'd been looking carefully at the skull as part of my dismemberment duties.

The human skull is a well designed piece of protection for the brain. There aren't that many ways in without damaging the bone. The stiletto could go through the ear directly into the brain and you'd hardly see any mark. It could also go up under the chin, through the lower jaw and through the palate, a relatively fragile piece of bone structure. You wouldn't see the hole when it was on the shelf. But I was afraid of getting the angle wrong and having to pull the blade out to try again. Of course, the eyes were another way in, but I didn't want to cause that kinda damage.

There was one obvious way round the whole armed coed problem: you had to be eighteen to get a concealed carry license.

I'd have to choose girls who looked much younger. Dulcie was eighteen. It wasn't too much of a stretch.

With everything that was going on – Hobo Joe, Buzzcut Dwight, Donahue – you might say I was feeling a little paranoid. The identification of the first and second girls had made the killings real in a way they hadn't been before. Before, they'd been something like a dream or an alternate reality for me alone to enjoy and replay. Now, other people were talking about them and using their names. Even if I'd known the girls' names from their IDs, I'd never thought about them as actual individuals. Our relationship had been beyond that. More profound. What importance did names have? And did a body without a head still have the same identity? Once I'd taken them, they were mine. I didn't want to share them.

Amber's words had struck me, also. "You wanna be careful with *your* history." Of course, my mother had said the same thing a million times, but that was just to needle me. Amber worked at the police station. She knew how they thought. My record was supposed to be expunged, sure, but all the paperwork would still be in a filing cabinet somewhere. How long before the Buena Vista police got desperate and started going through the records for juvenile crimes or mental health histories?

I realized I needed to be even more careful. I realized I needed alibis. If the detectives came round and asked me where I was when the first girl disappeared, what could I say? At home with my drunken, passed-out mother? Driving alone in the state park for pleasure? No, I needed people to back me up. Not Dulcie. I didn't want to involve her in any of this, though inevitably she would be.

What could be a better alibi than the police themselves? I decided to spend more time in the Holding Cell, especially if I was planning to go out driving later. The off-duty cops lost track of time after a couple hours drinking. They wouldn't remember any detail precisely. Sonny? Yeah, he was in the bar that night. About ten? Could've been. Ten, ten thirty.

I was in there one evening, standing at the bar, when I saw Dwight. I had Lieutenant Schumer to my left, his back to me, and a couple other detectives chatting to my right. And there was Dwight, standing in the doorway, looking around the bar. People were pushing to get by him, but he was oblivious.

He saw me. He waved. I think he actually shouted my name across the room, but it was pretty busy and it was lost in the voices. He started to walk through the tables to me.

Shit.

What if he was covered in blood again? What if he was carrying the .38 openly in his hand? I could see him walking right up to me at the bar and saying something like, "Hey, Sonny! I just shot a schoolgirl off her bike."

I had to intercept him.

The cops hadn't seen him and weren't looking at me. I left my beer on the bar and went to meet him in the middle of the room.

"Hey, Sonny!"

'You can't be in here, Dwight. The place is full of cops and they're all looking for you."

"But *you're* in here."

"That's different."

"How?"

"Let's go outside." I took his arm and felt the weight of his coat-pocket .38 knock against me. "Come on."

"Can't we have a drink together? I've been waiting for you to come up to the cabin. I even cleaned the place."

"That's great, Dwight." I was looking to see if anyone had noticed us together. Was it too obvious that I was trying to get him out of there?

We emerged into the cool air of the parking lot.

"Where's your car, Dwight?"

"It's right here."

I saw the blue Stingray.

"It's a new one," said Dwight, smiling like a kid at Christmas.

"Are you the one? The guy who killed the black rapist?"

"Uh huh. He was raping a girl when I met him."

"And you're driving his car? Do you know where you are, Dwight? This is the cop bar. All the town's cops are here and they're all looking for this car."

"It's right here!"

"Dwight . . . You have to get out of here *now*."

"We're not going to have a beer?"

I felt like I was going to have a heart attack. Schumer or one of the others could come out at any second and see the car. Excuse me, sir – is this your vehicle?

"No, Dwight. We can't have a beer tonight. I'm trying to help you. Do you understand? Let's walk to the Stingray. Come on."

He looked disappointed, like I'd told him he couldn't have a puppy.

"Got your keys, Dwight?"

He felt in a pants pocket. Nope. Not that one. He looked in another and another.

"Dwight. You need to get in your . . . get in the Stingray and go home. The best thing would be to abandon it somewhere. You don't want to be seen with it."

"You're a good friend, Sonny." It looked like he was going to cry.

"Okay. Go on, Dwight. I'm gonna walk away now. Get outta here."

I heard the engine start as I was walking back to the bar. I knew he'd pulled into the road when I heard the squeal of tires, a horn and an enraged yell: "Learn to drive, fuckhead!"

TWENTY-ONE

I went driving late that night after spending a little more time at the bar. It was late and I expected there'd be virtually nobody out hitchhiking, but there were quite a few. Maybe they felt bolder now the black rapist had been shot.

The truth was that he couldn't have been solely responsible for the 100 or more attacks over the last year. Guys were obviously coming out to Buena Vista from the city and from San Jose – maybe even from LA. It was an ideal hunting ground: hundreds of pretty young coeds and miles of remote forest to take them to, with hardly any police presence outside the downtown zone.

That was my problem. Most of the girls were obviously coeds and any one of them could've been an armed agent of PI Donahue. There were some very pretty young ladies thumbing rides and I would have stopped for them at any other time, but now their beauty was suspicious. They could've been chosen specifically as bait.

I probably should've gone home, but I'd drunk quite a lot of beer and didn't want to go back to Verdugo. I knew from experience that if both me and my mother were drunk, we'd spend the whole night yelling at each other. A neighbor had called the police once and I couldn't risk that again if I had a girl in my trunk. Unlike Dwight, unlike Joe, I was always thinking ahead. That's why nobody had even guessed.

Goddamn Dwight. If anything was going to get me caught, it was him. I could see him driving up to the station and showing me a dismembered body in the passenger seat. Or killing Tom right there in the office.

On the other hand, I had to stay rational. What did he really know? What could he prove? He'd seen me driving away from the spot where another girl had been found – the girl *he'd* killed. Okay, so he'd found the ear stud in the same place, but what did that prove? That the first girl had been there once and dropped her earring.

All Dwight could tell the police was that he'd heard voices and seen a fresh bloodstain after I'd been parked in that spot. It looked bad, sure, but it didn't prove anything. The girl's body, or parts of it, had been found elsewhere and I'd disposed of all other evidence. I could just stay I'd stopped to urinate and seen the blood myself. The noises? My car radio. Besides, he was clearly insane. Any lawyer could use that against him.

The bigger problem was actually Hobo Joe. He'd seen things that could send me directly to the gas chamber.

I was so occupied with my thoughts that I almost missed the girl. She was a little thing about the same size and age as Dulcie – either a very petite coed or a high-school girl. And very pretty, with delicate features like a porcelain doll. She was wearing a black dress with a white stripe around the waist like a signal. I pulled the car over just ahead of her and she ran up to the window.

"Hey," I said. "It's pretty late to be out hitching. Where you going?"

"El Bosque."

"Well, it's kinda the opposite direction for me . . . but seeing as it's so late. Get in. Here, let me check your door. It sometimes doesn't close right. Okay. That's it. Now you're safe."

She was made up, her hair glistening and her mother's

perfume filling the car. She was going to a party at a friend's house in the suburbs and chattering away.

"They said there'll be beer, but I hope someone'll have pot, you know? Do you smoke? My parents tell me I shouldn't, but *they* do. They think I don't know what it smells like! Say, is this the way to El Bosque?"

"It's a short-cut. They're digging up the road on Riverside."

"Oh, okay. And anyway, this guy is gonna be there who I like and he said he might have some mescaline, but he says a lot of things, you know? You ever tried mescaline? They say it's like acid but stronger. Hey, I think you're heading out of town. Are you from around here?"

"I'm afraid you're gonna miss your party."

She looked at the gun. "Is that thing loaded?"

"Yes, it's loaded."

"You know it's a crime to carry a loaded weapon in your car?"

I looked at her. "What do you know about it?"

"I'm pre-law. I was studying the Mulford Act just last week."

"How old are you?"

"Twenty. Yeah, I know – I look younger."

What was wrong with these girls? I'd just shown her a loaded gun and told her that she was gonna miss her party, but she was acting like I'd told her it was gonna rain tomorrow. Weren't they aware of the dangerous world they lived in? Didn't they read the papers?

"Don't you read the papers?" I said.

"Not really. I mean, the news is just an agenda, isn't it? It's the Man telling us his reality."

"Did you hear about that head they found in Hudd Canyon?"

"Yeah. Maybe . . . I remember something about a body. A leg? Was that the same thing?"

"Two different girls."

"That's it. The guy who takes women out of their cars and buries them in the woods."

"No. That's another guy. He strangles them with wire but doesn't cut them up."

"But they caught the rapist," she said. "The black guy. At least, that's what they said he was. It's easy to go with the stereotype of the black man as a sexual predator. The white cops are obviously intimidated by black masculinity."

"They found him dead, with his pants round his ankles and his victim next to him."

"It could've been a frame-up."

She was making me angry. I thought about putting a bullet in her just to get her attention. The stiletto dagger was on the other side of my seat, but I really wanted to try one of those quick-kill methods on her. I couldn't let her rile me. I deserved some respect.

"That head they found in Hudd Canyon," I said, "that was me."

She looked at me frankly. She shook her head. "I don't think so."

"I'm telling you: it was me."

"You don't look the kind."

"What's *the kind*?"

"I'd know. I'd be able to tell. You're a shy guy. A frightened guy. You show the gun instead of showing your dick 'cause really, you're afraid of women. You'd like to be that guy, cutting heads off or whatever, but what you really want is to talk to women without being afraid or ashamed."

I was gripping the wheel pretty hard trying to control myself. I pulled off Highway 9 into the forest and stopped at the first place I saw. I turned off the lights.

"What now?" she said.

"Turn around and put your hands behind your back. I'm going to cuff you."

"I don't think you are."

I pulled the gun, drew the bolt and aimed it at her chest. I could see her thinking about the next smart comment, but maybe she saw in my eyes that I was serious. She sighed and turned, putting her hands behind her back.

I got the cuffs from my pocket and clipped them round her wrists. I took the duct tape from the glove box and tore off a strip.

"Now face me," I said.

She did so with a real pissy expression and I put the tape over her lips.

"Now you're gonna get in the trunk."

"Unh-unh," she grunted, shaking her head but still calm, like I was trying to sell her insurance instead of killing her.

I reached across her and took the length of dowel out of the door mechanism. I'd have to get out and walk round to her side.

"Stay there a second," I said, showing her the cocked and loaded gun again.

I opened her door and took her under the arm to help her out.

"Here's the plan," I said. "I'm gonna put you in the trunk and we're gonna drive to my house. We can get to know each other there."

She just looked at me – insolent, not even trying to disguise her disdain.

Well, I opened the trunk and something changed in her. Maybe it was the smell. I mean, I'd decapitated a few girls in there already and I hadn't been so careful about cleaning it. Did she smell the blood? Or is it possible a place absorbs some substance of events it's seen? Fear. Desperation. Realization of death.

Whatever it was, her whole demeanor changed. She went stiff and sniveled a little, like, okay – this is real.

I offered her my arm. "I'll help you."

She ran. She just took off toward the highway, arms cuffed behind her, mouth taped up.

"Stop or I'll—"

The gun just went off. I'd forgotten the two-stage trigger. Having drawn the bolt, I'd set the trigger for a low-pressure pull and it just fired into the trees.

She kept on running jerkily. It was dark and she'd soon be out of sight. She was going to reach the highway and a car could come by at any time. I aimed along the barrel, thanking God I'd bought a target pistol, and fired at the center of her back.

The bullet hit her – not where I'd aimed, but somewhere. She stumbled and almost fell, but she kept on going. It was the main problem with the .22. I was too far away. I'd have to run.

"Stop!"

She wasn't going to stop. She was running for her life. I went after her through the darkness, wet leaves and damp soil underfoot. A twig whipped at my face, making my eyes water. Fortunately, I could hear her breathing heavily through her nose, so I knew which way she'd turned on the highway.

"I'm not gonna kill you!" I said, still running.

Her feet were slapping on the asphalt up ahead. I could see the white stripe of her dress moving against the night. Even in the heat of the pursuit, it occurred to me that she might have escaped if she'd chosen a different dress. I might have missed her entirely by the side of the road.

I was getting tired, but I was driven by fear. If a car came along from either direction, they'd see us: her cuffed and gagged, me with a gun. This had to end.

"Goddamn it! Stop!"

I aimed again and shot twice. I saw her fall.

She was crawling when I reached her. I couldn't see in the dark where the rounds had hit her, but she was lying on her side, moaning.

"Come on. You've made this much more difficult than it had to be. Come back to the car." I lifted her to her feet with a hand under each arm. She was surprisingly light and the weight of her body so close aroused me. I was imagining it headless and naked in my bed, even if there were a few bullet holes in it. "Walk ahead of me. That's it. No funny business. I've got my gun pointed at your spine, and there're plenty of rounds in the mag, so don't give me any trouble."

She was limping, but she could walk well enough, if slowly. Maybe she was exaggerating. We were almost back at the car when we heard a motor. Headlamps showed through the trees.

She set off running toward it and I started shooting. I think one of the rounds hit her head or her neck because she jerked and changed direction, running straight off the edge of the road.

I arrived two seconds after and saw that she'd fallen down a ravine whose depth was unfathomable in the darkness. I could hear her rustling about down there, either still falling or trying to hold on – it wasn't clear.

The car was almost upon me and all I could do was lie face down on the ground before it arrived, hoping it'd just sweep round the corner. I closed my eyes as if that was going to make me more invisible and the car went by, music playing loud inside. Probably a group of kids smoking pot and going to a party. Maybe the same party the girl was going to. Maybe it was the guy she wanted to meet who'd boasted about having mescaline.

The sound of the motor vanished into silence and I stood, brushing the dirt and dust from my front. I listened. Nothing.

"Hey! You down there?"

She was keeping quiet, or she was dead.

I stood there. There was no way I could climb down after her in the dark. *Was* she dead? I'd put at least three bullets in her and she'd fallen into the ravine. It was a question of whether she was going to survive the night and whether her body would be visible the next morning. My cuffs and my duct tape were on her.

Could I come back the next morning at dawn with some rope and try to find her? Shit! Shit! Shit! This was all her fault. Why'd she have to get so smart? All she had to do was get in the trunk.

I listened some more. Nothing. I went back to the car and got the flashlight, but its beam picked out only bushes and trash thrown by drivers. Cigarette packets. Beer bottles. The ravine was pretty much vertical. I couldn't see the bottom. She had to be dead. She *had* to be dead.

I drove back into town with my heart throbbing in my throat. This was the first time I'd messed up and left evidence. I'd left the actual body in the forest! If she was alive, she'd be able to tell them everything. I'd told her I was responsible for the Hudd Canyon head! I'd revealed the other killer was strangling his victims – something only the police and that killer knew. Shit! *Shit!*

It was about two in the morning. The streets were virtually empty. I was so preoccupied with the girl in the ravine that I didn't notice the other car following me.

Unmarked police? I was driving at the correct speed. My lights were all fine. But it was a Plymouth Valiant – not a standard police vehicle. I did a loop around the block and still the car was following. I couldn't see the driver clearly through the headlamp glare, but the shape looked like a man.

Could it be the PI? Donahue? Maybe he'd canvassed coeds I'd picked up and correlated accounts of a Ford Galaxie. Maybe he'd followed me up into the forest and heard the shots. With the girl in the car, I might have been distracted and not noticed a professional tail.

There was a stretch of open road between El Bosque and Verdugo. I could pull over and wait to see if the Plymouth did the same. I had my gun. I'd seen Donahue's picture in the paper. I'd recognize him. At the first sign of his face, I'd shoot.

I pulled off onto crunching gravel and saw the Plymouth do the same behind me. I cocked the Ruger and rolled down the window. I saw the driver's door open in my rearview and a silhouetted figure coming toward me. I gripped the gun.

"Hey," said Hobo Joe, bending to my window. I could smell him.

"You? Shit! I thought it was the cops or that PI!"

"Sorry, man."

This guy. Him and Dwight were gonna drive me crazy.

"Why're you following me?"

"I wanted to tell you I got your sign."

"What sign?"

"The next family for reaping."

"Did I give you a sign? How long've you been following me?"

"Few days. Ananiel told me to. You're King Abaddon."

"Listen, Joe – it's real late and I've had a hell of a night . . ."

"You lost that girl in the park, huh?"

"What? You were there?"

"Yeah. I parked round the bend and left the car. I was watching."

"Why?"

"For a sign. But then I realized: you already gave me the sign."

"What are you talking about, Joe?"

"The family up in Merluza. The young girl and her parents."

"No. No. That's not a sign. I didn't . . . Have you done anything?"

"Not yet. I thought we'd go together."

A truck passed, blowing its horn, rocking the car with the gust. Dust and litter chased it, swirling.

"You're not gonna touch that family, Joe. There's no sign. I've not signaled anything. You understand?"

"But it's written. The seals have been opened."

"There are no seals. Nothing is written."

He looked at me, all confused. I realized I was in dangerous territory. This one was caught between rationality and his fantasy apocalypse. You can't challenge the delusions of the insane. Their reality is different. Maybe I was King Abaddon, but Joe was acting on angelic authority. He had divine sanction.

"Listen, Joe. Now isn't the time for reaping. You need to wait a little and then we'll go together, okay? You, me and Ananiel."

"When?"

"Soon. But you gotta stop following me. It's dangerous for both of us."

"How will you contact me? I don't have a phone."

"You're in that shack on Cascade, right?"

"Uh huh."

A motorbike went by – a big Harley, growling. I waited for the sound to fade.

"I'll come see you. Until then, you gotta lay low. Stay out of town, okay? Stay in your shack." He seemed doubtful. "I'm the king, right? King Abaddon?"

"Yeah."

"Well, maybe you're following me for a reason. I lead the way."

"Uh huh."

"So go back home. We'll talk soon." A thought. "Say, where did you get the Plymouth, Joe?"

"Found it. Up in the park. Door was open, but no one was around."

Shit. It was probably another strangler victim. The police would be looking for it.

"You gotta ditch the car, Joe. Leave it in a parking lot somewhere and walk back to the cabin. Okay?"

"I guess so. I shouldn't be driving anyway. Ananiel said. It's lethal. But my feet are killing me with all the walking."

"I'm going now, Joe. Remember: stay away from Merluza and that family."

"Yeah."

I pulled out and left him standing there in the headlights of his stolen car.

Now what?

Should I call Dulcie and tell her to get out of there for a few days? With what reason? That the arson killer was coming for her family and that I knew because, well, he was kinda a friend of mine? If they all died, the police would be at my house within a day or two asking questions while Joe sat in his cabin talking to angels.

Then I remembered the girl up in the ravine. What if she was still alive? Maybe she'd be perfectly visible to traffic in the morning, wearing my cuffs and with a piece of tape that could be matched to the one in my car. I reached into the glove compartment and took out the tape, tossing it out the window into the ditch by the highway.

I wasn't gonna sleep well.

TWENTY-TWO

My mother woke me with the worst possible news.
"Sonny! Get up. The police are coming."
"What? Why?"
"I called them."
"Why?"
"I'm not going to talk to you through a locked door."
I unlocked it and stood at the crack in just my shorts.
"God!" said my mother. "You think I want to see that so early in the morning?"
"Why'd you call the police, Mom?"
"The phone line that was cut."
"But I fixed it."
"I know. But I was talking to Ruth and she said she read in the paper that this arson killer always cuts the phone line with a knife. What if he's planning to kill us next?"
"That's not gonna happen, Mom."
"How do *you* know? Do all the murderers belong to a club? Like the Shriners?"
"Look – you need to call them and tell them it was a mistake."
"They said they'd be here at nine. It's nine. You'd better tidy up your room in case they want to look in it."

"Why would they look in my room?"

"I have no idea. I'm just thinking of you – as usual."

"Goddammit, Mom!"

"You watch your mouth!"

I slammed the door and looked around my room. Normally, the police'd need a warrant, but my mother was inviting them right inside. It was *her* apartment, after all.

Thank God I didn't have a body in there. Destiny again. If the girl hadn't run the previous night . . . But I *did* have her handbag with her ID in it. If she'd been reported missing . . . No. It didn't seem likely. They'd either found her already or she was still unaccounted for.

The intercom chimed. They were here. I went to the window and looked out at their car next to mine. What if they wanted to look in the trunk? The illegal Ruger was in there. Also, it reeked of blood.

I pulled on my jeans and a creased shirt. I combed my hair with my fingers and opened the bedroom door. I told myself it was just like any psychiatric assessment. All I had to do was appear normal. Normal and slightly pathetic. The cops were all hyper-masculine types.

My mother was already talking to them in the living room when I entered. Two detectives in shirts and ties and light sports jackets.

"This is my son, Sonny. He's not combed his hair for some reason. He's the one who found the cut cable."

"Hi," I said. I recognized one of them from the Holding Cell, but we'd not spoken before.

"You didn't report it," said Tweed Jacket.

"Well, no. I thought maybe it was kids or something. I just fixed it myself."

"But the arson killer cuts the phone lines," said my mother. "Isn't that right?"

"Have there been any signs of an attempted break-in?" said Blue Jacket.

"Nothing I've noticed," I said, standing by the door.

"What about that broken window?" said my mother.

"I told you, Mom. I broke it by accident." The detectives were looking at me. "I was cutting a branch outside and, you know, just put the ladder through the window. Totally my fault."

Tweed Jacket wrote something in his notebook. "Noticed any suspicious characters hanging around?"

I shrugged apologetically. "I'm at work a lot of the time. It's a pretty quiet part of town here. I really can't say I've seen anyone like that."

"What about that Manson-looking wino who visited you?" said my mother, her face twisted in disgust at the memory.

The jackets turned to me.

"Joe? Yeah, I was talking to him about buying his car."

"But you didn't know him when he arrived."

Jackets were watching me carefully.

"He's a customer at the station. Came through one time and mentioned he might be selling his car. Then I didn't see him for a couple weeks. We get a lot of people coming through, you know. Hundreds. I can't remember them all. So, yeah, I was kinda surprised when he turned up here."

"How'd he know where you live?" said Blue Jacket.

"I guess I told him."

"You guess?" said Tweed Jacket.

"Well, sure. I mean, how else would he know to come here?"

"Don't get smart with the detectives, Sonny," said my mother.

"Did you buy his car?" said Blue Jacket.

"No. He told me he'd crashed it. Offered me a discount, but you never know with the chassis if it's bent. I didn't wanna get into that, so we agreed to leave it."

"Got a number for this guy Joe?" said Tweed Jacket.

"Sorry. No. He's not really a friend. I wouldn't expect to see him again unless he comes through the station."

They wanted to look at the window I'd replaced and saw I'd

put an iron grille over it. I think they were impressed with the work.

"You have a weapon in the house?" asked Blue Jacket.

"No, sir."

"Maybe you should think about getting one. Lot of crazies about right now. Did this Joe fella come into the house?"

"He went in Sonny's room," said my mother, visibly delighted.

"Mind if we take a look?" said Tweed.

"Sure," I said, my voice a little higher than I wanted. "Come right in."

They stood just inside the door looking around: the rapidly made bed, the shoes on the floor by the mirror, the bookshelf without a head on it.

"What's that smell?" said Blue.

"Is there a smell?" I said.

"Something rotten," said Tweed. "It's faint. You might want to check under the floor. Could be a rat."

"Is that your bag?" said Blue, pointing at the ravine girl's bag.

"No. It's my girlfriend's."

"Did you have a girl in your room without my permission?" said my mother.

"No, Mom. She left it in my car."

"What's her name, Sonny?" said Tweed, pen poised over his notepad.

I was getting pretty angry with all of this. What relevance did Dulcie's name have? Were they doubtful that I had a girlfriend? I gave them her name and address in Merluza. That was gonna cause problems if the detectives followed up on it.

Then they wanted to see the sawn branch I'd mentioned. I'll give them credit: they were good at their job. Fortunately, I'd anticipated this and sawn off a branch just after I'd fixed the window. It *had* been close to the building and sometimes hit the wall in a heavy wind. It was my insurance policy in case anyone had heard the window being broken by Joe.

The detectives left, probably thinking what a pathetic

specimen I was: living with my mother and not being allowed to have a girl over. They were hardly out of the parking lot before me and my mother got into it.

"Why'd you speak to me like that in front of other people, Mom?"

"Because you deserve it. Why do *you* keep so many secrets? You never told me about this guy Joe. You never tell me about this girl Dulcie."

"It's my private life, Mom."

"You can have a private life when you live in your own apartment. Under my roof, I want to know if you're associating with Manson-looking characters."

"He's just a customer, Mom."

"And this Dulcie. Some clap-ridden hippie tramp, I suppose."

"She's a nice girl, Mom."

And the rest. We could go for hours like this, round in circles of recrimination, blame and spite. Thank God it was early and she wasn't drunk.

I wasn't working that morning and I didn't want to stay home. I drove back out to where the girl had gone over the edge of the ravine and saw my cartridge cases glinting on the road. Some had been crushed flat by passing cars. I collected four.

I couldn't see any trace of the girl. The drop was almost vertical for about seventy feet and then it was all bushes. There was a lot of crap down there: packets, bottles and paper caught in the stiff foliage. People had no respect for the natural beauty of the state park. It wasn't possible to see if the ravine bottomed out into a trail or whatever. There was no way she could have climbed back up – even if the cuffs had broken during the fall. That was some relief.

I sat in the car awhile. I needed time to think and being behind the wheel made me feel I was in control. What was I going to do about Dwight and Joe?

You might think that killing them was the obvious solution. But killing men never entered my mind. That would have felt the same to me as murder for any regular person. Unthinkable. Even from a distance, with a good rifle.

Of course, I couldn't report them anonymously to the police. Both would mention me within minutes – not because they wanted to inculpate me, but because they both felt some deranged connection. I was King Abaddon. I was a focus in the oceanic consciousness. They couldn't separate me from their own totally unconnected crimes.

Neither could I simply do nothing. Both of them were going to get caught within a very short time. They were leaving evidence everywhere. They were both driving stolen cars connected to active investigations. They both seemed to be living as fugitives in the forest. At what point would their families start wondering, joining the dots, and contact the Sheriff's Department? Joe *smelled* like an arsonist and looked like Manson. Dwight walked around covered in his victims' blood and seemed insane to everyone who met him.

And what'd happen when they finally got caught? They'd talk.

What if . . . What if I could somehow engineer it so they'd kill each other? They were capable. That outcome would be perfect for everyone. We'd pretty much all used each other's guns by this point and there was probably enough ballistics evidence to pin my killings on one or both of them. Even better if they were dead and unable to face trial or answer charges. I'd be able to stop killing and live a normal life with Dulcie. I could move away from my mother . . .

It wasn't an unrealistic idea. We only hear about the serial killers who are caught. There are others who simply decide to stop one day. Who knows why? Maybe they find love or they've worked out their trauma, or they've simply matured, but they stop and live a normal life. And nobody ever guesses. Their family, their community knows them as the guy who helps out after church, who shovels snow for neighbors, who takes his boys to Little League – never imagining that he'd strangled and raped fourteen girls or hacked up bodies in his mother's tub. They're not all like Dwight and Joe. You can't always tell. You can't see it in their eyes when you shake the same hands that once wore gloves of glistening red. How many wives have lain under a husband and loved him, not knowing the homicidal abysses he's ranged?

There was just one problem: my mother had to die. It was as inevitable as the sunrise. I'd dreamed of it since I was eight years old. You can't do something like that and walk away, especially if you're living with her. You immediately become the primary suspect, whether or not you flee. There are two choices: face the penalty or kill yourself. That was how it had to end for her and me. There was a symmetry to it. She'd given me life and I'd end hers. I think she'd always known that. It was a kinda contract between us. Our version of love.

That night after work, I went to the Holding Cell for a few beers. The cops were nervous. The press was making it look like they were incompetent. People were joking it'd got so bad in Buena Vista, that there were so many murderers at large, that the killers were now killing each other. It wasn't literally true. I mean, the rapist wasn't a killer. But the killers *were* killing each other's victims. That poor girl Dwight had shot when she thought she was gonna be rescued. The newspapers loved that stuff. Drama. Tragedy.

I couldn't relax at the bar. I kept looking at the door to see if Joe or Dwight were gonna walk in and wave to me across the crowd with the severed arm of their latest victim. It could've happened. I really had to do something. I had to start taking control of this situation that was getting out of control. An idea started to form.

I left the bar and drove up into the state park. It was about ten-thirty and dark. There was quite a lot of moisture in the air so the headlamps were throwing beams through black tree tunnels. Dwight had said he had a shack up on Oban Drive. There wasn't a lot of property up there – only what'd been built before it'd become an official state park. I was hoping just one of the three or four places would have lights on, but in the end it was easy to find Dwight. He'd left the rapist's Stingray parked in plain sight where any passing CHP car could see it.

I pulled off the road alongside the Stingray and slammed my door a little harder than normal to give him some warning I was out there. You didn't want to surprise a guy like Dwight on home territory.

I saw a shadow move against a window. The shack door opened and Dwight came out onto the stoop, a cup of something in his hand and the .38 butt sticking out of his pants.

"Sonny! You came. I knew you would."

Sure. The oceanic consciousness.

The cabin was hideous. It smelled of body odor, rotten food and damp. He had two rifles on the dining table: a .22 Marlin and what looked like a Winchester – a very nice gun. Ragged-topped food tins seemed to be everywhere. Soup. Beans. Meatballs in tomato sauce.

"I did what you said, Sonny. I didn't go down to the cop bar."

"That's great, Dwight. You did the right thing."

"You wanna tin of something? I got some mushroom soup somewhere. But there's no more gas. You'd have to eat it cold."

"I'm not hungry." I sat on the edge of the mildewed sofa. "Listen – I wanted to tell you something. I think I might have gotten a message. You know, through the oceanic consciousness."

"Can you see through people? Like, they're transparent?"

"What? No. Well, sometimes."

"I knew it."

"Anyway, Dwight. This message told me I should come to you and tell you about a house in Oakwood, on Durero. There's a–"

"I know the place! I've been there!"

"Really?"

"Yeah. I picked up a guy and he wanted to go there."

"What'd he look like?"

"Long hair. Beard. But not like a hippie. More like a bum. He smelled of smoke. I think he's one of us. I gave him some acid."

One of us? "Okay. Well, the message said you should go there."

"We can go together. Right now."

"No. The message said you should go there alone."

"Yeah? And what should I do when I get there?"

"I think you know, Dwight. I think you've already received the same message."

He nodded, thinking. I had my hand in my coat pocket. I'd taken the ID from Ravine Girl's handbag and now I eased it slowly out of the pocket like I was changing position on the sofa. I stood, pushing the ID down between the arm and the cushion.

"Dwight – I have to go. I'm working early tomorrow. You have your message."

"You're right, Sonny. I've received the same message now. Will you come visit again? I promise I'll get some more gas canisters. Do you like chicken soup?"

"Sure. And lose the Stingray, Dwight. Get rid of it. It's attracting bad energy. The yin and the yang are way out of balance."

"Yeah?"

"Yep. I can see it."

I left him thinking about that and drove back to Verdugo. I had no idea what he'd actually do. I'd hit the wasps' nest a few times with a stick. Now it was time to stand back and see what happened. Wasps were pretty predictable. Stinging was in their nature. I used to shoot at their nests when I was with my grandparents, just to watch them go crazy.

My mother was sleeping when I got home. I drank some water in the kitchen and looked at the claw hammer on its hook. I took it and went to her bedroom door, which she'd left open as usual.

I stood just inside her room, avoiding the creaking floorboard. She was lying on her back, mouth open, a brown hairnet on, snoring lightly. I went to the side of her bed, the hammer seemingly heavier in my right hand. I made a deal with myself: if she wakes now and sees me by her bed, I'll do it. A single enormous blow to the forehead. She wouldn't be able to defend herself. Her arms were under the covers. The last things she'd see would be my face, and the hammer sweeping down in an arc.

The claw or the face? The claw was more brutal – a raptor's talon. But it might get stuck in the skull and I'd have to put my foot against her head to pull it out. The face of the hammer would be more devastating, driving a disc of bone deep into her frontal lobe.

This had always been my dream. Always with a hammer, always when she was sleeping. Maybe that was the coward's way, but she was my mother after all. She'd given me life. She'd raised me. Sure, she had to die – but she didn't have to suffer. I'm not a monster.

She didn't wake. She snored on, oblivious. I wasn't sure if I was happy or not.

TWENTY-THREE

Dwight pulled up outside the house on Durero Street in Oakwood. The windows were all dark, but that didn't mean anything. They might be hiding – the panoramic consciousness might've alerted them.

He sat in the car listening to music, realizing after a while that the music was in his head. It had happened a lot in the Tenderloin. He'd spent nights hammering on the floor of the room when he couldn't sleep, but the music just wouldn't stop. During the day, too. A kind of accelerated jazz with a lot of repeated phrases. Now he quite liked it. He could turn it up and down like on a hi-fi.

Finally, he decided to go in. He rang the doorbell and waited, the .38 in his hand. No answer. Was it the right house? Yep – he remembered bringing the bearded guy here because he'd watched them from the car. Maybe there was a back door.

He broke a glass panel in the door using the .38 butt and let himself in. It smelled clean – not like Joe. It smelled like childhood: good food, soap and shampoo. Detergent. He turned down the music in his head.

"Anyone home?"

No answer. He'd have to wait. There was probably stuff in the refrigerator to make a sandwich. He could do a tour of the place. Looking in wardrobes and drawers – that was always fun.

Joe climbed down out of the truck cab and thanked the driver. It seemed colder in Merluza. There was a brisker wind off the sea. He walked toward the house where the family lived. It was on the coast and he could hear the waves. He could smell and taste that salt-iodine tang in the air.

And the sea gave up the dead that were in it, and whosoever was not found written in the Book of Life was cast into the lake of fire.

King Abaddon had said to wait, but Ananiel was impatient. The seals had been opened and the locust creatures had been released. The reaping had begun. There was no stopping it. This family had been chosen as surely as the dead girl's family. King Abaddon had indicated them.

There were cars in the drive but no lights in the house. Joe crunched over the gravel and walked round the side to where the phone line came down from the post. He cut it cleanly with his knife then broke a bathroom window at the rear using the Magnum butt.

Rich people. They had a lot of art: paintings, sculpture, a grand piano. Joe sat on the little stool and pressed some keys, listening to the strings vibrate and the notes fade into silence.

Be patient, said Ananiel. *Soon they will return.*

I'd taken Dulcie's family out to dinner. It was partly to get them out of the house following my roadside conversation with Hobo Joe, and partly because I needed to do some work on making them like me. They were snobs. I wanted to show them that a gas monkey could be a responsible provider, at least until something better came along. With my record now officially expunged, I could apply to the police academy.

We were at Mamacita's, a fish place on Three-Mile Beach that Tom had told me served good food at reasonable prices. It didn't have candles on the tables or chandeliers, but it was clean and looked kinda sophisticated with the paintings of traditional fishermen and the nets hanging like a canopy from the ceiling. The clientele was apparently different at lunchtime and dinner. I wasn't expecting truckers or surfers.

I'd put on a new white shirt and Dulcie looked delightful in a flowery dress. She'd been cold in the car so I'd draped my buckskin jacket round her shoulders, figuring she wouldn't see the bloodstain in the dark. Her parents had sat in the back, not speaking to each other and kinda grimacing. It wasn't the smell from the trunk because I'd cleaned it all out with a pressure spray at the station. I supposed there'd been some kinda argument before they left.

Well, her dad didn't seem to like the place. He rubbed the paper tablecloth between his thumb and finger with an expression like, Do we need a hepatitis shot to eat here? The menus were a little sticky, it's true, but it smelled great and I decided to order a bottle of wine after asking his opinion.

"Should we go for red or white? White's for fish, right?"

"It depends what you're going to order, Sonny."

"I'm gonna go for the seafood soup and then the grilled octopus."

"Then I'd order red. Or maybe you'd really prefer a beer."

"Why don't we order one of each?" said Dulcie.

"Listen," said her father. "There's something we need to discuss before ordering any food."

This looked bad. Her mother seemed like she was either gonna faint or explode. Her face was a clenched fist, red and white.

"I'm afraid . . . " said her father, "I'm afraid that I've learned something very worrying. I'd really prefer not to go into the detail of it, but I think this relationship should end here. Tonight. In fact, I insist."

"Daddy!"

"He put his hand on hers, but kept looking at me, unblinking. "I'm doing this for your happiness, Dulcie. And for your safety."

I went cold.

"My safety? What are you talking about?" said Dulcie, pulling her hand away. "You think Sonny is dangerous? He's the kindest, gentlest man."

"I been in touch with someone in San Francisco, a private investigator, and he's uncovered–"

"You've been investigating my boyfriend? Mom? Did you know about this? I can't believe . . ." Her mother sat with arms folded and face pinched, staring at the floor. "Mom?"

I sat paralyzed.

"I'm really sorry about this, Sonny," said Dulcie. "I didn't know they'd been doing this. I'm sure there's nothing bad. I know you."

"This is for your own good, honey," said her father.

"Or is it because he works in a gas station?" said Dulcie. "You think a few unpaid speeding tickets or a broken window when he was twelve or whatever will change my mind about him? Because you're wrong, Daddy."

He sighed and I knew it was coming, whatever it was.

"Dulcie . . . he murdered his grandparents."

"What?" she said. "No. That's impossible. It's ridiculous. Sonny?" She'd seen my face. My eyes. I was falling into darkness. "Sonny? Say it's not true."

"He was fifteen," said her father, staring at me with loathing. "He shot his grandmother in the head with a rifle and then stabbed her. When his grandfather came home, he shot him, too – also in the head. This was in the newspapers, Dulcie. You can read about it in the town library. I've got copies at home. There's even a picture of him, your boyfriend."

"Sonny?" But she already believed it. I could see.

"Honey – your boyfriend spent six years in the state mental hospital at Atascadero as a convicted murderer. I can't make this any clearer. These are the facts. There are official documents."

Dulcie was staring at me, willing me to contradict him.

What could I say? That I had a certificate saying I was sane? That I'd served my time and was considered no danger to society? There was no changing the facts of my grandparents' murder. There was no explaining it away as an accident. I'd done it on purpose. I'd said at the time – I'd told my lawyers – that I'd done it just to see what it was like to kill a person. The papers had printed that in quote marks. I'd said it. That wasn't a robust defense. I was only a kid. It had been seven years ago. But murder is like a tattoo on your soul that you can never have removed. Once somebody's seen it, you're forever the murderer. Nobody wants the caress of the murderer. The murderer's smile is never just a smile. A murderer can't raise his voice, or move suddenly.

Dulcie was weeping now, still looking at me. It was getting through to her.

"I'm sorry, Dulcie," said her father, "but your boyfriend is a killer and I won't have my darling spend a second longer in danger."

"I wouldn't . . ." I started to say, but my throat was dry and I'd already lost Dulcie. I could see it in her face. Shock. Disappointment. Incomprehension. As if it all would've been okay if I'd mentioned it earlier and been more honest. "Just one thing, Dulcie – would you mind if I'd shot my grandparents to death on a whim? Would it affect our relationship?"

The waitress came and was about to speak, but felt the atmosphere at the table.

"My apologies," said Dulcie's father, "but we won't be ordering anything tonight. I wonder if we'd be able to call a cab to collect us from here?"

"I can drive you," I said.

They all looked at me.

"Let's go," said her father, standing. He glared. "Don't make any attempt to contact my daughter. I'm willing to keep this quiet, but only if you never see her again."

I nodded.

Dulcie looked back at me as they left – a look I'll never forget. Lost. Betrayed. Hurt beyond measure. She'd recover, sure, but she'd be scarred. She was the only person who'd ever truly loved me and now she'd seen a glimpse of the real Sonny Boden. I had to comfort myself with the idea that there was much worse to know, much worse to be revealed.

It was all quite a disappointment and embarrassing, for them as much as for me. They could have done this at their house, but I supposed they wanted a public place in case I flew into some homicidal rage. It showed just how little they knew me.

I stayed at Mamacita's. I had the soup and the octopus with the red wine. It was all delicious and very good value, as Tom had said.

Of course, now I'd have to find a replacement girlfriend.

Dwight was drinking milk in the kitchen when they came home. He heard two women's voices.

"I swear, if he touches me like that again, I'm gonna . . . I don't know, stamp on his foot and make it seem like an accident. I bet I could break a toe."

"It'd be better to stamp on his balls."

"He'd have to be lying down for that."

"So hit him with a skillet first."

They laughed.

"Did I leave the kitchen light on?"

They stopped, frozen, on seeing Dwight drinking milk.

"Hi," said Dwight.

"Who are you? Why are you in my house?"

"I'm Dwight." He waved with his non-milk hand. "The oceanic consciousness brought me here."

The women looked doubtfully at each other, deciding whether or not to be scared.

"He's an acid head, Sal," said one of them. "Probably thinks he's in his own house or somethin'. I'll handle this. Hey, Buddy!" she said to Dwight. "You popped a pill? Smoked some weed?"

"Sure," said Dwight, smiling.

"That's great, hon. But you're in the wrong house. You finish your milk and I'll show you the door. Okay?"

"Sonny sent me."

"Sonny?" She looked at the one called Sal. "You know a Sonny?"

Sal shook her head. She looked worried. She was looking to the other room like maybe there was someone in there.

"Sonny from the Arco station," said Dwight.

"Okay, you're really in magical Oz, aren't you, hon? Technicolor visions? Let's take you to the door and you can continue your mystical journey outside."

Dwight pulled the .38 from the back of his pants.

"LeeAnn," said Sal, gripping her friend's arm.

LeeAnn looked at him straight. "What do you want? If you're thinking about rape, I gotta tell you I'm on my period. Full flow. Pretty damn messy. And Sal here gave birth not so long ago – got a pussy like a suitcase. You wouldn't feel a thing."

"LeeAnn!"

"Shh. Leave this to me, Sal."

"I've had a message through the oceanic consciousness," said Dwight.

"Yeah? Me, too," said LeeAnn. "It said you should go home and drink plenty of water. Watch a little TV and your karma'll be all cool tomorrow."

Dwight cocked his head slightly. He *had* been thinking a lot recently about watching TV. There wasn't one in the shack. He liked the cartoons, but he preferred to watch them with the sound off. They were much funnier that way. You could imagine your own version of what they were saying – the cat and the rabbit and

THR3E

the mouse in the big yellow sombrero – and the coyote. The coyote was his favorite.

He shot LeeAnn in the chest and she went down.

"LeeAnn!' screamed the other one, *very* shrill, bending down below the counter out of sight. Dwight walked around to see.

Sal was on her knees pressing the hole in her friend with both hands, blood coming dark through her fingers. She looked up at Dwight and stood and backed away to the other room where she'd been looking before. She was shaking.

"Take whatever you want. Just leave me. I've got a baby. I'm a mother."

He shot her in the chest and she went down, too. She started crawling to the other room and he had to shoot her in the back twice to stop her.

There was a baby in the other room. It was in a kind of basket thing with a blue blanket around it. Sal had been crawling there. He laughed. She'd been crawling like a baby.

The baby was awake and looking around kinda stunned. Maybe the gunshots had woken it. Dwight reached into the basket and the baby grasped his index finger. Such tiny hands. Surprisingly strong.

"Wanna watch some cartoons?" said Dwight.

He turned on the TV and flicked through the channels. No cartoons. The baby seemed interested anyway, his little eyes watching the stuttering images. Maybe it was all a cartoon to him. Vietnam. Gas prices. 747s, 7-11s, 7 Up, the Chicago 7. Cambodian invasion. Aswan Dam. No mouse with a yellow sombrero.

Dwight left the TV on for the kid, but with the sound off. Always better that way.

I got angry after the meal. I was driving back to Verdugo and thinking about Dulcie's parents. It wasn't like they'd had any specific suspicions about my past, or that they'd heard any rumor.

They'd paid an investigator because they didn't want Dulcie marrying a gas monkey. Imagine the shame at Thanksgiving with all the family around! "And this is Sonny. He's . . . I'm sorry, but he pumps gas for a living. He also does something called a 'wax job.' Don't talk to him . . ."

I almost hoped I'd get caught for the other killings so that the shame would come back on them. MERLUZA FAMILY INTIMATE WITH MASS MURDERER – Coed slayer Sonny Boden said in court this week, "Dulcie's father was a good friend of mine. He taught me everything I know about cold-hearted psychopathy . . ."

I'd already passed the girl before I realized she was there. She lit up red as I slowed and pulled over about 100 yards further on. At this point, I didn't even know if she was my type. I rolled down the window and flicked on the ceiling light as she approached. Illumination gave them more confidence.

"Hiya! Goin' near El Bosque?" she said, with that confident air they had. She was a little older than the others and my first thought was that she might be one of Donahue's concealed-weapon girls. She was beautiful, too. I mean Raquel Welch beautiful but with darker hair. She knew the effect she had on men. I'm sure nobody had ever refused her a ride. I thought about saying no just to see the look on her face, but I wanted her in the car. I wanted her in the trunk and in my bed. Her hair was wonderful.

"Sure. Get in."

I knew I was taking a risk if she was one of the armed agents. To be honest, the impulse just came over me suddenly. Maybe it was the residual anger from the aborted meal at Mamacita's, but I felt powerful and decisive. I knew what I had to do.

As she was leaning over to pull the door closed, I took the stiletto dagger from the side of my seat and aimed the point where her ear was going to be as she sat back. She caught me in her peripheral vision as she moved and she gasped – more in surprise that I was closer than she'd thought.

I put the knifepoint against her head and just drove the pommel with the heel of my other hand. It was difficult to aim with my torso twisted like that in the driver's seat. In fact, the blade went right through her upper earflap, the pinna I think it's called, and about five inches into her skull.

I thought she'd die immediately from that, but she turned to me slowly with the dagger sticking out of her head and I saw her pupils had blown massively black – no irises at all. Just darkness. It frightened me a little. She twitched a little in the seat, her mouth slightly open.

I gently used the dagger as a kinda handle to turn her so she was facing forward again and I gave the pommel another colossal blow. This time, the blade went in up to the hilt and she slumped heavily away from me, her head and shoulder thumping against the door.

There was very little blood. I guess the dagger was like a cork in the wound. I'd be able to clean that up and there'd be no serious disfigurement to her beauty. Her lovely hair would cover it.

But that was for later. A more pressing problem: we were parked right on Highway 1, about halfway between Three-Mile Beach and downtown Buena Vista. There was still a lot of traffic. I'd have to drive a little further before I could get off onto a quieter road and put her in the trunk.

I awkwardly pulled her back into a sitting position and put her seatbelt on to keep her upright. The last thing I needed was a traffic stop from the CHiPs because my passenger looked dead. I debated with myself about removing the dagger. I didn't want a sudden spray of blood all over me and the inside of the car. Better to leave it where it was.

So we drove together, my hand on the warm skin of her thigh and her hand on mine. I was highly aroused. Maybe it was the rapidity of the kill, or maybe it was her smoldering beauty, but I couldn't remember being so excited with the other girls. The only bummer was that dagger sticking out the side of her head – a real insult to her looks.

I got off the highway as soon as I could and put her in the trunk, leaving the dagger in place. Then I went directly to the Holding Cell. It was part of my new commitment to having a solid alibi. I'd been at Mamacita's and then I'd be at the bar. The time in between would be typical on the highway.

But I surprised myself at the bar. I had to look at her one more time before going in. I was there in the parking lot with the trunk lid open and I had a powerful urge to behead her right there and then. The boning knife was under the blanket. I'd have to be quick because cars were coming and going all the time and passing on the main road beside the Holding Cell.

So I did it. With practiced cuts, I had the head off in about twenty seconds, all the while feeling the exhilaration of standing there, openly in public, my back to the bar and people moving around. They didn't know what I was doing. I was just a guy getting something from his trunk. A jacket, maybe. Nothing unusual. Nobody would ever have guessed.

I wiped off the blood on the blanket and went in for a few beers, shaking hands with the cops I knew and letting them gently mock me.

Joe pulled up outside his house on Durero. He'd taken the Merluza family's car because it was just too far to walk and he was tired. Ananiel had warned him again about the lethality of driving, but Ananiel had also told him to follow Abaddon so . . . He rang the bell and waited. There was blood on the back of his hand. He wiped it off on his pants leg. There were lights on inside and he could see the flashing colors of the TV screen through the half-drawn drapes. He rang the bell again. Something was wrong.

He walked round back and saw the broken glass, the open door.

"Sal?"

LeeAnn was on the kitchen floor. There was a lot of blood. It looked like she'd tried to crawl to the living room. He squatted to look at her face and an eye flickered.

"LeeAnn? What happened? Where's Sal? Where's the baby?"

She tried to speak but it was just a breath. She wasn't moving. The eye closed and was still.

He saw the other blood trail and went toward the living room.

"Sal? Sal!"

She was face down, three holes in her. He turned her over, her limbs heavy, head lolling, eyes fixed open.

"Sal!"

He sat on the floor beside her. He took her hand in his. He looked at the phone.

No, said Ananiel. *You have to burn it all,* said Ananiel.

Joe wept.

TWENTY-FOUR

MERLUZA FAMILY SLAIN – Fire teams were called to the house of Dr. Patrick Mulholland Friday, when neighbors reported a huge fire burning on the coast. Police investigators arrived after firefighters discovered the bodies of three people in the ruined home, each killed by gunshots. The three are believed to be Dr. Mulholland, his wife Laine and his daughter Dulcimer, though formal identifications have yet to be made . . .

ARSON KILLER STRIKES IN OAKWOOD – Two women and an infant were killed on Durero Street in Oakwood, Buena Vista, Wednesday night. Their bodies were discovered in the remains of the burned-out house. Sheriff's Department detective Lt. Schumer said that the crime bears all of the hallmarks of previous crimes committed by the so-called Arson Killer, who has struck multiple times in recent weeks. One unusual piece of evidence in the case is that a car belonging to a family slain in Merluza the same night was found parked in front of the house. Lt. Schumer did not rule out the possibility that the same perpetrator had struck twice within a short period.

BODY IS IDENTIFIED – The sliced portions of a human body that drifted into shore last week at Las Arenas have been positively identified. The UCBV coed has been named as 20-year-old Juanita Cortez, who had been reported missing August 1, one day after she reportedly hitchhiked to a party being held in Las Gambas, Buena Vista County.

Of course, ballistics would show that a .45 had killed Dulcie's family and a .38 Joe's family. It was possible that the suspect had changed guns, but it was an added complication for the police.

I bought copies of the *Examiner*, the *Chronicle*, the *Sentinel* and others to get the full story on Dulcie's death. There wasn't much detail. They'd been found like most of the others: bound and sitting in a row on the sofa.

I tried to imagine the scene. They must have arrived home in a black mood after the disastrous non-meal at Mamacita's. Dulcie would have cried in the car, comforted by her mother and lectured by her father. Maybe she fought back and defended me, but the facts were compelling and she believed them. I'd seen that in her eyes. She knew it was over. She just needed some time to forgive her parents and also wonder whether they'd do the same with every future boyfriend.

So, they arrive home and maybe there's a light on. "Did you leave the den light on, Laine?" Dr. Mullholland might have said in that accusatory tone of his. Because *he'd* never leave a light on. Then they'd see Hobo Joe sitting in an armchair holding the .44

Magnum. Of *course* it was Joe. Who else would it be? Him and Ananiel.

"How dare you enter my house, *etc*!" from Dr. Mullholland – too superior to be afraid. I like to think he got it first. The papers didn't say where the gunshots were, but I imagined his forehead. The .44'd take the back of his skull off at that range. Brains out, everything. He'd probably died with an outraged expression. Killed by a stinking long-hair! The indignity!

Dulcie would have gone quick. She was so delicate – like a bird. A.44 round would finish her immediately. There'd be no pain. Just the jolting shock of the impact and the fleeting realization that she was dying. I wonder if I was in her thoughts during those last seconds?

Anyway, my intention that Dwight would kill Joe had backfired pretty badly. Now the police were looking for Joe – not necessarily as the main suspect in the killing of his own family, but as someone they needed to eliminate from inquiries. I mean, he seemed to have no motive. They'd done some digging and discovered he'd been having some mental problems. The wife's brother said something about mescaline and a car crash. Joe'd left work and left home and gone off-grid. He had guns.

It was bad news for me. When they found him – as they surely would – he'd start blabbering about King Abaddon, who had headless girls in his room. "Can you take us to King Abaddon's house, Joe?" *Real* bad news. I'd need to see him before the police did.

It bothered me less that they'd found parts of the third girl, the Mexican-looking one whose father was a Capricorn and who'd damn near broken my nose as I asphyxiated her. I'd been pretty sloppy disposing of her because I'd been in a hurry. Most of the bits I'd simply thrown off a cliff up near Las Gambas – kinda ironic since that's where she'd been heading when I picked her up. The parts had taken quite a while to move south, completely bypassing Three-Mile Beach for some reason. Something to do with currents. Amber told me the bits were so eaten by sea life that the only way to identify her had been an ankle tattoo. How had I missed that?

It had been a page-one story. Again, it was dramatic: parts washing up on the beach as people licked their ice creams and kids built sandcastles. "Daddy? What's this?" Well, it was a human thigh with just a few scraps of meat left on it around the joints. There was a very good chance that other pieces – hands, feet – had been swallowed whole by sharks and were now moving around the coast of Catalina Island or as far south as Baja. It was a curious thought.

I'd spent the day up around Oso Grande and Redwood Creek, disposing of the most recent girl. It was getting difficult to find new places. I'd typically been cutting each girl into around twelve pieces if you count the torso, and I tried to keep the disposal sites separate. It really adds up.

The latest girl – Raquel, as I thought of her – had been hard to let go of. Her head on the shelf was like a sculpture. I'd even gone to the library for information on how to preserve it permanently in its pristine beauty, but mummification would have negatively affected the lines and I didn't know where I'd be able to get formaldehyde, or how to apply it. Some type of pump was necessary and I didn't want to raise suspicions asking around for that sort of thing.

Her body, too, was spectacular. I mean, every young man's dream. But for some reason it had started to decompose faster than I'd expected. The temperatures had been a little higher, it's true, and I'd left the window open a crack to aerate the room. Maybe some insects had blown the body? I don't know. I just had to dispose of it sooner than I wanted. I still had the Polaroids and her personal belongings, though – a guilty pleasure.

It was inevitable that they'd come for me in connection with Dulcie and her family. I was a known associate. We'd been seen together. I just didn't expect it to happen so quickly. Later, I'd put a few things together and realize that Amber must have said something to someone at the Sheriff's Department as soon as she heard about Dulcie. I could see the scene: "Hey, listen, Lieutenant – can I have a word? About this arson killing in Merluza . . . I think you should talk to my brother. The daughter was his girlfriend and, well, he does have a homicide record."

I knew it was the police when I saw the unmarked car in the parking lot at home. My first thought: the Polaroids and Raquel's stuff. They were hidden, but if the detectives had a warrant . . . The gun and the boning knife were in my trunk. Would a warrant cover that too?

I had to stay cool. I'd faced the police before. I knew how they thought, their processes. And it was true that I genuinely had nothing to do with Dulcie's killing. I mean, I was sad about it. Sure. It was a tragedy. That was the script.

They weren't in their car, so they had to be inside talking to my mother. God knows what she was saying. She'd been waiting for me to trip up since I got out of Atascadero. Once a murderer, always a murderer. She'd like to see me out of her apartment even if that meant going to the gas chamber. In fact, she'd probably come to watch them drop the pellets. I guarantee it. I was pretty sure she already had an outfit picked out. She'd be there on the front row, turning wild-eyed and drunk to harangue the governor and the press and the red-eyed relatives – "I said he'd do it again and, by God, I was right!" – never stopping to wonder why any son of hers would turn out like I did. She never saw the irony of calling me a son of a bitch.

They were sitting in the living room with cups of coffee: two detectives and my mother. She gave me the evil eye, thinking, What'll the neighbors say? Why are the police coming to the Boden place all the time? What kind of delinquent family are they? And why do the grandparents never visit?

"Sonny," she said, mouth like a trout. "These gentlemen from the Sheriff's Department have come to interrogate you."

I recognized them from the Holding Cell. I raised a hand. "Hi, guys."

"It's not an interrogation," smiled Plaid Tie. "Just a few questions."

I held up my hands as if in surrender, smiling. "Do I need a lawyer?"

"This is purely informal, Sonny," said Horrible Tie. "But you can call your lawyer if you like."

Purely informal. Sure. If they could put me at the Merluza house at the time of the fire, I'd be in cuffs and in the back of their car within seconds.

"It's okay, guys. Haven't got a lawyer anyway." I sat in the armchair facing them. "Ask away. And could I get a coffee, too, Mom?"

She glared. Any other time she'd spit something like, "Am I your goddamn servant? Get it yourself!" But, you know: manners. Appearances. She went to the kitchen.

"So, Sonny," said Plaid Tie, his pad and pen ready. "I guess you heard about the house fire up at Merluza and the family killed there."

"Yeah." Somber face. Look down at hands. "It really broke me up." Look up, make eye contact. "You already know that Dulcie was my girl, right? That's why you're here."

"That's it, Sonny," said Horrible Tie. "What can you tell us about that night?"

That meant they already knew something. Maybe the Mullhollands had mentioned to someone that they were going to Mamacita's that night – a kinda insurance in case they didn't come back. Maybe these two detectives had already asked questions at the restaurant and wanted to see if they could catch me in a lie.

My mother banged cups in the kitchen: her Morse code of anger.

"Well, we all went out for dinner together," I said. "I picked them up around seven and drove them to Mamacita's on Three-Mile Beach. The three of them went home by taxi and I came into town for a few beers. In fact, you both saw me at the Holding Cell, right?"

"What'd you eat?" said Horrible Tie.

"I had the seafood soup and the octopus. Fudge brownie with vanilla ice cream for dessert. No, sorry – it was whipped cream."

Plaid Tie didn't write that down.

"Why'd they go home in a taxi, Sonny?" said Horrible Tie.

Awkward hand-wringing. "Well, I don't know how to put this. We had . . . I suppose you'd call it an argument. It was very tense. They didn't even order. I offered to drive them back but Mister . . . sorry, *Doctor* Mulholland insisted on a taxi."

Horrible Tie: "What was the argument about?"

"They didn't think I was good enough for Dulcie. You know, the father a big-time professor of music, a lot of money in the family and me just a gas monkey. Me and Dulcie were happy, but they insisted we end it. I mean, she was angry with them."

Horrible Tie: "And how did *you* feel, Sonny?"

What was he expecting I'd say? That I was enraged? That I wanted to blow them away with a .45 and burn their house down?

Look down at the hands again. "I was sad. And disappointed."

Plaid Tie: "What time did you arrive at the Holding Cell?"

"About nine? Lieutenant Schumer was telling that joke about the two nuns on bicycles."

They laughed. They'd both been there.

Horrible Tie: "And where'd you go after?"

"Home. Here. Watched some TV. I think it was a re-run of *Police Story*."

Plaid Tie: "Can your mother corroborate that?"

My mother came in from the kitchen, where'd she'd been listening to everything. She put the coffee in front of me. Half full and probably lukewarm.

"I was asleep," she said. I swear she was trying not to smile.

Horrible Tie: "Didn't hear the TV? The door?"

"Nope," she said, imagining me in the gas chamber.

"I'm very considerate if my mom's sleeping. I keep the volume down." I looked at her. "Also, she's a very sound sleeper." After four or five glasses of brandy. I thought she might explode right there, but she kept it together. Manners. Appearances. "You could ask the neighbors," I said. "There were a few lights on when I got back. They might have heard or seen the car." For sure, they didn't see me carrying the headless girl up the steps and into my room.

I was getting pretty irritated by this point. They were giving me the third degree for a crime that Hobo Joe had committed. Where was *he*? And where was oceanic Dwight?

"Just one more thing," said Plaid Tie. "Do you ever pick up hitchhikers?"

Shit.

Where was this coming from? Amber? My mother? Had somebody uncovered my expunged record? Had they actually run a ballistics test on the Ruger I'd handed in? If .22s were being used in murders . . .

What did they know? Or were they fishing?

"Yeah, sure. I mean, sometimes."

"You pick anyone up August first?"

The Mexican girl. Now in sharks off Catalina Island. Note how they said 'anyone' – not specifically 'a girl.' Clever guys.

I blew out some air, trying to remember. "The first? What day was that?"

Horrible Tie: "Sunday."

I'd picked her up out of town. Nobody around. But if someone had seen her get in my car . . .

"I mean, I guess it's possible. I like to drive on a Sunday and if there're people hitching I like to help 'em out, you know? If it's not too out of my way."

Plaid Tie: "Girls? Boys?"

"Whoever. I mean, I'm a red-blooded male. I'd prefer a pretty girl to chat to for ten minutes, you know?"

They laughed. I laughed. All the guys together.

My mother snorted like, That's the only kind of relationship you're ever gonna have: ten minutes.

Horrible Tie: "So did you pick anyone up or not?"

"Let me think . . ." I looked down and to the side: the sign of someone remembering rather than fabricating. But I was trying to think if they could possibly have any evidence that would put me with the girl. I'd not shot her, so there was no bullet in the brain for ballistics. I'd removed the duct tape from her mouth so they couldn't print that. She'd been in the sea awhile, so any traces of me would've gone, and, anyway, I'd washed her before dismembering her – like I always did. It was just a question of if someone had seen her getting into my car and I was almost certain there'd been no other cars or buildings around.

"You know, I didn't pick anyone up that day," I said. "But I almost did. I saw this girl – a pretty little thing – up ahead. This was a little north of the UCBV campus on Amador. Around there, anyway. She had her thumb out and I thought, Why not? But someone two cars ahead stopped instead and she got in. Pity. She looked like a lot of fun."

Plaid Tie was writing.

Horrible Tie: "How'd she look?"

"Dark. Could've been Indian – either from India, or native. Kinda small but curvy, you know?" I drew her shape with my hands.

Horrible Tie: "And the car she got into?"

"A silver Chevy. It was a Chevelle Malibu."

"A Malibu? You sure?"

"Pretty sure. I like cars."

Plaid Tie was writing it all. This was gold for him. I'd given the make and color of the car being used by the guy who took girls from their cars and strangled them. This hadn't been in the papers; Amber had told me. Sure, it wasn't his MO to pick up hitchhikers, or to dismember them, but it was a lead. I was just a suspicion.

It kinda confirmed in my mind that this whole thing was from a tip-off rather than any compelling evidence or a witness statement. Someone had talked to them. Maybe it was the PI employed by Dulcie's father. If they were asking about the Mexican girl, it was because she was the most recently discovered. Anyway, I'd know in a few minutes what was up. If they walked out of there with a friendly, "Have a good day!" I'd know they had nothing but a rumor.

The two detectives looked at each other, trying to hide that I'd given them a key piece of information. Whatever else they were rooting for was now less important. They stood and brushed down their slacks.

"Thanks, Sonny," said Plaid Tie. "And thank *you* Missus Boden for the coffee."

That put a smile on her face – a scrap of courtesy in her ravaged life.

"If you remember any more details," said Horrible Tie, "you give us a call." He handed me a card.

"You both have a good day," said Plaid Tie.

My mother waited until they pulled out of the parking lot before she started.

"It's you, isn't it? This monster cutting up girls – it's you."

"Mom . . ."

"That's three times the police have been here sniffing around. They never came here when you were in the wacko hospital. Maybe you didn't burn that house, but you're just the type to go cutting heads off."

"Mom . . ."

"I want to look in your room. I want you to unlock it and I'm gonna look around. It's my apartment and it's my right. I don't need an excuse or a warrant."

"And what about my privacy?"

"You've got no privacy while you're living in my house. Let's go. You open that door right now or I'm calling those detectives back and telling them there's blood all over your walls."

"Blood on the walls, Mom? What are you talking about?"

"Right now, Sonny Boden! Open that door *right now*."

I sighed. There was nothing in plain sight. I couldn't see my mother lifting the floorboard under the rug to find the Polaroids. I walked to the door with her close behind. I unlocked the door and pushed it open.

"Knock yourself out, Mom. Don't forget to check the walls for blood."

I'd done the right thing. She went in, but she just stood there impotently, looking around. The bed was made. The floor was clean. Everything was in order.

"Look under the bed, if you like. Check for bodies."

She did, too. Maybe she thought I was bluffing. She got down on her knees and bent to look. Nothing there.

She went to the closet, looking back at me for some sign that she was getting warmer in her search.

"No, Mom! Not the closet!" Mock serious. "That's where I keep their bodies!"

Oh, she was angry. She was volcanic. She opened the twin doors and looked inside. Clothes on hangers. Bed linen folded on the upper shelf. Shoeboxes in the bottom. I had Raquel's stuff in the inside pocket of my buckskin jacket and I'd already decided: if my mother found it, I'd strangle her there in my room with my bare hands. Believe me – I was ready for it. I *hoped* she'd find the stuff.

My mother got on her knees again to open shoeboxes, finding shoes.

"I hope you're gonna tidy all this up, Mom."

"You shut up! You always had a smart mouth."

"Check all the boxes. There might be a head in one of them that I forgot about."

She stood glaring at me. "You're gonna trip up and when you do I'll be there waiting."

She was right about that, but she wouldn't be waiting. She'd be sleeping.

"Good talk, Mom. 'Preciate it."

"Fuck you, Sonny!" and she was out.

"The mantra of good parenting!" I called after her.

I heard things clashing in the kitchen. Plates would be broken. This wasn't finished. It'd start up again later after she'd had a few sherries and thought of more insults.

Meanwhile, my problems with the other two weren't quite over.

TWENTY-FIVE

Joe was in the forest. He'd tried to go back to the shack, but there'd been cars parked outside, two of them marked city police vehicles. He'd sat on a wet log, its bark peeling off to reveal bone-white wood, and waited to see if they'd leave. Instead, a van arrived and more people went in. He'd have to get some distance.

He walked for a couple hours northeast, avoiding tracks and cutting across roads only when there was no sound of traffic. His plan was to build a lean-to shelter with sticks and fronds in some remote corner of the forest. He'd done it often as a kid. In the end, he found something already ninety percent built, beer bottles and joint butts lying all around. The labels on the bottles had faded or completely fallen off and blown away. The joint butts were only flattened flecks of paper. He'd just have to add a fresh layer to the roof. He set to work with his knife.

Don't light a fire, said Ananiel. *It will bring men.*

Joe was getting tired of Ananiel. Light a fire. Don't light a fire.

Do not think about the woman and child, said Ananiel. *This is the end of times.*

"That's not Sal," said Joe.

The mother of harlots and abominations of the earth, said Ananiel
"No," said Joe.
You have the mark, said Ananiel. *You are chosen.*
"I don't wanna be chosen."
You know who did this, said Ananiel. *Who knows where you live?*

Joe thought. *Did* he know who? The guy with the acid who picked him up. Buzzcut guy. *Dwight* – that's what King Abaddon had called him. And Dwight had said he lived up around here in the park. He had a shack. On Oban. Dwight knew where Sal lived. He'd parked outside the house.

Right, said Ananiel. *Right.*

Joe waited until dark. The problem was, he couldn't retrace his steps through the forest. He'd have to find a road and hitch. His flashlight was dimming, but he was able to follow the trail of litter the partygoers must have left before. It led to a road and a turn-off that smelled of piss.

He squatted by the side of the asphalt. No cars came. It was late and this was a pretty remote spot north of Redwood. Finally, he heard an engine and stood with his thumb out.

The car swerved around him, accelerating. Well, he did have a Manson flavor about him.

He squatted again, his breath steaming now in the forest night. He must have waited an hour, dreaming flames. When the next motor sounded through the trees, he stepped into the center of the road with the Magnum pointed.

The car slowed and stopped. A silver Chevy.

Joe walked around to the driver's side, aiming the Magnum all the while.

"Take me to Oban Drive?" he said.

The driver was a pale-faced blond man wearing wire-framed glasses. He looked like an accountant or someone who'd know what a computer was. He had his hands up like it was a robbery. He had a fresh cut on his upper lip like someone had recently socked him. He said, "I'm . . . I'm not really going that way."

"You are now," said Joe. He got in the passenger seat and kept the gun on Accountant Guy. "Drive," said Joe. "I'm not gonna hurt you."

They drove, the headlamps on high beam illuminating categories of darkness through the trunks into black.

Dwight wasn't home. He was driving the blue Stingray into town. He hadn't seen his family in a while and thought it was time to pay a visit. He had his two new rifles in the back seat and the .38 on the passenger side.

His father answered the door. "Dwight?" He saw the rifle slung over his son's shoulder. "What do you want?"

"Hi, Dad! Long time. How you been?"

His father looked at his face. "Are you hallucinating right now? Look, Dwight – it's better if you leave. I don't think your mother can handle–"

Dwight pushed through the door. "I wanted to watch some cartoons. Can we watch some cartoons together like we used to?"

"You were a child, Dwight. You're not a child anymore. Where are you going?"

"Mom? Mom?" called Dwight. "I'm home."

His mother was in the dining room. She was clearing away the plates and cutlery. "Dwight?" A fork slipped off a plate and fell on the floor. "Why do you have that gun?"

"I found it. Hey, Dad – why not come in here where I can see you?"

His father came in. "We don't want any trouble, Dwight. It's better if you go. I'm sorry, but you're not welcome here anymore. There's nothing we can do for you. The best thing would be to check yourself into the psych ward. I can drive you there. We can go right now. I'll get my coat."

"Sit on the sofa," said Dwight. "Both of you."

"Don't be a horse's ass, Dwight. Let's go to the hospital."

Dwight unslung the rifle from his shoulder and cranked the bolt, loading a cartridge.

His father sat on the sofa. His mother started whimpering.

"It's you, isn't it?" said his father. "It's been you killing all these people recently. I told her. I just had a feeling. You're crazy enough. If only you'd kept taking your pills, or listened to Father McLeish's advice. It's you, isn't it?"

"Not all of them. Just some."

His mother was weeping. Father put his arm around her. "Do we deserve this, son?"

"'Son?' That's funny. Have you considered it's your fault, everything that's happened? All I wanted was a strict macrobiotic diet. My yin and yang have been all over the place. The equilibrium needs feeding properly. It's your fault I can't see through things."

"He's out of his mind," said father, holding mother.

"But thanks for mentioning Father McLeish the child molester. I think he should join us. Shall we give him a call, what?"

Dwight had lapsed into his English accent. Mother sobbed gently.

He held the rifle loosely and consulted the handwritten list of numbers by the phone before dialing. "We can ask him if he's ejaculated on any other boys, the rotter." He listened to the tone.

"Hello, Father McLeish. Awfully sorry to bother you at this hour. It's Dwight . . . Very well, thank you . . . Yes, I'm at my parents' place. We wondered if you'd like to come round for a chat – maybe watch some cartoons and talk about ejaculating on boys . . . Yes. Uh huh . . . Well, that's wonderful – we expect you momentarily."

Dwight put the phone down and winked at his parents. "He's coming."

"Are you going to kill us?" said mother, her cheeks shining.

Dwight thought about it. He *had* quite expected to kill them, but the oceanic consciousness was now being a little ambiguous on the matter. Perhaps the arrival of Father McLeish would help clarify. In the meantime, he bent to the TV set.

"Excuse me, but I'm desperately keen to see what's on the telly."

Joe and Accountant Guy were still driving through the state park.

"What happened to your lip?" said Joe.

Looking sidelong at the gun. "I hit it. On the car door. I was in a hurry."

"You wanna get some ice on it. To reduce the swelling."

"Thanks. I'll do that."

A thump.

"I think you hit something," said Joe, looking in the wing mirror.

"Yeah, maybe. There's a lot of animals out on the road at night."

Another thump. It was inside the car.

Joe looked at Accountant Guy. "You got someone in the trunk?"

"Look . . . I don't want any trouble."

"You got a gun in the car?"

"In the glove box."

"Why didn't you go for it when you saw me?"

"I almost did, but you don't look like a cop."

Joe popped the glove box and took out a silver Colt .38 auto. He slipped back the slide a little to see brass shine in the chamber. It was loaded. Nice gun. He put it back. "Stop the car. I wanna see what you got in the back."

"Can't we just get to Oban and go our different ways? I don't care what you're doing out in the forest with your Magnum. I didn't see you."

"Stop the car." Accountant guy sighed and pulled over. "You get out first," said Joe.

THR3E

They stood together at the rear, illuminated red. A length of brown hair was caught in the trunk lid. Its ends brushed the license plate.

"Open it," said Joe.

Accountant Guy opened it. The girl was on her side, mouth taped shut, her arms tied behind her back with cord and her ankles bound with tape. The whites of her eyes gaped.

Kill her, said Ananiel.

"Let her go," said Joe.

"Come on, man," said Accountant Guy. "This is my thing. I'm not messing with your thing, whatever it is. Let's just get to Oban."

Joe took his knife out of its sheath.

"Whoa," said Accountant Guy. "This doesn't have to get violent."

"Stand back. There, where I can see you." Joe leaned into the trunk and cut the girl's bindings. He sheathed the knife and offered his hand. "Come on. Take my hand. Climb out."

"She's seen our *faces*, man! What are you doing?"

The girl climbed out and looked between them, wild-eyed. Mouth still taped.

"Go on – run," said Joe.

She took a few steps, looking behind her.

"Go!"

She started running, crying as she went.

"Shit, man!" said Accountant Guy. "You know she's gonna run right to the police."

"Let's go to Oban."

Accountant Guy watched the girl disappearing into the night.

"Hey!" Joe waved the Magnum toward the front seats.

"You're crazy, man."

Dwight was in the armchair, moving the rifle between his parents on the sofa. His mother was a mess, sniveling and sobbing and dribbling snot. His father was pale and defeated, all out of reasoning and pleading.

Dwight was waiting for a sign from the oceanic consciousness. It could be anything: an image on the muted TV set, a chiming clock, a sudden storm. He'd know it when it happened.

The doorbell rang.

"That'll be Father McLeish," said Dwight. "I'll get it. Don't you move."

He opened the front door to see two men in crouching stances pointing pistols at him.

"Drop the rifle, son," said one.

"Where's Father McLeish?" said Dwight. "Is he with you?"

"Help us!" shouted father. "We're inside!"

"Quiet, Dad! I'm talking to these men."

"Drop it, son. Nice and slow."

"I didn't steal it. I found it." The two men flicked glances at each other like, This guy's a fuckin' fruit loop. "Did you bring Father McLeish with you? Is that it?"

"Sure. We got him in the car. He'd like to talk to you, but the rifle's too big to fit in the car. That's why you gotta drop it."

That made sense. Dwight lowered the rifle by its strap until it was on the floor. The two men rushed him, one of them kicking him behind the knee so he fell. An instant later, he was on his front and his wrists were cuffed behind his back.

"I'll check on the parents," said one of the men. "Stay with him."

"Can we go see Father McLeish now?" said Dwight, twisting to address the remaining cop. "I wanted to ask him about other boys he ejaculated on."

Joe and the Accountant Guy passed the shack on Cascade. No cars were parked outside and there were no lights in the windows, but they'd probably left someone on guard.

"This is Oban Drive," said Accountant Guy, still pissed off.

"Okay. You can stop here," said Joe.

The car came to a halt on crunching gravel. They sat inside listening to the engine running. Moths flickered in and out of the headlamp beams. The exhaust breathed red through the rear window.

"Will you go looking for that girl?" said Joe.

"What choice have you left me?" said Accountant Guy. "She's seen my face and the car."

"Why do you do it?" said Joe.

"Do what? Kill girls?"

"Uh huh."

"I just do. Are you gonna shoot me?"

Joe looked at the Magnum resting on his leg.

Kill him, said Ananiel. *Burn the car.*

'Don't kill him,' said Sal. 'He's a violent abuser, but you're no murderer.'

'Don't kill him,' said the baby. 'You've killed enough.'

The trumpet has sounded, said Ananiel. *These things must come to pass.*

Joe covered his ears and closed his eyes, the gun still in his hand.

Accountant Guy was sweating, his hands gripping the wheel.

Joe got out of the car and started walking down Oban.

Accountant Guy sighed and watched the Manson-looking guy in the beams. Run him down? Eliminate at least one witness? No. This one had his own problems. The girl was more important. He turned the car and accelerated back the way they'd come.

Joe didn't know which place was Dwight's, but he'd seen Dwight's car before. He walked through the darkness, his breath pluming, and folded up his collar. The gun was too big to fit in a pocket, so he kept hold of it.

The car was almost out of sight beside the cabin, but no lights showed. Joe tried the door. Locked. He went around back and found another door, kicking it open and splintering the lock out through the jamb.

Silence. Nobody inside. It smelled bad. Furniture cast dark shapes in the darkness. Joe moved the weak eye of the flashlight around the space. A chair. A table. Empty tins.

He sat in the chair and switched off the flashlight. Now to wait.

He realized he smelled of smoke and gasoline. He saw flames when he closed his eyes. He saw blood and smelled it.

A whirlwind came out of the north, said Ananiel. *A great cloud, and a fire infolding itself, and a brightness was about it.,*

"No," said Joe. "Stop talking to me. Get out of my head."

The book cannot be resealed, said Ananiel.

Joe remembered the acid Dwight had given him. It was still there in his breast flap pocket. He swallowed it.

A hundred years or three seconds later, Joe saw blue and red lights. He saw them on the ceiling because he was part of the floor. Footsteps and voices came vibrating to him through the timber. A rapping on the door provoked stars sparkling across the room.

"Police! Anyone at home? You see anything through the window?"

"Nothing. It's too dark."

"Use the flashlight, numbnuts."

Light cut through the black, shadows shifting, things glinting. On the floor behind the sofa, Joe smiled. God had a lot of angles.

"It looks abandoned. Just a lot of shit and litter."

"There's a car, isn't there?"

"Someone could've dumped it. There's leaves and shit all over it."

"Okay. There's no one here now, anyway. We'll run those plates and come back tomorrow when it's light."

"Fine by me."

The naked ceiling bulb spoke, despite a blown filament. It spoke with Sally's voice. "You saved a girl from being raped, just like you'd save me . . . Things just got out of hand. You're a good person. It's like a dream you had once. Hush now and try to get some sleep. Put your arms around me."

He tried, but he couldn't reach her.

Somewhere in the endless night, two shots cracked. Could've been a .38 Colt auto. Accountant Guy must've got his girl.

TWENTY-SIX

MAN HOLDS PARENTS HOSTAGE – Buena Vista police arrested Dwight Paulson, 22, yesterday after he held his parents at gunpoint in their home on Roble Avenue, El Bosque. Family friend Father Dominic MacLeish alerted police when he received an erratic call from Paulson, who has a history of serious mental illness, asking him to visit the Roble Avenue address. Sheriff's Department detective Lou Jackson said that Paulson was also being held for questioning regarding a number of other cases . . .

Well, I could hardly sleep. I spent a day at the gas station scanning every car to see if it had two guys in it, waiting for detectives to arrive and pick me up. A few times, I almost called Amber to ask her what was going on. They had to be interrogating Dwight non-stop. If they had his guns, they'd be running ballistics tests. How long before he mentioned me with that goofy grin of his?

I needed answers, but I couldn't be sure if Amber was the one who'd sent the detectives round to my mother's apartment. I didn't want to be the one who suggested any connection to Dwight. *She'd* have to bring him up. I didn't know him.

I took some consolation from the fact they'd not mentioned any other crimes in the papers. Of course, they could have been withholding information as usual, but it looked like his main crime was threatening his parents and probably illegal possession of weapons. With his mental health and arrest record, he should never have been able to buy guns without being flagged. That made me angry. They'd discovered my sealed record when I bought the Ruger, but Loony Tunes Dwight had walked right into Scott's and bought one without any problem.

There were three outcomes that I could see. He'd say nothing about his killings and just ramble incoherently about the oceanic consciousness. Or he'd tell them everything, delightedly, like he was talking about a camping trip. Or he'd reveal it all piece by piece and accidentally, as they tried to pick through the pieces of his splintered psyche. The third one would buy me the most time. They'd have to follow all the leads, no matter how crazy they sounded.

The guys in the Holding Cell were being more tight-lipped than usual. Since the arson killings in Merluza and Oakwood, there'd been more reporters in town and they were all looking for leads.

Was it one killer or two? Who'd killed the rapist Wendell Holmes and the kids in the forest? Who was taking women from their cars and strangling them? Who was leaving female body parts in bags all over the state park? Was it two killers or three? Or four? Basically, what the shit was going on in this small town? Someone had written that, per population, Buena Vista had seen more murders than any other place in America. Was it something in the water?

Amber came round at the weekend, full of gossip to tease me with.

"So you've read about the crazy guy they arrested?" she said.

"The one who held his parents at gunpoint? Yeah."

"Well, they're saying he might have committed a lot of the recent crimes. I mean *a lot.*"

"Which crimes. The house-burning ones?"

"That's not clear. But that hitchhiking girl – the one who survived the family car crash."

"The miracle girl."

"Yeah. And possibly also the rapist, his victim and those boys in the forest."

"So he's talking, then, the crazy guy?"

"Yeah, he's talking. He won't stop. But it's all bullshit. He's an acid head. Spent the first four hours in custody explaining something about the global consciousness and how we should all eat beans made with a glass spoon."

"But he's not actually confessed to anything. I mean, is there any evidence?"

"He drove to his parents' house in the dead rapist's car. Is that evidence enough, Sonny?"

"He could've found it somewhere."

"What're you, his defense attorney? The guy's totally *loco.* Says he found the guns but one of the rifles belonged to the murdered kids. They're testing his handgun against other crimes."

"I guess it looks bad for him."

"No shit, Sherlock. It's just a matter of time until they match the ballistics."

"And those two house fires? In Merluza and Oakwood?"

"The Oakwood one, they're looking for the husband. Seems he went feral a few weeks ago after taking a lot of mescaline. But . . . *Shit* . . . She was your girl, right? Dulcie? I'm sorry about that, Sonny. Were you still together?"

Sorry my ass. Amber hadn't called or anything when that news broke. She would've heard the names and realized immediately that it was my Dulcie. How many Dulcimer Mullhollands were there in Merluza?

"Her parents wanted to break it up," I said.

"They find out about the grandparents?"

"What do you know about that? Did you–?"

"Come on, Sonny. I didn't say a thing. Why would I? But they were always gonna find out sooner or later. It was in the newspapers, for Chrissakes. It was on TV. Somebody always remembers."

I looked hard at her. "The detectives were round here pretty quick after that fire at Merluza."

"What'd you expect? It's their job. You were her boyfriend. They have to talk to all potential witnesses and eliminate suspects. Anyway, I can see you're not especially sad about the brutal murder of your girlfriend. You're not *grieving*."

"Sure I'm sad. She was innocent."

"What does *that* mean? The parents *deserved* to die?"

"You know what I mean. She was just a young girl: kind, simple. Never hurt anyone." I hoped maybe a tear might come to my eye, but there was nothing. Amber could see it.

My mother shouted from her room: "They also asked him about those chopped-up girls!"

"They did?" said Amber, staring.

A shrug. "They asked me if I picked up hitchhikers, is all."

"They asked him about the one washed on the beach!" shouted my mother.

Amber studied me.

"Really, Amber? You think I'm cutting girls into pieces?"

"Don't you remember what you did to the cat when we were kids?"

"I was a kid. Kids do stuff like that. And it was already dead."

"Because *you* shot it."

"A cat isn't a person, Amber. And a grown man isn't a boy."

"A grown man would brush his teeth before going to bed!" called my mother.

"We're not talking to you, Mom!" I said.

"Well, I'm talking to *you*!"

"Don't look at *me*," said Amber, hands raised. "I already told you to move out. It's like you actually *want* to be here – like you *need* her shit."

"I can *hear* you, Amber!" called my mother.

It was the last time I ever saw my sister.

I mean, I read her comments in newspapers later and she was in court on the first day of the trial. I waved to her, best I could in my chains, but she just shook her head slowly. She was embarrassed and I guess I can't blame her for that. I don't know why she came. Maybe just to make it real, or reassure herself then try to forget it. She changed her name and moved away to Utah not long after, probably because she got married. I couldn't find any more details and she never wrote. Again, I couldn't really hold any of that against her.

I've thought often since about those final words of hers. Seems like she understood me better than I gave her credit for. That's something.

I wasn't happy about the Dwight situation, but I had to remain rational. What did he know? He'd seen me buy a gun illegally? No problem – I'd returned it to the Sheriff's Department. I'd given him a .38? Okay, that was technically illegal, but it wasn't a jail term. The truth was that Dwight didn't know anything concrete or probative about any of the girls. He'd seen nothing. Nor could he say I'd told him to kill anyone in Oakwood. He'd done that on his own initiative. The worst he could say was that I'd known about his killing of the rapist and the miracle girl. Did that make me an accessory? I could say I thought he was just a fantasist. I mean, he also said he could see through people.

Joe was something else. He'd seen two of the girls' heads on my bedroom shelf. He could identify them if someone showed him pictures. It's not like I could say I just found them. Even worse, he might think I had something to do with the death of his family. He'd told me where they lived. What if the experience had shocked him into lucidity and he'd put a few things together? Would he come for me? He knew where I lived. He'd even cut the phone line that time as if he was preparing to kill the inhabitants. Maybe Dwight had told him where I worked.

Well, all this was preying on me. It was a question of time. The cops could roll up to the station or the apartment at any moment – not because they had anything on me. *I'd* been careful. I'd handled every piece of evidence with care. Not one of those girls could come back to me.

Okay, maybe the last one: Raquel. I should've destroyed the Polaroids and her belongings, but I couldn't. She was the only one I'd photographed with her head attached. I mean, I'd actually gone up to my room to get the camera just to take a picture of her posed in the trunk, her blouse open, looking right at me like, Wait 'til I get you home!

Of course, I'd removed the dagger from her skull for the shot. I'd kinda teased it out like a champagne cork, expecting an eruption of warm matter, but it came out clean once I gave it a jerk.

It was the photos that gave me the idea. I was at the station and about to go on my lunch break the day after Amber had visited. I'd sold a lot of stuff that morning – spark plugs, couple fan belts and three oil changes – and Tom was happy. I told him I was gonna go run a few errands and he didn't give me the usual line about returning exactly on time or it'd come out of my wages *etc*.

I had the photos under the driver's seat in my Galaxie, mostly for security. I figured they'd get a warrant for the apartment before the car. My plan: drive up to Oban Drive and leave the photos and Raquel's belongings in Dwight's cabin. It would be compelling evidence, even if he denied it. He was going to prison whatever happened.

I hadn't expected there'd be police up there. They'd set up an actual checkpoint and were stopping cars. A line of them was waiting where Cascade joined Oban. Lieutenant Schumer was talking to a uniform, but he didn't see me.

My first thought: they'd found another body part. The third girl's head was buried off Cascade, but I'd put it deep enough that animals wouldn't go rooting for it. At least, I'd thought so at the time.

I could reverse and approach Dwight's place from the other side, but they were watching the line of waiting cars. If I turned, one of the police motorcycles would come right after me.

Shit.

I looked to the side. Could I toss the Polaroids and the ID out of the window without anyone seeing? Then I told myself: calm down. Nobody knows anything. You're just a guy in a car like anyone else. You've got through worse.

What was up with all the traffic in the park on a weekday? The press. The press and the rubberneckers who went up there hoping to see . . . What? Limbs hanging in plastic bags from trees? People are pretty gruesome.

"License and registration," said the uniformed cop at the head of the checkpoint.

I opened the glove box and handed them through the window. Everything was perfectly in order with my papers, but Schumer was still there talking. He'd recognize me if he looked.

"Why're you up in the park today, sir?"

Smart question. If I said I was on my way anywhere, he'd ask me why I wasn't using one of the three highways that were faster.

"I'm on my lunch break," I said, indicating the branded shirt I was wearing. "I work at the Arco on Sloat in El Bosque. I like to get out for an hour if I can, you know? Eat my lunch in the forest. I didn't expect all of this."

"Got your lunch in the car?"

Good cop. I pointed to the brown bag on the passenger seat. "Pastrami and lettuce. I always take the pickle out. Guess I should just tell them not to put it in, right?"

He looked at me like, You think?

"Say, officer, what's going on up here?"

"Routine checks." He handed back my documents. "Cascade is closed until about three. You'll have to take Oban and Redwood if you wanna get back on the highway. Or you can turn around here and go back the way you came."

"Thanks, officer."

I took Oban, watching in the rearview to see if he was paying any more attention, but he was on to the next car. Schumer was gone, probably down Cascade.

The rapist's car was gone from Dwight's drive, but I could see his other car further in. I checked the mirror again. Nothing behind. I'd have to be real quick with so many cops around.

I was on the stoop when I realized I'd left the Ruger in my car. Too late. If anyone was inside, they'd already heard my footsteps thudding on the wood. I knocked on the door. No answer. I went to the nearest window and looked in.

Joe.

I ducked. Had he seen me? Hobo Joe was sitting motionless in an armchair. His eyes were open, but he seemed totally catatonic. He hadn't reacted at all to my knock or my shadow at the glass. Was he dead?

I rose slowly and looked again. Still the same. I tapped gently at the glass with a fingernail. No reaction.

I tried the door, but it was locked. The back door was smashed open and I entered over splinters, pushing part of the lock aside with my shoe.

"Joe? It's me. Sonny? King Abaddon?" He didn't turn his head to look. I stood in front of him. "Joe?"

He blinked and I almost jumped.

"What's up, Joe?"

He wasn't looking at me. He wasn't looking at anything in that room or that world. He spoke in a low monotone. "They're all dead. The reaping has begun . . . but Ananiel said their names weren't in the book."

I knew the signs. Sanity hangs on the weight of a single hair.

That night I'd walked up the stairs with a girl's head in a bag and met the young couple, I'd known which side I was on. Joe was lost somewhere in the middle, in the gray abyss. Horror. Desolation. The voices in his head. Ananiel – whoever. He wasn't coming back.

"Listen, Joe – I've gotta leave a few things here in the shack. I'll just . . ."

I'd just seen the Magnum on his knee. His finger was on the trigger.

A shot from that cannon at this distance would cripple if it didn't kill me.

I moved out of his immediate line of fire. I took the photos of Raquel in their envelope from my inside pocket. "I'm just gonna leave these things, Joe."

He sat staring.

Watching him the whole time, I put the envelope inside a kitchen cupboard. Now the ID and her ring. I knew I should really make more of an effort to hide them. I needed to increase suspicion. But Joe's Magnum and the heavy police presence in the park were on my mind. I put the ID and ring in the drawer of a wooden cabinet that was thick with dust, the wooden runners scraping dryly in the silence.

"Okay, Joe. I'm gonna go now. I'll see you around."

He raised the gun slowly as if in a dream. I froze and started to put my hands up, but the gun continued rising until the end of the barrel was under his chin, touching the soft part below the jaw. His eyes were blown black gems.

Every TV show I'd ever seen told me what to say. I said nothing.

The top of his skull blew off in a darkly glistening spray and he fell backward, his head lolling over the back of the seat. The Magnum banged onto the floor. I heard dripping on the floor.

It'd been loud. They'd probably heard it over on Cascade.

I had to get out of there *fast*.

I reversed onto Oban, worrying about the tire treads I was

leaving in the damp earth. No time to do anything about that. I needed to get to Redwood Creek and onto Highway 9. The next time I'd be on that road would be with Lieutenant Schumer, but a lot needed to happen before then.

I needed to get back to work.

I needed a few beers.

I needed to kill my mother.

TWENTY-SEVEN

I spent that evening in the Holding Cell. It was busier than ever in there, with all the journalists trying to overhear something. I picked up amid the chatter that the checkpoint earlier had been about a shack Joe'd been using. The gossip was that cops had been looking for evidence and they'd found the body of an older man shot in the top of the head with a hunting rifle. Locals were saying he was an ex-cop who'd gone missing up in the forest.

I also heard a rumor they'd found Joe's body in Dwight's shack. There was quite a buzz about that because the details were so scarce. Nobody at the Sheriff's Department was talking. There'd been no statement. But somebody had heard something about the corpse and how it looked like suicide.

I could only imagine how it had played out. The cops over on Cascade must have heard that massive .45 blasting through Joe's skull. They pause. 'You hear that? What was that? D'you hear a shot? There's a few cabins over on Oban. We checked them last night, but one was empty . . .'

They probably sent a car, the uniformed cops approaching the cabin with weapons drawn, nervous because at least two mass murderers were known to be loose in the area. 'Police! Anyone in there? Come out with your hands in the air!' An anxious glimpse through the window . . . the body with its gaping mouth and the black gore dripping . . . The cracklestatic of the radios. 'We got a body here on Oban!'

Then the detectives and the coroner and the realization that something weird was going on here. Whose cabin was this? 'Lock it down. Everybody out!'

How long before somebody wearing gloves held up a Polaroid of a headless girl, nude and willing? 'Gents? You gotta see this!'

I sipped my beer. I knew more than all of them. I imagined standing and turning to address the room. 'Hey! You wanna know what's *really* been happening in Buena Vista the last few months? Listen up – I got the whole story.' The jukebox'd go dark and a hundred faces'd turn my way.

But no. I wasn't finished yet. I needed to stay invisible a little longer: me, the uniformed gas monkey who sold wax jobs and asked 'Regular, special or sport? Clean your windshield, madam? Is this your daughter? Beautiful girl.' She'd be a credit to my bookshelf.

Well, I was pretty drunk when I left the Holding Cell. I mean, I could drive, but I was definitely pretty woozy. I did think about picking up another girl. I passed a few of them. But I'd always been strict about not doing it when drunk. That's how accidents happen. Killing is its own intoxication. You get caught inside that bubble and *nothing* else exists. Someone could walk by and stand there watching you at work, but you wouldn't notice a thing. I couldn't risk combining that level of distraction with being drunk.

Look what happened with the petite girl, the porcelain doll who fell down the ravine. I thought I was in control of that situation and it still got away from me. You've gotta be 100% on top of these things. That's what marked me apart from the total crazies like Dwight and Joe and the rapist Wendell, who never imagined he'd get caught. The only other one who deserved respect was the guy who kidnapped and strangled and partially buried the girls. The Accountant Guy? He was smart. True story: they never caught him. The bodies just stopped appearing in the state park. I imagine he moved territory and started somewhere similar. Colorado would've suited him. The Appalachians, maybe.

I must've got home about midnight. Only one light showed in the building. I was feeling nostalgic. I stood there in the parking lot looking into my empty trunk and remembering the times I'd beheaded my girls. You might think it sentimental or exaggerated, but I'd climbed mountains, I'd discovered continents, I'd won gold medals. I'd gone further than most other humans had ever been – to a different place. Call it a higher place or a lower place, brighter or darker, but I'd been further.

I'll repeat: I'm not talking about the false, chemical illusions of acid or mescaline or peyote. I'm talking about *reality*. I'd gone to the outer limits and into realms from which most had never returned – and I'd survived there. I'd *thrived*. I'd walked confidently on the abyss's edge and looked deep into it – to its absolute bottom. Those people sleeping in apartments around me were ants who'd only ever known their immediate nest. Me – I'd walked on the moon without a suit, without oxygen, without being burned by the solar glare.

My mother was sleeping. I heard her snores as soon as I came through the door, closing it gently behind me. I knew I was going to do it. I'd known for days. I'd been looking at the claw hammer on its hook above the garbage pail and telling myself, Yeah. OK – soon.

Don't think it was an easy decision. Don't think that. We're talking about my mother here. There's a bond of blood. She nursed me as an infant. She bought my clothes. She also tortured me and poisoned me against her. But even I, who'd traversed remotest peaks and descended blind depths, faced the ultimate challenge in a mother's murder.

I sat in the kitchen awhile. She'd left a bottle of red wine uncorked and I finished it. I was going to have a hell of a headache the next day. I weighed the hammer in my hand. It felt heavier – almost too heavy to lift. I went into her room, avoiding the floorboard that creaked. I stood beside her and looked down at her sleeping, her mouth slightly open. Ugly. Most people are beautiful when they sleep, all expression erased – just their true nature. My mother was bitter and disappointed, even in sleep.

I raised the hammer, holding the end of the shaft for maximum force. I looked at the impact point in the exact center of her forehead, crossed by the hairnet's brown elastic band.

But I couldn't. Something wouldn't let me. I could visualize the act. I could physically swing the hammer. But still there was some barrier.

I'd felt it as a kid. Perhaps you did, too. You're standing at the edge of a cliff and some wild thought comes into your mind to leap into the void. Or you're at school or church and the priest tells everyone to pray, and you have this upswelling urge to yell – just to disturb the intensity of silence. And something in your mind says NO. A steel shutter comes down. A moral failsafe.

I went back to the kitchen and I drank a glass of her brandy. The hangover was going to be brutal. I thought about all of her comments, her malign presence, the way she snorted mucus when she was reading. I *wanted* to kill her – let's be clear. It was a volcanic urge that was ready to blast through the crust of self-control: a molten red jet a mile high.

I went back to the bedroom, avoiding the creaky floorboard. She was sleeping on her side now. That made it easier somehow, like she wasn't looking. If the hammer blow woke her up, eyes staring, there'd be nothing to see but her bedside cabinet and the clock telling her it was just after 5am. Then the red curtain descending.

I realized I was ready. It was easy now. I looked at the spot just above her ear. I raised the hammer, light as air, moving my left foot a little to give me maximum clearance for the swing. I held the shaft loosely, remembering out of nowhere something Corsican Tony had told me at Atascadero. When you punch someone, you should keep your hand relaxed until the very moment when it strikes – *then* you make the fist. It's more devastating that way.

Well, I brought the hammer down with such force that its head pretty much disappeared into her skull. I believe I screamed as I did it: a raw, despairing yell. I certainly wept a little. I remember because my vision was blurry. I blinked. Blood welled up out of the wound and flowed over her face. She didn't move, but was still breathing – a thick gargling deep in her throat. Evidently, there was a massive amount of bleeding going on inside her head.

I heard later in court that the hammer was found on the other side of the room. It had apparently hit the wall, leaving a bloody imprint, and fallen to the floor. I have absolutely no recollection of throwing it, but the timelessness of murder is like that. You live minutes within milliseconds. Consciousness is dilated to a pinpoint.

What I do remember is that I threw up immediately afterward. Right there, next to her bed. Maybe it was the mixture of alcohol I'd drunk, but more likely it was something psychological. I'd finally done the thing I'd dreamed about since I was a kid. It wasn't a joyful thing, a triumphant thing, like the killing of the girls. It was more that I'd been possessed with this urge for more than half my life and now it was erupting from my body. My soul was vomiting.

Of course, I had to be sure. I went to the kitchen to get a knife and a garbage bag. I would've preferred to use the boning knife, but it was in my trunk and I was in no condition to go outside. I put the bag over her head and cut right through her neck until the head came off. I don't know exactly why I put the bag on.

There was a lot of blood, mostly from cutting her head off. Her nightgown was black with it and the wall above the bed was sprayed with it. I hadn't thought this far ahead, to be honest. Killing her had always been the end – as far as I'd ever got. There were no more steps beyond that. Now I looked at the scene and thought, What if Amber came round and saw this?

I was being irrational; Amber wouldn't come round at five in the morning. But it sobered me. I took my mother under the arms and dragged her to one of the two closets in her room. I kinda folded her into the bottom where the shoes were and I piled all the bloody bed linen on top of her. It was a bad job. Sloppy. The mattress was pretty badly stained, so I turned it over. That left the blood on the wall, which had run down and soaked into the carpet. It was really never-ending and I could hear her commenting that I'd not cleaned everything well enough. 'You've got to *scrub* it, Sonny – not just wipe at it!'

It was past dawn by the time I'd got everything more or less back to normality. Or so I thought. I went back into her room after eating some dry toast with cold coffee left over from the previous day and I realized that the smell of blood and vomit was very strong. I'd have to air the room and hope the stink didn't carry to other apartments.

I should have gone to work that day, but I guess I knew this was the end. There was no coming back from this. They'd come for me as soon as my mother was missed. Primary suspect. Nobody'd be surprised. They'd just remark that it took me a long time to get round to it.

I didn't even bother to call Tom and tell him I wasn't coming in. I felt bad about that because he'd given me a job and never been unfair with me. He'd be disappointed. The only consolation was that maybe his bitch sister might have to take my shift. I imagined her breaking a nail on the pumps – the worst thing that could possibly happen to her.

In the end, it was an opportunity to spend some time with my mother and tell her some home truths. I took her head out of the bag, washed it off under the kitchen faucet and put in on a tray on the dining table.

"So here we are, Mom. This is what you brought me to. Are you satisfied now? All those girls that died? Your fault. Yep. Didn't they say that I should never live with you after Atascadero? That you were the trigger for my aggression? Couldn't accept that, could you? As if you were the perfect mom! Well, you raised a murderer. You *made* me a murderer. That's on you. Huh? What? Nothing to say? No acid comeback? No belittling insult? Is this what I had to do to get the last word? I guess *your* apartment is mine now, huh?'

I punched the head – knocked it right off the table and along the floor. I felt something break in it. The nose? An eye orbit? I had to humiliate it. I had to demonstrate my mastery over it – my power, its silence. Standing over it at my feet, I was a giant – finally grown to independent adulthood.

About eleven, I had to get out of the house. I took a shower and put on fresh clothes and drove to a bar I'd passed a few times but never visited. I realized later I'd chosen it because it was on the same street as the Sheriff's Office. At one point, I even walked down there and stood on the opposite side of the road. If Amber had come out and seen my face, she would've known in an instant. (Turned out she wasn't at work that day anyway.)

I thought about going in there and walking up to the desk and telling them: 'I've murdered my mother. She's in the closet in her apartment in Verdugo with a pile of bloody bed linen on top of her. I also killed five girls and disposed of their bodies in pieces. Sure, I'll take a seat. Got nowhere else to be.'

I mean, it was inevitable. The only question was when and how. At least if I walked in there, it'd be my choice. I'd be calling the shots. But I couldn't do it then. I wasn't ready. Besides, a plan was forming that might buy me more time to do it all my way.

I should've said that this was a Saturday. My mother didn't have to go to work until Monday. I could call them and say she'd caught some bug, but I couldn't risk anyone coming round to check on her. My idea: I'd say that she'd gone away with a friend for a week. It didn't matter if she'd booked any holiday time or not – she'd be unavailable for a week. And, anyway, she'd never be coming back.

It was over. No more deaths.

Now I had to run.

TWENTY-EIGHT

I hadn't planned anything beyond my mother's death, so I was pleased when I saw her friend's car in the parking lot. She left it there sometimes and took a cab if she was too wrecked to drive through the city. I moved the Ruger into the glove box of her Chevy Impala.

I changed my clothes, choosing the same outfit I'd used for most of the hitchhiker killings: the buckskin jacket, my Levis, the dark shirt, the cowboy-style boots. There were still bloodstains on the shirt cuffs and jacket, but you had to look real hard to see them. It was a look that gave me confidence.

I went to her room again before leaving and I was surprised. I thought I'd done a great job cleaning it up, but now I saw that the wall above the headboard was still smeared brown. I'd missed a lot of spatter. The side of the mattress was stained black even though I'd turned it over. No time to fix it. Instead, I scribbled a quick note:

> Sorry, guys! I know I've not left you much evidence to go on, but I just don't have the time!!! It's 9:00PM Tuesday. My mother's been

> dead about 16 hours if you want to tell the coroner. She never felt a thing. It was quick: asleep – no pain. Just <u>the way I wanted it.</u>
> Sonny.

I would have written it differently if I hadn't felt so pushed. I could have told them about the hammer. I could have saved them a lot of evidence-gathering work. I mean, I wasn't thinking straight. I'd not slept for two days at this point and was running on pure adrenaline – literally trembling with it. I knew it was all gonna catch up with me somewhere down the road, so I cleared out my mother's bathroom cabinet. She had Benzedrine pills and an unopened pack of No-Doz, which was basically pharmaceutical caffeine.

Then I took the Impala and I set off with no destination. We were on the West Coast; the vast continent of North America stretched to the east. That was as far as I could go in a car without a passport.

I went first to Watsonville on Highway 1, then cut east on 129 to somewhere near River Oaks, taking 101 north toward San Jose. It was a very roundabout way of getting there. I could have gone through the town and straight up through the state park, but I didn't want anyone to see my face. The Watsonville route was one I hardly ever took.

From San Jose, I took Interstate 680 to bypass San Francisco and went through Pleasanton, Danville and Walnut Creek before I realized I was heading north. I was just driving. Just putting distance between myself and Buena Vista. Something was drawing me toward Sacramento, across the Benicia-Martinez Bridge and through Fairfield.

Fate's a funny thing. We see it only in retrospect. Living is chaotic – things come at us randomly from all directions and we're blind to the future. The ironies and hidden meanings make sense only when time allows sorting and selection to take place. Look at that miracle girl who survived the family auto wreck against all odds, only to be murdered by Dwight in a different car. Look at Hobo Joe, whose life was saved by medics after his crash so that he could go on to end and ruin other lives.

I didn't see the irony when I drove through Vacaville, about thirty miles east of Sacramento. I just passed through an unremarkable-looking town without stopping, but I was within two miles of the state medical facility where, after sentencing, I'd shortly be imprisoned for the rest of my natural life. I could have driven anywhere in the whole of the USA, but I drove unerringly to the town that was going to be my home forever. Can *you* explain that?

Well, I reached Sacramento and there was no reason to stop, so I just kept on driving east toward Nevada. I'd been on the road four, five hours and I was starting to feel the lack of sleep from the night before. It seems absurd now, but I was angry she'd made me lose sleep. I popped one of the bennies and a No-Doz and they kept me going, but I was struggling to think. I was trying to get control of a situation that had got completely out of hand. How was this gonna end? Who was gonna end it?

I decided at one point, maybe somewhere after Roseville, that I'd ask for the gas chamber. The idea had always made a big impression on me. The drama of it. There'd been a high-profile case in the news when I was a kid: Caryl Chessman. Remember him? He was a robber, kidnapper and sodomitical rapist who spent twelve years on Death Row at San Quentin arguing that the kidnapping part of his sentence – the part that had got him the death sentence – was unjust because he'd taken a victim just a few yards from her car.

Chessman wrote books in his cell. One of them was even made into a movie. I mean, the guy was a celebrity. People like Marlon Brando, Aldous Huxley and the Pope pleaded his case and hailed him as an eloquent evangelist for survival and the enduring human spirit. He turned his crimes into art, into philosophy. Each appeal, each stay of execution brought him even more attention. He was on the cover of *Time* magazine. No joke. A few times they were actually strapping him into the chair when the judge's call came through.

I was just thirteen or fourteen at the time, and about to murder my grandparents within a year, but I was reading it all in the papers. All the details. I imagined being strapped in with leather bands at chest, waist and forearms. They'd attach the heart monitor, whose rubber tube passed through the chamber wall to an adjoining room where the doctor could hear the final stuttering heartbeats and put a time on the death certificate. The curtain to the viewing room would be pulled aside and the twenty-two invited guests – journalists, officials, victims' families – would wait anxiously to see the effects of the gas pellets dropped into their acid bath beneath the seat.

The chamber itself looked like a rocket ship or a lunar landing module in the pictures – like the prisoner was going on an interstellar trip. Not to death but to fame and immortality. I remember getting Amber to tie me to a dining chair with belts and how I practiced the convulsions. There was something sexual in it: being bound, having an audience for the most intimate moment of your life.

The pellets had already been released when a stay of execution came through for Chessman's final trip to the chamber. The judge's secretary had tried to call before but had the wrong number. In the time it took her to find the right one, Chessman was already dying. They probably could have ventilated the space and pulled him out of there alive, but the prison governor decided to let it go ahead. Irony. Fate. Call it what you like.

It's what I wanted for myself. It seemed like an ending. My story, my successes, were still unknown. They'd found only a few body parts and nobody had any idea that the killer had been Sonny Boden – the guy who stood at the bar with his beer in the Holding Cell, next to the cops spending their days trying to figure out who was killing coeds. The same Sonny Boden they mocked and called Joe Friday, who actually had a pretty good understanding of police procedure and how to conceal evidence. It would all come out.

The point was that I'd been the author all along. I'd dictated it from the beginning and I was going to control the ending as well. People would respect me as they'd respected Chessman. I wasn't some out-of-control psycho like Dwight or Joe. I'd acted consciously throughout and carefully managed every part of the story. Only I knew where the rest of the heads were. Only I could show them the disposal site. Only I could inform them which of the missing girls were mine. I had all the answers.

I wish I could tell you more about the scenery as I drove across the states. I remember a pine-lined highway ahead of Reno. Mostly, I was just gripping the wheel, trying to put distance and trying to think logically. I was running and running, but nobody even knew my mother was dead. It was Sunday. I hadn't called her employer to mention that she'd gone away with her friend. It was the sleep deprivation. It was impairing my ability to think.

I stopped in Reno for gas and I ate in an Italian restaurant with candles and checked tablecloths. Spaghetti with meat sauce. I remember thinking it would've been a nice place to take Dulcie. Eating helped. Being out of the car helped. It gave me an idea.

I drove the Impala a little out of town and left it near the Nevada University campus. Then I strolled into town and called Hertz rental out at the airport to book a car. I called from a hotel lobby just to leave a confusing trail and buy myself more time. The idea of the airport was that departing travelers don't rent cars. I took a cab out to the airport and collected the car – another Impala, but a newer model. I'd kinda got to like the way it drove.

Anyway, I took the rental car back to the university and moved my stuff – gun, ammo, knife – from the old car and into the new one. Now, if they put out an APB for the friend's car, it'd take them a helluva long time to find it in Nevada and I'd be nowhere near it. I thought about leaving a note in the glove compartment: *Sorry guys! Missed me again!* But I didn't have a pen or paper.

I took Interstate 80 out of Reno and just headed east. I didn't have a plan. For some reason, I turned south on Highway 50 and drove pretty much non-stop for the next twenty hours across Nevada and Utah toward Colorado, popping bennies and No-Doz and drinking from bottles of orange juice I'd bought at a gas station.

There was a lot of sky, a lot of desert, a lot of nothing through the middle of Nevada. I think another night passed. I'm surprised I even stayed on the road. At one point, possibly somewhere around Eureka, I kinda woke up and thought someone was in the passenger seat. In fact, there was a police car right behind me with its lights flashing.

I pulled over. The Ruger was in the trunk. I was thinking maybe I could smash one of the OJ bottles in his face through the window and grab his gun. But I stopped myself. I considered the situation: nobody knows anything. Nobody's looking. There's no possibility anybody could know about a rental Impala in the middle of Nevada.

"Could I see your license and registration, sir?"

"Sure, officer." I got them from the glove box. "It's a rental out of Reno."

He looked at the documents, then at me. "Do you know that you were speeding?"

"I honestly didn't know that, officer. Truth is, I'm not used to these desert roads. They give you the sensation you're not moving. You ever get that?"

"Been drinking, sir?"

"Only this OJ."

He looked at the bottles. "Your vehicle was all over the road. You drifted over the center line twice while I was behind you."

"I guess I'm tired. I've not slept in a while."

"I suggest you pull over and get some rest. There's a hotel just down the highway."

"Thanks, officer. I'll do that."

"There'll be a fine for the speeding and the erratic driving."

"A fine? How much?" I had only seventy-five dollars in cash.

"Twenty-five dollars, sir. You can face the charge in court tomorrow and argue your case, or you can accompany me now to a postbox and pay the fine in cash."

Shit. "I'll pay it now."

So I had to follow this cop into town and wait for him to fill out the citation on the hood of his car and get me to sign it and give me a copy and put the notes in an envelope and post it – all under his observation. All the while, I was bursting to say something like, "How dumb are you gonna feel when they tell you that you stopped a mass murderer for erratic driving and got him to pay a twenty-five dollar fine while the police forces of multiple states were chasing him down?" I mean, I was rehearsing it in my mind while he was scratching away at the citation and I was seconds away from just coming out with it.

Now I had only fifty dollars. How far could I go on that?

I drove clean across Utah. Eskdale, Hinkley, McCormick, Scipio, Saona. Red earth and hills. Eroded bluffs and mesas. Cisco. Agate. Loma. I was in Colorado and I didn't even know it. Somewhere just after the state line, I pulled off in a desolate, rocky canyon and blacked out. Just instant unconsciousness. I hadn't slept in three, four days? I don't know how long I was gone for. Could've been an hour or twenty. I didn't dream. It was the nearest to death I've ever been. A meteorite or an earthquake could've struck and I would've slept through it.

It was the cold that woke me. I guess I must have been a few thousand feet above sea level and it was dark. I could see more stars than I've ever seen in my life. A wash of stars. I felt happy at that moment. That was freedom. There'd been so few glimpses of it, most of them through a windshield.

I was still tired. I felt heavy. There seemed to be a delay between movement and my recognition of it. I guess I knew it was all coming to an end. Sure, I could hole up in a hotel for a couple nights and plan my strategy, but I knew there had to be a final page and that I had to write it. It had to be *my* way.

I went on through Colorado, watching the fuel gauge sink. Rifle, Gypsum, Beaver Creek. I turned south at Frisco because I took it as a sign. A little further along the highway after Leadville and Granite, I thought I was hallucinating again when I realized I was in a town called Buena Vista. Buena Vista, Colorado.

I pulled over and stopped. It was like the Vacaville thing again. Of all the thousands of towns and cities in America, I'd driven blindly across four states to finish in the same place. I'd done it all without once looking at a map – just following highways and interstates and turning according to the flow of traffic. This was it. This had to be the end. That was when I decided.

I went to a pay phone and asked the operator to connect me with the Sheriff's Department in Buena Vista, California.

I hadn't really thought it through. I was so tired. It was dark, but I didn't know what time it was. The operator put me through and I asked for Lieutenant Schumer. I don't know why. I guess I respected him more than the other detectives. I'd seen his name in the papers a lot and the other cops seemed to look up to him. Well, the operator connected me to, I guess, a guy on the switchboard or the front desk at the Sheriff's Department. I was briefly afraid that Amber might pick up.

"Hi," I said. "I'm calling from Buena Vista long-distance, so I gotta make this quick."

"Whaddya mean long-distance? We're *in* Buena Vista."

"Buena Vista, Colorado. Look–"

"There's a Buena Vista in Colorado?" A palm rustled on the receiver. "Hey, Bud! Did you know there's a Buena Vista in Colorado?"

"Hey! Listen!" I said. "I've got important information for Lieutenant Schumer. Can you put him on the line?"

"Ed Schumer? Here's not on duty for another ten hours. You'll have to call back."

Shit. I had no idea what day or time it was. "Can't you call him and tell him to come into work? This is important. He's gonna wanna know about this and he's not gonna be happy if he finds out someone didn't call him to tell him."

"How about you give me the message and I'll pass it along to Lieutenant Schumer?"

"This is important! You're looking for me. You're all looking for me, but you don't even know it. I'm not saying I'm gonna turn myself in, but I need to tell Lieutenant Schumer some things he needs to know. I *have* to talk to him. Nobody else."

"Can I take your name?"

"No! Just call Lieutenant Schumer and tell him . . . tell him I know where all the pieces are. No . . . tell him . . . Look – just call him. I'm only gonna talk to him. I'll call you back in thirty minutes and you'd better have him on the line waiting."

"Lieutenant Schumer comes on duty in ten hours, sir. If you'll just–"

"*Fuck!*"

The operator came on the line. "Sir, I'll have to disconnect the call if you continue using curse words."

"Sorry. Sorry. Okay, I'm gonna call back in thirty minutes and I expect to talk to Lieutenant Schumer."

I hung up. I punched the payphone's metal side repeatedly, denting it. The whole thing was wobbling. I was shaking.

I spent the next thirty minutes just pacing and pacing and thinking how I could say what I needed to say. I mean, what was I even trying to do? Was this a confession? I didn't want to turn myself in. I didn't want to go to jail. But I wanted everything to be known. I wanted credit for it. I wanted my version to be out there. I felt like I was gonna die of exhaustion and frustration in the next thirty minutes and nobody would ever know what I'd done. They'd pin my mother on me, but the hitchhikers would go unsolved after all my hard work.

I called back through the operator. A different guy picked up.

"Yeah. Buena Vista Sheriff's Department."

"I called half an hour ago to speak to Lieutenant Ed Schumer. Is he there?"

"Lieutenant Schumer will be on duty in around ten hours. You'll have to call then."

"Wait! I just called. I said he should be ready for my call."

"This is supposed to be an emergency line. You'll have to–"

"Wait a minute! This is about a crime."

"What's your name?"

"I'm not gonna tell you my goddamn name! . . . Sorry. Sorry for my language. I just wanna speak to Ed Schumer. This is about an active investigation you're conducting over there."

"What investigation?"

"The coeds."

"The coeds?"

"Yeah, the coeds!"

"You'll have to give me more than that."

"I'm talking about six people in total."

"There are six people involved in this crime?"

"No! There are six people *dead*."

"And you know about these crimes?"

"That's why I wanna talk to Schumer."

"Look – I told you – the lieutenant won't be in until–"

"Call him. Call him at home. I guarantee he'll wanna take the call."

"I'm not calling him at home for this. You'll have to give me more."

"You think I'm bullshitting?"

"I got no idea, do I? I don't know who you are, where you are or what you're talking about. Are you under the influence of any substances? Are you drunk? Because this is supposed to be–"

"I'm not drunk! I've just not slept in four days. I'm in . . ." I honestly couldn't remember for a second where I was. "I'm in Buena Vista, Colorado. I'm in Colorado. I think I'm an hour ahead of you. Look . . . it's Sonny Boden."

A pause. "Amber's brother? Joe Friday from the bar? What're

you doing way over in Colorado, Sonny? Listen, you can't be making pranks like this. I'm serious."

Well, I hadn't been planning to give them all the details over the phone. I didn't really know *what* I was planning. I was just so tired. More than anything, I just wanted everything to end. I wanted this call to end. I was so frustrated. So angry. It felt like one of those arguments with my mother that went on for hours, faded out and started up again.

"Okay, listen," I said, leaning my head against the payphone's gray, dusty metal. "What's your name?"

"Jerry."

"Jerry. Couple days ago, maybe three or four, I killed my mother. Smashed her head in with a hammer and cut it off. She's in the closet. You'll find her there. Her head's in the kitchen cabinet by the toaster."

Now I had his attention.

The line echoed. I wondered if the operator was still listening in.

"Where, Sonny?" said Jerry. "Where are the closets?"

"313 Heliotrope in Verdugo. Apartment One. Her apartment. Didn't I say that?"

"And the body's still there?"

"Unless someone moved it, but I doubt it."

"You said something about coeds."

"Did I?"

"Yeah, you said coeds and six people dead. There are five coeds?"

"Yeah, that's right."

"And did you kill them?"

"Uh huh." I was gonna go unconscious any second. I could feel my legs going.

"Can you give me any detail about those?"

"I can't remember the names. Gimme a sec . . . Miller. The first one was Miller. You found her torso above Three-Mile Beach. That was me. I cut her up. I suppose you'll want some, er, what's it called? Corroborating evidence. Something that wasn't in the papers. Okay. There were two stab wounds on the right side of her front, but no wounds to her breasts. There might also have been a bruise just below her collarbone where the knife hit the seatbelt. There're more injuries, but you haven't got all the parts, so you can't check."

I could picture him rapidly scribbling all of this onto a yellow legal pad while the other guys gathered around him. I waited while he wrote.

"Sharleen Miller," he said, finally.

"That's her. I don't really know the names."

"Her family was shot to death and their house was burned down."

"Yeah. That wasn't me."

"Do you know who it was?"

"No. Maybe."

"Could you tell me?"

"I've said too much already. Will you call Schumer now?"

"Sure, I'll call him. But listen, Sonny – I think we'll need to pick you up. Where are you now? I mean, exactly where?"

I realized I *wanted* them to pick me up. I didn't want to drive anymore. There was nowhere to run and nowhere to turn. I looked around for a street sign. There was a billboard advertising a restaurant and an arrow pointing down the road.

"I think I'm on the corner of Crossman Avenue and Highway 24. Buena Vista, Colorado. Did I say that already?"

"You stay there, Sonny. Okay? Don't move from that spot."

"I'll stay here. Will you call Schumer now?"

"Right now, Sonny. I'm calling him now."

I hung up the phone. There was nobody about. A car passed occasionally on the highway. I was confused about what'd just happened. Was Ed Schumer gonna drive down here and pick me up? It was at least thirty hours away, even if he didn't stop.

I imagined the detectives rushing to the apartment in Verdugo, breaking down the door and finding my note, the blood, the bodies. My Galaxie in the parking lot.

I suppose I could've just got back in the Impala and kept on going, but I didn't have the will. I was still standing there, kinda dazed, when a patrol car showed up with the lights flashing. A uniformed cop got out with his gun already pointed. A young-looking guy. He was tense, nervous.

"You Sonny?"

"Yeah." I swear he was trembling.

"I got take you in, Sonny. I want you to turn around, kneel on the ground and put your hands behind your back. Got that?"

I felt pretty sorry for the guy. He must've got a call about five minutes before, telling him to go out to the edge of the highway and single-handedly arrest a mass murderer from California who'd just slaughtered his mother and was waiting by a payphone. He didn't know if I had a gun or if I was insane.

He cuffed me and we went to his car.

And I guess that's everything.

TWENTY-NINE

My lawyer complained I appeared too sane for an insanity defense. Not so Dwight, who was about as messed up as any human could be. He confessed to all his murders as naturally as he might've confessed to eating a cheeseburger, and they put him away for life. He never mentioned me to the police, by the way. You might call it loyalty – or maybe he wasn't sure if I'd ever been real. Or maybe he mentioned me as some figment of the oceanic consciousness and they ignored him. We'll never know.

Long story short: I was convicted of six counts of first-degree murder with a life sentence for each to run concurrently. Why didn't I get the gas? Funny story: the state of California ruled it unconstitutional shortly before I came to sentencing. It just wasn't an option. Instead, they sent me to CMF Vacaville for the rest of my life and I guess I couldn't hold any bad feeling against them for that. They were just doing their jobs.

I'd experienced a sort of happiness at Atascadero as a kid and I'd quickly learn to be happy at Vacaville. Order suits me. I'm useful here. The only thing I miss is driving. But you don't want to hear about any of that. Let's get to the most important question in all of this – the thing everyone always wants to talk about.

Why.

Why did I do what I did? Is a person born evil? Is it genetic? Is it social? Is it cultural? There certainly seem to be other American serial killers. Maybe it's just a part of the American dream – killing on a bigger scale for fame. It's a subject I've thought and read a lot about, having skin in the game, so to speak.

Look at Dwight. His case is highly specific to the period. You might not guess it, but Dwight was a jock at high school and popular. He was on the football team and a few others. He was a captain and a leader. He got good grades. He went steady with a girl for a few years. He was voted Most Likely to Succeed in the class yearbook. Seriously. Then he started on the weed, which led him to acid.

That was where the real problems started for Dwight. The fact is that LSD psychosis is practically indistinguishable from paranoid schizophrenia. Abnormal thoughts, mood disorders, bizarre behavior, memory problems, a sense of connecting with the divine combined with intellectual alertness . . . Acid, or mental illness? It didn't help that everyone else in the city was dressed as a monk or wearing an orange velvet top hat. Dwight was weird, but he wasn't out of place.

Chicken and egg. Did the drugs cause Dwight's condition, or mask it? Did he start on the drugs due to the trauma caused by Father McLeish's molestation? Lots of kids are molested by priests, but they don't all become murderers. By the time he was suffering from echopraxia – copying other people's movements – his brain was clearly damaged. We know now that the condition is connected to the so-called mirror neurons behind our empathy function. We see a sad or a happy face and we feel sad or happy whether we want to or not. We observe and replicate. Dwight's mechanism was faulty to a colossal degree.

There were more allegations about Father McLeish, if you want to know. He killed himself with a hose attached to the car exhaust in his garage.

Trust me when I tell you that echopraxia is a symptom of acute psychiatric illness – one of the signs of a catatonic state. It's often seen alongside psychosis and mania. Ring any bells? Sufferers of these kinds of illnesses can become highly frustrated that nobody understands their version of reality. It seems everyone else is deluded or pretending. Dwight had to show people the truth. He'd already passed to a higher plane and he was helping people to join him there. They were asking him to. There was never a moral question. He was beyond morality. His empathy was broken.

Dwight was insane. His identity had come undone. He was Mexican. He was British. He was a monk. He heard the voices of his victims begging for death. He burned himself on the penis without knowing why.

It's also interesting that Dwight had a bad car crash when he was sixteen, just before he started on the drugs. Could've died. Quite a few serial killers suffered serious damage to the frontal lobe, which controls our impulses and empathy and the other good things that stop us killing. Me, too.

You'll remember that's what started it all for Joe. Sure, he'd had a delinquent childhood, but he's not alone in that. He was never a victim. He was a fighter. He might've told Sally about the guy he and his friends killed, but I've not found evidence of it being true. And killing someone isn't enough in itself to trigger wholesale psychosis, though many of our servicemen have come home with PTSD.

No, it all started for Joe with that massive injury to the frontal lobe followed almost immediately by the mescaline trip. He wasn't the first and won't be the last to go permanently cuckoo from a single trip. It's rare, but it happens. The evidence is clear in his case: a normal, loving relationship and a young family . . . then hearing voices and killing families. It was like a switch tripped in his head: sane to insane.

Am I saying Dwight and Joe somehow weren't responsible or guilty? Dwight wasn't. He didn't know *what* world he was in. I met him again after we were both sentenced and we chatted a little. He was at Vacaville for a short time before being transferred and he was still just as nutty, though heavily medicated. He'd sing to himself at night and try to kiss sleeping inmates until they moved him for his own safety.

But I think Joe realized what he was doing toward the end. Some part of his damaged brain woke up and told him. It was probably the death of his family. He loved them and love is hard to kill. He did the right thing.

Which leaves me.

The psychiatrists keep coming up with labels. Way back when I killed my grandparents, it was supposed to be paranoid schizophrenia. They said at my second trial that I was a sex maniac. These days, the popular diagnosis is antisocial or paranoid personality disorder. They also say I have a high IQ, which is nice. Nobody's sure of anything. The problem is: I seem to be pretty normal, all things considered. You've probably had colleagues that seemed crazier.

Do I lack a degree of empathy? Well, I'll give you that. Does it mean I'm psychotic? If so, that's me and a few hundred thousand people who *aren't* killing coeds.

The easy answer is that my mother made me kill. That's what they said at Atascadero and after. I was full of bitterness and resentment, so I killed other girls instead. So far, so Freudian. But I didn't want to have sex with my mother and I really wanted to have sex with those girls. Have sex with them and kill them, though not necessarily in that order.

I never had sex with Dulcie. I kissed her maybe once. It was a totally chaste relationship. Why? Because I didn't want to kill her. And this is the point. This is my theory.

But let's take a quick step back to my early teens. I was an avid reader of crime magazines back then. Titles like *Detective Stories* that reported real-life crimes as entertainment for a male audience. They especially chose crimes that involved attractive young women or salacious detail about rape, sexual torture and sadism. I mean, they published actual crime scene photos and if the victim was really attractive there'd be a large photo of her beside the description of her ravishment. The stories overtly sexualized the murders. Stuff like, 'The blond's shapely body had been slashed multiple times,' or, 'Her disarranged underclothes left no doubt that the long-legged coed had been raped, possibly after death,' or, 'Even in death, the brunette maintained her voluptuous beauty.'

And on the covers of these magazines was almost always an artist's rendering of a girl in a tight sweater or cleavage-baring, unbuttoned blouse or hitched-up skirt, gaping in horror, her mouth wetly open and her legs parted, like being murdered was top of her Saturday-night list. Of course, the murder weapon was usually something long and hard: the gun barrel, the bludgeon, the dagger, the brandished fist. The magazines also ran ads for lingerie catalogs, for Chrissakes, and I'm pretty sure the readers weren't ordering these for their wives.

And where was the murderer in all of this cultural mythology? Invisible. Unknown. Dangerous. Sought by the detectives through the few clues he left. He walked among the normal populace, appearing to be one of them, but he knew more. He was smarter. The police had to painstakingly reconstruct the patterns wrought by the murderer. They might even interview him and not know who they were dealing with. He was an artist. He was a *hero*. Woman secretly wanted to feel his brutal grip around their necks. And when he was caught, even if he fried in the chair, we remembered *his* name. Not the victims. Not the detectives.

That's what I grew up with. Then I spent my years between fifteen and twenty-one in a mental hospital surrounded by sexual deviants of all kinds who spoke adoringly, nostalgically and in great detail about their crimes.

Is it any surprise that my young sexuality was twisted? That I came to associate sexual satisfaction with voyeurism, fear, death and decapitation? The system made me. The culture made me. America made me what I am.

But what am I? A monster? Am I evil?

Don't worry, I'm not gonna talk about state-sanctioned murder or Vietnam or Afghanistan. Political stuff and sociology don't interest me. If we're gonna look at me, I'm more interested in something we've not addressed. Another guilty party.

You.

Yeah, you. The reader, the viewer, the avid consumer of serial killer narratives. What fascinates you so much? Why have you followed me to this point? Have you asked yourself that?

What attracts you to the details of these crimes? Where does it come from, that compulsion to know who did what and how it looked? Don't tell yourself it's just some disinterested academic sense of trying to understand aberrant psychology. Don't call it a guilty pleasure like it's a chocolate truffle or a milkshake. Be honest – you like the darkness. You like the salt of cruelty. It's the thrill, the spark, of imagining for just a second the depths you're afraid might also be in you. Are *you* capable?

Sure, you feel revulsion at the detail. You might turn away. But you always come back. You look again. You seek more. Dahmer. Bundy. Ramirez. Gacy. Gein. Ridgeway. Kemper. Why do you know those names? You've seen the movies. You've read the books. They're all anti-heroes – the same anti-heroes I found in my teenage magazines: guys who went beyond normal human experience, but who appeared normal among us. Monsters. Devils. Why do they attract you? Why do you want so badly to see through their eyes as you've seen through mine?

Have you considered that I see also through yours? When I spoke to victims and potential victims, when I searched for headlines, when I disposed of bodies, when I imagined reactions – there was always an audience. Murder is performance. Murder is art. It's *entertainment* for you. It's what draws you to these stories. *You* came to *me*, remember. You chose this journey and you stayed to the end.

If I've learned anything from more than fifty years among murderers, it's that there's a black seed in all of us – a part of what makes us human. It grows in some with dense and twisted roots then breaks through with a burst of cloying purple-black flowers. In others, it lies dormant. It's in you. You know it.

Well, I'm here in the state medical facility: safely behind bars. The justice system put me here because I'm not fit for society. I accept that. Maybe I've learned things in here. Maybe I've found Jesus or become a better person. Maybe I help others. But you don't care about that. All you want to know about are the worst things I've ever done – those people I killed, how I did it, and why. It's like an obsession with you, isn't it?

Take some time. Think about why.

I'll be here. Waiting.

ALSO BY MATT STANLEY
NOT PUBLISHED BY BLOODHOUND BOOKS

A Collar for Cerberus

I Am the Sea

A NOTE FROM THE PUBLISHER

Thank you for reading this book. If you enjoyed it please do consider leaving a review on Amazon to help others find it too.

We hate typos. All of our books have been rigorously edited and proofread, but sometimes mistakes do slip through. If you have spotted a typo, please do let us know and we can get it amended within hours.

info@bloodhoundbooks.com

Printed in Great Britain
by Amazon